THE ILLUSION OF ANNABELLA

JESSICA SORENSEN

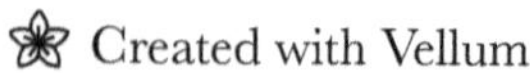 Created with Vellum

PROLOGUE

A SEA OF GLASS

I'VE ALWAYS BEEN A HAPPY PERSON. AT PEACE WITH MY LIFE. Always wearing a sparkling smile, I was the kind of child who dreamed about catching rainbows and drinking glasses of sunshine. There wasn't a day I didn't wake up thinking how wonderful it was to be alive.

I was fortunate enough to be born into a loving family. I grew up in a small town in the center of suburbia where life stood still in comparison to larger cities, but I loved the comfort it brought, that hometown feeling I got whenever I walked around. But my favorite part was how everyone celebrated the holidays. Christmases were dusted with handfuls of holiday magic, and everyone who lived on our street decorated their homes so the entire block was lit up. Fourth of Julys were spent at the park with neighbors, eating popsicles and pies, and gazing up at an explosion of fireworks painting the dusky sky, like fireflies. When I was younger, I truly believed they were fireflies.

"I want to catch them," I shouted while pointing at the

sky. "Please, Daddy, let me catch them. I think they might secretly be fireflies."

"That's not a wise idea, Annabella," my father, who was going through his overly protective phase, said. "You could get burned if you actually caught one."

I sulked, and my mom chimed in, "Oh, come on, honey, let her go play for a while." She urged me forward, and I ran across the grass with my hands in the air, watching the sky in awe.

My younger twin sisters, Alexis and Zhara, and my older sister, Jessamine, joined me while my brothers, Loki and Nikoli, stayed by my father, pretending to be uninterested. I felt sorry for them. They didn't realize how much fun we were having, even if we never caught a single firefly—they always fizzled out before they hit the ground. Over the years, my father stopped being so paranoid and joined in, even going as far as buying us our own box of sparklers every year.

Despite the magic of the Fourth of July, birthdays were always my favorite time of year. When I was younger, birthdays were solely a family holiday, where the seven Bakers spent the day together doing whatever the birthday girl or boy wanted. It didn't even have to be mine. I was always happy on birthday mornings, so thrilled to celebrate the day together, days that promised endless magical possibilities. My parents would do crazy things like pull us out of school to take us to concerts, let us spend a day on the beach sculpting sand statues—which they'd judge at the end—or my personal favorite, shopping at secondhand stores to see who could come up with the best find. I always felt so lucky all the time, and maybe that's where I made the mistake.

"I found a vase that belonged to a princess," I proclaimed to my mom on my tenth birthday.

The vase was black and pink with jewels and a small crack down the center. In reality, it didn't belong to a princess. I just believed pretty vases were supposed to belong to princesses.

"Anna's lying," Nikoli said, pointing at me. "She's making stories up again."

"It could've belonged to a princess." I cradled the vase to my chest. "Mom, tell him it could."

"It can be whatever you want." My mom smoothed her palm over the top of my head.

She always encouraged me to be whoever I wanted to be and believed whatever I wanted her to believe. She was the same way, full of ideas that didn't always make sense. I dreamt of being like her one day.

All of that changed the day I turned seventeen. The day that had held so much promise when I woke up, carried so much despair when I shut my eyes to go to sleep. Maybe it was because I knew nothing was ever going to be the same. That Christmases, Fourth of Julys, and even birthdays would never be magical again. Those days would be less promising. That the happy, sunny days of catching rainbows were dead.

Because it was the day I learned that I had been, and always would be, living my life in a sea of glass. That my life was a distorted reflection of what I wanted to see, and when that life shattered, I was left trying to figure out how to put the pieces back together.

ONE
A GLITTER RAINSTORM

I'M NOT THE PRETTIEST GIRL IN THE WORLD OR THE MOST popular. I don't have a fantastic talent that sets me apart from others. I rarely rebel. I do smile more than most, and I love to dance. I enjoy a lot of things, like books that you can get lost in, movies that make you happy, and music you can dance to. Most days, I'm average at best. Most days I'm okay with that. Today, not so much.

It's my seventeenth birthday. Although I used to spend the day with my family, now that I'm older, my parents are throwing a party for me and my friends. And Ben Winsington, a guy I've crushed on since grade school, is coming. It took me days to work up the courage to invite him and all my willpower not to faint when he said yes. Ben, the star quarterback and one of the hottest guys at school, said yes!

The party hasn't even started, and I'm already a bundle of nerves over what I'm going to wear, what I'm going to say to Ben, if I'll be able to act semi-cool. Since it's still early, I have another seven jittery, nausea-filled hours to suffer through before the actual fun begins.

The music in my bedroom is cranked up, a string quartet floating from the speaker, as I yank all my clothes off the hangers and toss them onto the bed. In the midst of the madness, my mom sticks her head into my room then snaps her fingers at me. "Annabella Baker, we need to go now, or we're going to be late." Her urgent tone doesn't match the huge smile on her face.

"I'm hurrying as fast as I can." I fasten my lengthy brown hair into a ponytail then put my hands on my hips and stare at the mound of clothes piled on the bed. "I just can't figure out what to wear."

"Since when do you care about clothes so much?"

I hope my heated cheeks don't give me away. "I don't know."

But she can read me like an open book. "Is this about a boy?"

I shake my head, but eventually I'll cave and tell her about Ben and my huge crush on him. Hopefully she'll give me some advice on how to chill out and act cooler than I feel.

"All right then," she says skeptically. She starts digging through my clothes and holds up a pink, knee-length dress. "How about this one? You look cute in it."

I scrunch up my nose. "I don't want to look cute today."

"Then what do you want to look like?"

"I don't know . . . like you maybe."

My mom is anything but ordinary. Her wild, brown curls that frame her heart-shaped face and cat-shaped eyes surrounded by long, dark eyelashes remind me of an

Egyptian princess. She's an amazing cook, too, the kind who can make cakes look like works of art. Plus, she wears a lot of edgy outfits that make her standout.

"Most daughters would never say that," she remarks as she sifts through the clothes on the bed.

I dramatically flop down on the mattress. "Most daughters don't have mothers that wear studded leather jackets and glittery heels."

She glances at her black dress, plaid overshirt, and knee-high studded boots. "I probably should start dressing more mother-appropriate, right?"

"You really want to be like everyone else? Because let me tell you, being ordinary isn't always great. I mean, sometimes I'm cool with walking with the crowd, but sometimes," *like today*, "it kind of sucks."

She laughs, her blue eyes crinkling around the corners. "Oh, Annabella, sometimes you can be the silliest girl on the planet." She pats my head. "But that's okay."

"Why? I didn't do anything weird."

She just smiles. "You'll understand one day."

"You're being super weird right now."

She hums under her breath as she sorts through my clothes, but gives up and backs away from the bed. "Get your hair and makeup done. I'll be right back." She taps the skip button on the iPod on her way out. The song switches to "Elastic Heart" by Sia. "Stop sulking and dance, my Ballerina Annabella," she says before waltzing out of the room, twirling at the door.

As stressed out as I am over Ben, I feel a tiny bit better as I move my feet and spin in circles all the way to the mirror. The more I dance to the rhythm, the smaller my worries about guys and birthday parties become. For a moment, I feel calmly still in life.

I run a brush through my hair while shimmying my hips. I squeeze in a pirouette between tracing my hazel eyes with a dab of liner and applying a drop of lip-gloss. By the time I'm finished with my makeup, I've spun at least fifty pirouettes and one very over enthusiastic brìse.

"Feeling better?" My mom returns to my room with clothes in her arms.

"Yes," I admit as I stretch out my legs and point my toes a few times. "You did that on purpose, didn't you?"

"Did what?" she asks innocently as she drops the clothes onto the bed.

"Left me alone in my room so I would dance and chill out."

"Well, I had to get you to chill out somehow. I figured I could either let you take some time to dance and mellow out, or get you to fess up to whatever's got you all depressed on your birthday." She waits for me to offer up the answer, but my lips remain sealed, too afraid to tell her that I, Annabella Baker, the girl who dreams of chasing rainbows, is stressed out over a guy. "Not going to tell me, huh?" She pouts disappointedly. "Okay, well maybe you'll feel like telling me during the car ride."

"Car ride to where exactly?" I pick up the short, red and black patterned dress she brought in with her.

"It's a surprise." Her eyes sparkle with a secret.

"What kind of a surprise?" I eye the dress, studded bracelet, and strappy heels she put on the bed.

"The good kind." She backs toward the door. "Now get

dressed. We need to get going if we want to make it back in time for the party."

"Can't I have a hint?" I plead, clasping my hands in front of me.

"Music," she says. "Any particular birthday wish this year?"

"How about a unicorn?" I joke. "You know I've always wanted one of those."

"As much as I love giving you whatever you want, I just don't think we have room for a unicorn," she says almost mournfully.

I love that she doesn't say it's not possible, that unicorns don't exist. It's probably why, when I was younger, I wished for a glitter rainstorm and believed it would come true.

"How about a glitter rainstorm, then?" I ask, hopeful. "That would be pretty amazing, too."

She chuckles that oh-Anna-you're-so-silly kind of chuckle. "I've always envied that imagination of yours." She whisks out of the room, leaving me to obsess over what she said.

My mom envies *me*? Really?

While the idea seems impossible, I feel all glowy inside. I start to get dressed as my nerves about Ben abruptly shift into excitement over whatever my mom has planned for today. My bet is that it has something do to with dancing, my one and only passion.

I've been taking ballet classes since I was six-years-old. Eleven years later, I'm still in love with every aspect of it; how easy it is to get lost in the music, how I feel so at peace whenever I'm dancing, like it's exactly what I'm supposed to be doing. Sometimes I get so caught up in it, I'll dance for hours, until my muscles ache and my feet are covered in blisters. I love it so much that I plan on majoring in dance. I've started looking into colleges that have good dance programs so when I graduate, I can live out my dream of dancing onstage and performing with a major dance company.

Hmmm . . . maybe that's what the surprise is? Taking me to check out college campuses?

I peel off my pajamas, squeeze into the dress and slip on the heels. As I'm putting on a few bracelets, I hear my phone vibrating on my dresser. I smile when I see my sister's name on the screen.

Jessamine: Hey bday girl! Can't wait to c ya tonight!

Me: Me either! It's been too long.

My sister's been attending culinary school overseas now for almost a year, and I haven't seen her since she left, so I was super excited when she texted me, saying she was coming home and staying for over a week.

Jessamine: U haven't told Mom and Dad that I'm coming, right? I want it to be a surprise!

Me: Whoops! I forgot. U know I suck at keeping secrets.

Jessamine: Oh, Anna! U didn't!

Me: J/k. It's still a secret. But u totally owe me. I HATE keeping secrets.

Jessamine: I know. That's why I have about a pound of chocolate in my suitcase.

Me: Woo hoo! Can't wait!

Jessamine: Me either. C ya tonight!

Putting the phone down, I do a quick check in the mirror

before skipping down the stairs way too eagerly, and I end up tripping on the final step.

"Shit," I curse as my hip bashes against the counter.

Damn heels. I'm not used to wearing them, and they make me less coordinated than I am.

My dad, scrambling eggs and frying bacon on the stove, shoots me a look from over his shoulder. "Anna, watch the language. At least when you're in front of your brother."

"Why? You and Mom swear all the time." Nikoli, my youngest brother and the baby of the family, chimes in. He's munching on a piece of toast and reading a playbook. Even though he's only thirteen, he's already decided to devote his life to sports, mainly football.

My dad reels around toward Nik, trying to appear stern, but with the floral apron he's sporting and the greasy spatula in his hand, he misses the mark. "Your mom and I are adults; therefore, we can say whatever we want."

Nik drums his fingers on the table. "That kind of seems unfair. I mean, yeah, you're adults, but you influence us. We look up to you. If you swear, then we view it as an okay thing to do."

My dad's gaze darts to me. "Did you tell him that?"

"No, but he has a point." I grab a piece of dry toast from the toaster. "Although, I'm not sure where he got the point."

"Where did you get that theory from?" my dad asks Nik, flipping over the bacon.

Nik turns the page of the playbook, shrugging. "I had to write a report on heroes for English class. I did a lot of research on parents as heroes, because I used one of you guys, and there was an article that said that."

"You used one of us as your hero?" Hope fills my dad's eyes as he distractedly reduces the heat of the burner.

Oblivious, Nikoli examines the plays. "Yep."

I cross the kitchen to get the butter from the fridge. "Niki, would you please just tell Dad that you did the report on him before he ends up burning breakfast."

"What . . ." My dad trails off as smoke funnels from the pan of bacon. He curses as he swipes up the pan and rushes for the sink as the smoke alarm starts screeching.

Nikoli and I look at each other then erupt with laughter.

"I think he just totally made it okay to swear," I say through my laughs.

We high-five each other, then I butter my toast while my dad fans the smoke alarm with a dishrag.

My mom strolls into the smoky kitchen right as he gets the alarm to shut off. "I'm seriously starting to wonder if your cooking skills are ever going to get better," she teases, giving my dad a quick kiss on his scruffy cheek.

For as long as I can remember, my parents have been completely and one hundred percent in love. Their story is pretty ordinary, but I think their love is an epic fairytale.

High school sweethearts and first loves, they got married not too long after they started college. They struggled to make ends meet, living in a tiny apartment that had practically no furniture and a neighbor that liked to sing show tunes during odd hours of the night. Add that to finals and part-time jobs, they were under a lot of stress.

Although most people spend their time in college figuring out what they want in life, my mom wanted to share the journey with my dad. And my dad . . . well, he remembers those days as "some of the best."

Eventually, they both graduated and found steady jobs. Two years later, the first of the Baker clan was born. My brother, Loki, who's off at college studying philosophy and dating girls who wear lots of black and, in my opinion, seem really sullen about life. Loki seems happy, though. Well, about as happy as any other philosophy major.

I dream of one day finding what my parents have. If I'm lucky, maybe I'll end up having it with Ben.

"You about ready to go?" my mom asks me as she scoops up the car keys from the counter.

"Yes siree." I munch on my toast while my parents exchange a look. "I'm starting to get really curious about where we're going. And if I had known Dad was in on the secret, I would have wiggled it out of him before you got down here.

"All I'm going to say is you're going to love it." My dad returns to the stove with his back turned to me.

"Are you going to be able to take the day off?" my mom asks my dad as she gets an energy drink from the fridge. "So you can go with us?"

"Yep. I told Maggie she'd have to hold down the fort on her own," my dad replies as he screws the cap on a gallon of milk. "But I have to run in and help her open up first, so I'll be about another hour."

My dad owns a quaint bookstore in one of the quieter areas of town. During the summers, I spend a lot of time there, helping out and reading the inventory. I love everything about the store, love the smell of new and old books, the atmosphere, and I love spending time with my dad.

"An hour sounds perfect. I have to run a few errands first, anyway, which may or may not have to do with presents and cake." My mom smiles at me, then gets her purse from the table and hugs Nikoli goodbye. "How about I go run my errands then pick you up at the store?" she says to my dad. "That way Anna won't be late for her party."

My stomach somersaults at the mention of the party, but my mom leaves me hardly any time to tumble back into stress mode. She waggles her fingers, waving goodbye, then motions for me to follow her.

I start to leave, but my dad snags my elbow and draws me back. "This is for later." He hands me a rectangular box decorated with pink paper and silver bow.

"Thanks, Dad." I circle my arms around him. "You're the best."

He hugs me back then we say goodbye, and I chase after my mother, the heels of my shoes scuffing against the hardwood floor.

"Why are we going this way?" I ask, because we usually use the back door.

"Because I have something for you that requires us going out the front door." Right as she says it, I hear giggling from above me.

I tip my chin back and look up at the banister right as a rainstorm of silver and pink glitter showers down on me. A laugh bursts from my lips as I span my arms to the side and spin in a circle.

"It's a birthday miracle," Alexis and Zhara singsong from above me as they continue throwing handfuls of glitter down.

I twirl around until they run out of glitter. Then I give my mom a ginormous hug. "Thank you."

"You deserve to get what you want on your birthday."

She smiles as she smoothes her hand over my head. "Now, come on. Let's get this fun-filled day started.

Beaming from ear to ear, I follow her toward the front door. As we're passing through the foyer, I catch my reflection in the mirror on the wall. My dress, cheeks, and hair are covered with sparkles.

"I look like a unicorn threw up on me," I remark with my head angled to the side. "But in the best way possible."

My mom chuckles as she opens the door. "How you make such a gross sentence sound so appealing is beyond me. But then again, you always did have a gift of making sunshine out of rain."

"You're really stroking my ego today."

"Nope, I'm just telling the truth."

I brush the glitter out of my hair before getting into the car. My mom cranks up her favorite classic rock station, and a little Pearl Jam plays through the speakers.

"What errands are we running?" I ask. "Something fun, I'm hoping."

"Unfortunately not. As much as I hate to do it, this is an unbirthday related stop," she admits as she brakes at the stop sign at the end of our street.

"Well, I'll let it slide just as long as you tell me where you, Dad, and I are going." When she remains silent, I sulk. "You're really not going to tell me where we're going?"

"No way. It'll take all the fun out of the surprise."

"Oh, fine," I huff, pretending to be more irritated than I am.

She drives down Main Street, past all the shops, the second hand store, the bank, and finally stops at the grocery store. "I just have to grab something real quick." She reaches into her purse and tosses me a bag of M&Ms and a Snickers bar. "Eat up."

"Thanks." I dive in, stuffing my face with chocolate while she runs in.

I kick the heels off, prop my bare feet up on the dash, and relax in the seat, cranking up some tunes. I tap my feet and sing along, observing all the people walking in and out of the grocery store. Honeyton has more people around in the summertime than in the wintertime, mainly because it's a tourist town. Since its June, it makes people watching super fun.

After ten minutes, I grow bored and open the present my dad gave me. I know what it is before even getting it open, considering it's been a tradition for four years now. Just like I guessed, under the wrapping paper is a small box of sparklers and a lighter.

Glancing around, I take one out of the box, shove open the door, and plant my bare feet on the hot asphalt. Flicking the lighter, I move the flame to the tip of the sparkler, igniting a shower of sparks. Laughing, I jump to my feet and dance around in a circle, giggling even harder when people gawk at me.

After the sparkler dies, I return to my seat in the car and drum my fingers against my thighs to the beat of a Pink Floyd song. By the time my mom walks out of the store, I'm giggling at a mom who's scolding her teenage son for wearing a hoodie when it's ninety-five degrees out. He keeps glancing in my direction, as if he's embarrassed. I don't know why. His sunglasses hide his face so I can't tell who he is, but I'm guessing he's a tourist since I don't recognize his mom.

"Whatcha laughing at?" my mom asks, tossing a plastic bag onto the backseat as she climbs in.

I point at the guy. "That . . . I kind of feel sorry for him."

My mom laughs, shifting into gear. "See how lucky you are to have such awesome parents?"

I wave goodbye to my sunglasses, hoodie wearing friend and shove the rest of the candy into my mouth. "You guys are super awesome, but FYI, I've heard Dad yell at Loki like that. Remember when Loki put gauges in his ears?"

"I almost forgot about that phase. Thanks for reminding me." She's all sarcasm.

"No problem." I'm all smartass.

She shakes her head, grinning, and I sit back and enjoy the drive.

We pass by houses and businesses, driving toward the outskirts of town. The sun sporadically reflects through the paper-thin clouds, and my eyelids flutter against the short, fleeting flashes of light every time one of the rays hits my eyes.

"It's going to rain today," I comment as thunder rumbles in the distance while the clouds brew up an early summer storm.

"Only in the morning," she says. "It should be completely rain free by the time your party starts."

Great, now I feel jittery again, and my excitement over the surprise dwindles.

Noting my frown, she turns down the volume of the radio. "No being sad on your birthday. You have to be happy today. It's a rule."

"I'm not frowning because I'm sad. I'm frowning

because," I pick at my fingernails, an anxious habit of mine, "I'm nervous."

"About?"

"Um, a . . . Never mind. I can't tell you."

"Oh, come on, Anna. I'd like to think that I'm a cool enough mom that you feel like you can tell me these things." Turning the wheel, she makes a sudden right down an unfamiliar dirt road.

"What things?" I sit up straight and peer out the window. "And where are we going?"

At the end of the road, enclosed by a field of dry grass, is a blue and white two-story Victorian home. Beside the house is a faded red barn with a painted sign, *Honeyton Antiques and Things*.

"I wonder what 'things' stands for," I joke.

"Who knows," she says with a grin, playing along.

"Is this my surprise?" I wonder, getting super excited. "Wait. Are we playing the antique game?"

"Nope, not this time. And stop changing the subject." She parks in front of the narrow path decorated with roses and leaves the engine idling. "Now, tell me what's with the frown, Charlie Brown."

"I don't want to . . . It's so stupid . . . you're going to think I'm stupid."

"Try me."

"Fine." I heave a dramatic sigh. "It's about a boy."

She muses. "It always is, isn't it?"

I lift my shoulders, shrugging. "I don't know. This is the first time I've felt this way about a guy before."

She gives me a *really?* look, because I've probably said the same thing to her at least a dozen times. "I'm guessing the guy is coming to your party tonight?"

"How'd you guess?"

She glances at the dress I'm wearing. "Because of the fashion meltdown you had this morning."

"Was I that obvious?" I hope Ben doesn't pick up on my crush on him.

She thrums her fingers against the console. "Give me, like, five minutes to run inside and then you and I are going to have a very long talk." She reaches for the door handle and opens the door.

I lower my feet from the dash. "About what?"

She swings her feet to the ground. "About the World of Women."

"It sounds like the title of a book. World of Women, a secret society built on gossip, shopping, and a lust for men." I pucker my lips and flip my hair off my shoulder.

She points a finger at me as she gets out of the car. "Sounds like someone's been spending a little too much time in the romance section of your father's store."

"He made me stock the shelves, and I can't help it. I get bored and read the blurbs."

"Well, I'd rather not hear you say the word lust again." She starts to close the door, but pauses. "From now on, you'll call it an adorable little crush, because you're seventeen-years-old, and you aren't allowed to be lustful or whatever the books are calling it."

I laugh at her, and smiling, she bumps the door shut. Instead of heading to the barn, she hikes up the path to the house, but I figure that's probably part of the store, too.

I flip through the radio stations, and start obsessing over all things Ben.

Settling on the alternative station, I sing along until my phone vibrates. I retrieve it from my pocket and open the message from Cece, my best friend since kindergarten. In some ways we're similar in the sense that we both love to dance and take a ballet classes together, but she's not as passionate about it as I am. She's also a cheerleader, last year's homecoming queen, and a self-proclaimed fashionista, all things I'm not nor ever will be.

Cece: Hey, bday girl! How's it goin'?

Me: Super great. Headed somewhere with my mom right now.

Cece: That's so cool! I can't wait for the party tonight. I heard a lot of people r coming.

My nerves skyrocket through the roof. I'm not that popular. Sure, I have a handful of close friends and can float through the social circles, but unlike Cece, there aren't people lining up to hang out with me. Plus, I devote a lot of my time to dance and most people don't seem to understand my obsession with it.

Me: How does everyone know about it???

Cece: I may have told some people.

Me: How many people did u tell?

Cece: I don't know. I sent out texts to like half our class.

Me: Ok, now I'm really nervous. We're not even doing anything fun. Just hanging out and watching movies.

Cece: We'll make it fun :) We always do.

She's right. I relax a little until I read her next message.

Cece: Ben told me today that he was excited about it.

Me: U are such a liar, but I luv u for trying.

Cece: I'm not lying! I swear he did. While I was waiting for my sister to pick me up from cheer practice, he came up to me and started asking me about the stuff u like. He said he needed ideas for a bday present, but I think he wanted to be prepared.

Me: For what?

Cece: To put the moves on you ;)

My cheeks heat. Thank god, my mom's not around to hassle me about it.

Me: What'd u tell him?

Cece: That the way to your heart is through dancing, glitter, and magical kisses.

Me: U so did not. Cece, tell me u didn't.

Cece: Whoops. Was that a secret?

With Cece, there's a fifty-fifty chance she's kidding, and if she did tell someone, I'd have to hide forever.

Me: Please tell me u didn't.

Cece: Oh fine, I didn't mention the magical kissing part, but I did tell him about the dancing. My bet is he buys you something music related.

Me: He doesn't need to buy me anything.

Cece: Why? Presents are awesome, but getting presents from guys is even better.

Me: I'll have to take your word on that.

Cece: Not after tonight. I'm betting you'll not only have your first present from a guy, but your first kiss!

My heart rate speeds up, and my palms dampen with

sweat, all because she implied it. I feel silly that I've never kissed a guy while all my other friends have, partly because I'm too shy but also because I haven't really had a lot of time to date with all the dance classes I take on top of practicing at home and performing in recitals. It seems like the older I get, the more nervous I am about kissing, which makes the possibility of ever losing my kissing card dimmer and dimmer.

Maybe it could happen, though. After all, it did rain glitter today.

Cece: Gotta go! My mom's yelling at me to help her with lunch. C u later tonight bday girl.

Me: C ya!

Fighting back a goofy, Ben-induced smile, I put the phone down. I manage to keep my elation contained for a whole ten seconds before the smile wins and breaks free.

Grinning like a goof, I tap my feet to the beat of the song and sing along with the lyrics. Five minutes turn into ten, and ten into fifteen. Almost a half hour later, my mom still hasn't come out of the store, and a dark, thunderous storm has taken over the partly cloudy sky. Rain splatters down against the windshield, and the wind howls and kicks up debris.

The forty-five minute marker passes, and I finally text my mom. When she doesn't message back, I reach for the door handle to get out. Right as I'm preparing to make a sprint through the rain, the front door of the house opens and my mom hurries out.

She peers back at the house and runs her fingers across her lips. Then she barrels out into the downpour and clambers into the car. Her hair and clothes are soaked, her lipstick is smudged, and her cheeks are flushed.

"Man, I disappear for ten minutes, and it starts raining cats and dogs out there," she says, wringing out her wet hair. Her voice is shaky, and she's out of breath.

"Ten minutes?" I gape at her then at the clock. "You've been in there for over forty-five minutes."

Her brows knit as she looks at the time. "Oh, my word, I didn't . . ." She sighs. "Anna, I'm so sorry. I was looking at antiques and lost track of time. You know how I get."

"Yes, I do." I fasten my seatbelt as she flips down the visor and runs her fingers through her hair. "Why didn't you answer my text, though?"

"Oh, I forgot I turned down the ringer because I didn't want anyone bothering us on this little trip." She seems distracted as she reapplies her lipstick. With a pop of her lips, she drops the tube into her purse and puts it on the backseat. Then she briefly places her finger to her lips as she stares almost dreamily at the house.

"You're acting weird." Why the hell is she staring at the house like that? *Stop, Mom. Just stop.* "Well, weirder than normal."

"Not really." She lowers her fingers and shoves the car into reverse.

The tires splash through the puddles and murky water sprays all over the windows as she backs up. A middle-aged man wearing a t-shirt and jeans walks onto the porch barefooted and watches us drive away. When my mom spots him, she flushes again.

I think about asking her who he is, but fear the answer

might have to do with why her clothes are on funky. "Your shirt's inside out," I mutter.

"Shit." She slams on the brakes at the end of the drive, jerks the emergency brake, and starts to slip her arms out of the sleeves of her overshirt.

I stare out the window, trying to remember if her overshirt was like that when she went inside the house. I don't think so. But maybe I'm remembering things wrong.

"I tried on an old dress," she explains, as if reading my mind. "It was an old Victorian dress I wanted to wear for Halloween."

"Halloween isn't for, like, four more months." And why is she shopping for Halloween clothes on my birthday, anyway? Usually the day is all about me.

"I know, but this kind of dress is hard to find."

I glance at her then at the grocery bag on the backseat. "But you didn't buy anything."

She struggles with what to say as the rain pours down so violently that I can't see the trees and fields around us. "I did, but I'm picking it up later . . . It's a surprise for your dad actually. He's been wanting to do this couples costume thing since forever—you know how excited he gets over holidays. I've always told him no, but decided maybe it's time." She places her hand on my knee and looks me straight in the eye. "You have to keep it a secret, even though I know you hate keeping secrets. Otherwise, you'll spoil the surprise for him." The pitch in her voice is too high, her smile too fake. "Anna, this is really important, okay?"

I don't like what I see. Liar, liar, her expression reads. But I can't work up the courage to call her out on it.

I swallow the lump in my throat and nod my head once, silently agreeing to something I don't want to do.

"Good." She loosens up as she pulls onto the road. "I love you, Anna. You know that, right?"

"Yeah," is all I say.

I don't speak to her during the ten minute drive to my father's store, guilt knotting in my stomach with every passing second.

My mom wouldn't have an affair.

She loves my father.

My family is too happy.

Right?

How did the day go from magical and glittery to guilty and disgusting?

By the time my dad ducks into the backseat, that guilt and disgust has formed a giant, twisted knot in my stomach.

"How's my girl?" he asks, shaking his head, making rain spray everywhere.

My mom squeals, shielding herself from the water, even though her clothes and hair are still damp. "Sweetie, easy on the dog shaking."

"Why? You know you secretly like it." My dad slides forward and kisses my mom's cheek.

She subtly winces from the kiss, something she's never done before. Or maybe she has and I never had a reason to pay close enough attention to her reaction.

"Did you two have fun running errands this morning?" he asks, sitting back. "You never did say where you were going."

My mom gives me a discreet sidelong glance, and panic

flashes in her eyes. "I actually just had to stop and drop off some bills."

"Really? On her birthday?" My dad looks at me, and I swear I see a question in his eyes, like he's waiting for me to disclose the truth.

I force a smile. "I didn't mind."

"That doesn't sound like a very fun birthday morning." My dad winks at me. "Good thing you're about to get one of the best birthday presents ever."

I feel sick to my stomach as my mom maneuvers the car onto the street. I want nothing more than to blurt out what happened. Tell my dad that something doesn't feel right. That I have a gut-wrenching feeling my mom might be having an affair.

But I fear that I might be wrong. Or that I might be right. That my wonderful life could change if I open my mouth.

Despite my internal tug of war, I never get the chance to say anything. Don't get a chance to say anything to them ever again.

As my mom merges the car onto the highway, the earth is practically drowning in the rain. Maybe that's why she doesn't see the car coming. Or perhaps she was distracted by whatever happened in the blue house. But moments later, our car is sideswiped.

The impact knocks the wind out of me, and my head bashes against the door. The car flips over. And over. And over. The metal caves against the impact and glass shatters everywhere. Someone screams. Maybe me. Maybe my mother. Maybe my dad.

When the car finally stops moving, it lands on the roof.

I'm still strapped in the passenger seat, hanging upside down. Thunder booms and lightning claps. It's dark, cold, wet. The stereo is still working, but the speakers are cutting out so I can't tell what song is playing. Blood rushes to my head and drips into my eyes. My entire body aches, and my leg is wedged under the concaved dash. My pulse pounds. The world spins around. Strangely, though, I can't feel any pain.

"Mom . . . Dad . . ." I crane my neck toward the driver's side then at the backseat. The left side of the car is smashed in, and all that remains is balled and broken metal.

Shock seeps deep into my bones. I don't cry. I can barely breathe. I wait for my parents to answer me. I swear the sun fleetingly pushes through the clouds and reflects against the shards of glass and rain, causing the world to briefly sparkle like the glitter this morning. But as quickly as the sunshine surfaces, it fades.

And all that's left is a rainstorm.

TWO
FAIRYTALES ARE JUST ILLUSIONS

Light. Dark. Rain. Sun.

"Stay with us."

Beep . . . beep . . . beep . . .

"Stay with us. Come on."

"Anna, can you hear me?"

Loki, is that you?

"Anna, please don't go. We can't lose you, too."

Who else did we lose . . . Loki, please answer me.

"God, I can't do this."

Sobbing, sobbing, so much sobbing.

"What am I going to do?"

I want to hug my brother, throw my arms around him and tell him everything's fine, but I can't see anything. And I don't have any idea what's making him sad. Plus, I'm so tired. So very, very tired.

I think I'll go to sleep now.

Beep . . . beep . . . beep . . .

Beep . . .

I FEEL LIKE I'M SWIMMING IN A SEA OF GLITTER.

I open my eyes and see the monitors, tubes, and cords attached to various places on my body. Shock ripples through me. *Where the hell am I?*

"You're in the hospital, sweetie." An unfamiliar voice scares me half to death. "Just relax. Everything's going to be okay."

I jerk to the right but immediately regret it as pain radiates through my skull.

A woman is standing beside the bed that I'm lying in, holding a clipboard. She's wearing scrubs with penguins on them, her auburn hair is pulled into a tight bun, and a stethoscope hangs around her neck.

"You need to take it easy," she says, setting the clipboard down.

"Who are you?" I croak, my throat feeling as dry as sandpaper.

"I'm your nurse. My name is Marcia." She points to the nametag pinned to her shirt. "I've been taking care of you for over a week."

My eyes snap wide, and the heart monitor beeps wildly. "For over a *week*?"

She nods, studying the monitor. "Sweetie, you need to relax. Your body's been through a lot."

My body? Been through a lot?

I throw the blanket off my body, but the movement yanks the IV in the back of my hand. I cry out but, determined to see the damage, use my other hand to lift off the blanket. My knee and thigh are wrapped in a bandage, and my leg is elevated, but my toes and everything else appear intact.

"Thank god." My hand falls to my stomach, and I relax against the pillow. "For a moment there I thought I was missing a leg or something."

Marcia smiles rigidly. "No, everything's still there. You did have to have surgery, though."

"But I'm going to be okay, right?"

Her smile dwindles. "I think I'm going to go call your brother and tell him you're awake. The sweetheart's been here day and night waiting for you to fully wake up." Her shoes squeak against the floor as she heads for the door, and she forces a high-pitched laugh. "Figures the moment he left, you finally decide to wake up."

"My brother? What about my—"

She hurries out of the room before I can finish, leaving me alone with monitors and cords and a ton of questions. I try to recollect the last thing I can remember. My birthday. *Glitter rainstorms.* The car ride to the store. *Real rainstorms.* My mom lying to me. My dad looking so happy to be in the world. *Deadly rainstorms . . .*

A lump forms in my throat, my pulse accelerates, and the monitor announces my panic. Panic that's painful. Hot. Sweltering.

"I can't breathe," I gasp, clasping the base of my neck. "I can't . . ." My vision spots as the room crumbles and fades.

I hear the thudding of footsteps. Someone mutters something about a sedative. Cold liquid spills into my veins and submerses the panic inside.

Life feels like a dream.

I kind of wish it were.

When I open my eyes again, my head feels groggy and my eyes are droopy. But the panic has dissipated, and I calm down even more when my brother's face appears above me.

Loki's here. Everything's going to be okay.

This is all a dream I'm going to wake up from.

"Thank god, you're awake." He lowers his head into his hands, and his shoulders tremble.

I think he's crying, but that can't be right. Loki doesn't cry. Loki, the philosopher who once said that crying was a pointless emotion people use when they're lost.

Is that why he's crying?

Is he lost?

"It's going to be okay." My voice sounds faraway, like an echo.

I reach out to him and put my hand on his shoulder.

He trembles even more.

The monitor beeps numerous times before he sucks in a breath, mutters something about sucking it up, then wipes his eyes with his hand and lifts his head back up. He looks like hasn't slept in days, making him appear older than his twenty-one years.

He takes my hand in his. "How are you feeling?"

Such a simple question, but it throws me off.

"Good . . . but where is everyone?"

A strangled sound gets caught in his throat. "Zhara, Alexis, and Nik are at home with Jessamine.

"Oh, good . . . She made it here." I skim the white walls and ceiling, trying to piece together what happened. "But why am I here?" I nod downward at the foot of the bed. "And what happened to my leg?"

"You don't remember what happened?" He rubs his red, puffy eyes with his free hand.

"I remember there was an accident. And the nurse said I had to have surgery on my leg, but she never explained why. She also said I've been out for, like, over a week, which just seems crazy. I mean, it's just a leg injury, right? How the hell does that knock someone out for over a week? And why the hell aren't Mom and Dad here . . . Wait, are they in the hospital, too?" An image of a mangled car briefly flashes through my mind. "Are they okay?"

"You weren't knocked out, Anna . . . They had to keep you heavily sedated for surgery and then again after you woke up because you . . ." He summons a deep breath, dragging his fingers down his face. "I don't even know how to tell you this."

His voice cracks, and my heart races. Loki frowns at the monitor then gives me the same look he wore when he had to tell me our dog had been run over.

Tears spill down my cheeks. "Just spit it out," I whisper. "Just say it!"

"I'm sorry, Anna. I'm so fucking sorry."

He never actually says the words aloud, but I figure out what happened on my own. I think I might have known the moment I heard the semi truck hit our car, but my head was crammed with glitter and rainbows and unicorns, fairytales and illusions. I didn't want to believe what I saw and heard. That my parents could be dead.

"I don't even know what I'm going to do," Loki whispers. "I don't think I can do this."

"Do what?" My voice is hollow, empty.

"This . . . take care of Nikoli, Zhara, Alexis, you . . ." He slips his fingers from mine as his head falls forward.

"Why would you have to take care of us?"

"Because," he says, his voice cracking, "there's no one else but me."

There's no one else?

No one.

Else?

Reality is brutal. Mean. Harsh. The reality is my parents are gone. I never got to tell my mom about Ben. I'll never get to tell her about another boy again. I'll never get to pick out outfits with her or hang out with my dad at his store, listening to old rock songs and chatting about books. The last memory I'll ever have is my mom lying to me. The last time I ever looked my dad in the eyes was when I withheld the truth from him—when I betrayed him.

There's no one else.

No more glitter rainstorms. No more burnt breakfasts. No Fourth of July picnics or crazy birthday trips. No catching imaginary fireflies.

I want to scream. Cry and yell until there's nothing left inside me. Get out all the anger and guilt that I can feel rotting inside me.

This can't be real.

It just can't.

Instead of screaming, my lips remain sealed, and the pain, guilt, and anger remains stuck inside me.

THREE

THE PROMISE OF RAIN

SIX MONTHS LATER...

"Anna, open the damn door!" Nikoli hollers, banging on the bathroom door. "I'm going to be late for practice!"

I crank up the volume of my iPod so the lyrics of Rise Against suffocate his hounding. Definitely not dancing music, which makes the song that much more perfect.

Leaning over the sink, I check my reflection in the mirror. My eyes are heavily framed with liner, but I need more to cover up who I used to be. I pop the cap off and trace the pencil around my eyes a few more times. Satisfied, I move on to the lipstick—dark purple to match the streaks in my hair. Then I slip on a leather jacket and sit down on the closed toilet seat to lace up my combat boots. The car accident left me with a shitty knee scarred from surgery and a thigh with muscle deterioration thanks to a smashed artery and a blood clot. I don't dance, and I can't walk without a limp, something the doctors and therapist say is probably permanent.

I was lucky, though, or so everyone says. Lucky to walk

away from such an accident with only minor injuries. Lucky. Lucky. Lucky. Sometimes it feels like my entire body is a scar that will never heal.

Shifting my weight, I clutch onto the edge of the counter and hoist myself to my feet.

"What the hell is wrong with you?" Nikoli snaps when I open the door and hobble past him.

I trip over a lip in the flooring and brace my hands on the wall to stop myself from falling on my face. I grind my teeth in frustration. God, I hate this.

"I've been knocking for, like, ten minutes," Nikoli whines. "I'm going to be late now."

"Good for you," I snap, squeezing my eyes shut.

After a night of partying, I'm too drained to hash anything out with anyone. My head feels like it's been drilled into, and my stomach is temperamental, every movement making it churn. I'm hungover, worn out, and in so much physical pain that I can barely focus on anything else, including the grief, anger, and sadness inside me, which is exactly how I want to feel.

Pushing away from the wall, I limp down the hall toward the stairway.

Nikoli yells after me. "Nice outfit! Halloween was two months ago!? You're seriously getting creepier by the day!"

He's right. In all black clothes, except for a neon pink belt, I stand out like a cloud in a sky covered in rainbows. But that's okay. Rainbows suck. Lie. Disappear when you really need them.

I flip him the middle finger from over my shoulder then begin the excruciating journey downstairs. By the time I make it to the kitchen, I'm panting, my leg is throbbing, and my brain is pounding from all the memories hiding in every nook and cranny of the house, reminding me of what was and what will never be.

We received enough insurance money from the accident to pay off the house, and Loki decided to keep it because he thought it would help us all cope better. Same house, same lives, right? Despite that the walls, floors, doors, and counters all look the same, everything feels different. Colder. Emptier. Hollow, like an empty grave.

Zhara and Alexis are lounging at the table. Alexis, who used to be as cheery as me, is now the biggest downer I know. She never smiles. Never says anything positive. The girl who loved expressing her happiness through art has died.

Zhara decided to go the opposite route, to the point where you can't even tell they're twins anymore. She's upbeat all the time, like sunshine on crack. She's always been a little extreme on the positivity, but she's even more intense now. I think she believes she's supposed to take on the role of our mother or something. She looks a lot like my mom, too, with her brown curls and cat-shaped eyes. Sometimes it's hard to look at her.

"You look like shit," Alexis says to me. "No. I take that back. You look like someone who had way too much fun last night."

"I look like I always do." I get a few painkillers from the cupboard to take for my hangover and leg.

Zhara glances up at me with a cheerful smile plastered across her face. "Are you feeling any better than you did last night?

"I'm fine," I mumble.

"Anna, you're not fine. Your screaming woke me up

again. I think your nightmares are happening more often . . . Maybe you should tell Loki about them."

"You need to chill out and stop worrying about me." I swallow the pills then rest against the counter, waiting for them to kick in.

"Oh, all right then." She fights to keep the smile on her face. "Did I tell you Jessamine called last night and said she's coming home this summer? Isn't that exciting? An entire summer with all of us together. It'll almost be like old times."

I turn my back to her so I don't have to watch her pretend she's okay when she's not. "No, it won't."

Even when Jessamine is here, the life we knew no longer exists. So she might as well stay off at college where she doesn't have to be around the fighting and stress and complete and utter chaos our lives have turned into.

"I don't know why she's coming back," Alexis mutters. "She chose to leave us."

"She didn't choose to leave us," Zhara insists. "She just didn't want to drop out of school. You can't blame her for that."

I don't dare turn around, knowing they're going to be at it for a while.

"I'm not blaming her for anything. You're just freaking out." Alexis rolls her eyes then violently flips the page of the book she's reading. "Have you been snorting crack again or something?"

"Hey, I don't do drugs," Zhara gripes, slumping back in the chair. "God, I can't even be nice without you insulting me."

"Maybe you should stop being nice then," Alexis

suggests, flipping her hair off her shoulder and smirking. "There. Problem solved."

They start arguing. Alexis says something mean, and Zhara bursts into tears and runs out of the room.

"Good riddance," Alexis mutters under her breath then redirects her attention back to the book in front of her.

I should probably tell her to be nice. It's kind of depressing to see them this way when they used to be so close, but I don't—can't—find the will to care anymore. Just like I don't care enough to bother waking Loki up even though he'll be late opening the store if I don't. Waking him up means talking to him, and if I had my way, I'd be a ghost in this family, dead with my parents where I sometimes feel I belong.

After grabbing a granola bar from the pantry, I leave the house without making a sound.

It's a late Saturday morning. The cool December breeze nips at my skin, and the cloudy sky above me makes silent promises of rain. I'm supposed to be going to physical therapy to help regain more mobility in my knee, but I'm not feeling it, just like I wasn't last weekend. It doesn't really matter if I go. Yeah, maybe I'll be able to walk better, but because of the injures to my thigh that deteriorated my muscles, I'll never be able to dance again, at least not like I used to, and therapy reminds me that my dancing, ballerina, dreamer life is over.

I trudge down the driveway, noting a large yellow moving truck parked next door. I'm curious what kind of people they're going to be. If they have kids. If it's a family.

A woman in her mid forties wearing a hot pink dress and a leather jacket suddenly appears at the back of the moving truck. Her outfit reminds me a lot of my mom, and I momentarily feel angry as a web of memories spin around me. She lied to me and made me lie for her and part of me hates her for that, which only makes me hate myself even more. She's dead. I shouldn't hate her—shouldn't be angry with her—yet I am.

The woman jogs down the ramp with a box in her hand and a huge nice-to-meet-you smile on her face. "Hi there," she says. She sets down the box and rounds the chain link fence.

I contemplate bolting back to my house, but not wanting to go back inside there either, I pick up the pace and make a beeline for the sidewalk.

She blindsides me at the end of the driveway and sticks out her hand. "I'm Tammy Benton, your new neighbor."

Begrudgingly, I shake her hand.

"And you are?" she asks as I pull away.

"Annabella," I reply dryly, hoping she'll take the hint to leave me alone. I'm not in the mood to talk, never am.

"Annabella. What a pretty name," she says thoughtfully. She stands on her toes, waving at someone over by the moving truck. "Luca, come meet our new neighbor. She looks about your age," she looks back at me, "seventeen . . . or eighteen?"

I almost say twenty-one so she won't try to force her son to be my friend. But she reminds me so much of my mom that I get a little lost in the moment and end up uttering the truth for the first time in months. "Seventeen."

"What a crazy coincidence. Luca's seventeen, too." She seems so elated about the fact that I have to question if maybe she's blind, since, right now, I look like the kind of girl mothers definitely don't want around their sons.

Luca walks toward us with his hands stuffed in his pockets. He's tall and lean with softly tousled brown hair. He's rocking a plaid shirt and jeans with square framed glasses. He's cute, sure. Completely crush worthy for someone normal. And I'm sure my parents would approve of him, that is, if they were here.

I clear my throat at the painful reminder, ignoring the way my chest constricts.

"Luca, this is Annabella," Tammy says. "Our new neighbor."

When he gets a good look at me, shock flashes across Luca's face, but I tend to have that effect on people. But the look promptly erases, and he offers me a lopsided smile and a tentative wave. "It's nice to meet you."

I force a grin that's as fake as my dyed hair. "Sure."

"So, you're a junior at Honeyton High?" he asks, crossing his arms, seeming the slightest bit nervous.

Even with the painkiller I took, my leg is still killing me, and I have to readjust my weight. "Yep."

"That's cool. I've heard it was a small school," he says. "Like, maybe five hundred people, which seems crazy to me considering the school I used to go to had triple that."

"*Triple?*" I ask, taken aback. "Where the fuck did you move here from?"

Tammy winces at the f-bomb.

There you go. You can see me now. See me for who I really am.

But her wince hastily shifts to a smile again.

Seriously, what is she on? Or maybe one of the neighbors has warned her about me. Told her my family's sob story.

"We moved here from LA," Luca explains, sliding his finger up the bridge of his nose to position his glasses back into place.

"Oh . . . okay, I get why you think Honeyton is small then." I tuck a few strands of hair behind my ear and steal a peek at the corner of the street, calculating how long it would take me to get there if—when—I decide to flee from this conversation.

"Your hair's cool." He extends his fingers toward my head and pinches a strand, totally invading my personal space and sending my heart into a fitful frenzy. "It kind of reminds me of grape Skittles."

I tell my heart to chill the hell out, that I'm not that silly girl who gets giddy over guys anymore. Then I drop my head and the strand falls from his fingers. "No, it doesn't."

"I don't mean that in a bad way," he adds hastily. "In fact, the grape ones are my favorite."

"Grape isn't anyone's favorite, no matter what kind of candy you're eating." Ready to get the hell away from them, I open my mouth to tell them bye.

"I have an idea." Tammy's eyes light up as she turns toward Luca. "Maybe Annabella could show you around town. You said you wanted to have an adventure and go exploring."

"I didn't say exploring or adventure." His cheeks redden. "I just said it'd be nice to walk about and see what's around." He smiles at me, as if waiting for me to agree to go *exploring* on an *adventure*.

"Maybe . . . if I have time." I won't make any promises I

can't keep, and I know I won't be doing anything with Luca because he seems too nice, and nice isn't what I need anymore, what I deserve.

"Oh, okay . . . Well, hopefully you can find the time." She fiddles with a silver hooped earring in her ear, growing fidgety. "It'd be really great if Luca had someone to hang with."

I search for an out while Luca stares at me, his eyes roving all over my body, unsubtly checking me out. I loathe that he's noticing me and I despise how much I like the attention.

"Are your parents around? I'd love to meet them." Tammy looks at my two-story home that resembles every other house on the street

There goes my theory of her already knowing my family's history.

My lips part to tell her my parents are dead, to just throw it out there and watch her squirm. But the words get lodged in my throat along with a thousand emotions I refuse to let out.

I limp away without saying a word. Someone else can tell her.

I feel their eyes on me as I hobble down the sidewalk. At the end of the street, I veer to the right toward the bus stop. By the time I make it to the bench, my knee is sore and my phone has rang at least ten times.

I wait for the bus, letting the phone ring about ten more times before answering it.

"Where the hell are you?" Loki fumes before I can even get out a hello.

"Going to physical therapy like I'm supposed to," I lie, slumping back on the bench.

"And how the hell are you getting there?" he seethes. "You can't drive. Not with that leg. You know that."

"I'm not stupid. I'm taking the bus."

"You're not supposed to be walking around like that. You're going to fuck up your leg even more."

"I just thought I'd take the bus since you're going to be late opening the store."

He fires off a sequence of curses. "Dammit, I forgot about the store."

Loki forgets about the store a lot. Between taking online college classes, paying the bills, and keeping an eye on the four of us, he's losing his mind and is completely unlike the Loki before the accident. We've all changed. Me, the rainbow turned raincloud. Alexis, the thunder grumbling at everyone. Zhara, the sunshine refusing to fade despite all the rain. Nikoli, the lightning shouting out at everyone. Jessamine, the distant wind. And Loki, the rain struggling to wash all our pain away.

"Why don't you just sell it, then?" I ungracefully stagger to my feet as the bus rolls up to the curb.

"You're joking, right?" he asks. "Please, please tell me you're joking."

"Why would I joke about that?" The bus doors swing open, and I struggle to get up the stairs. "It's just a store, and it's stressing you out." It's not just a store, though. It's my father's store that reminds me of the last time I saw him, looked him in the eyes, and lied to his face.

Swiping my bus card more violently than necessary, I limp down the aisle to the back, noting everyone's stares.

Who are they staring at, though? The girl with purple hair wearing too much makeup? Or the girl with a limp? Which one is it? Who do they see? Because I have no idea anymore.

"Will I ever dance again?" I ask the doctor with false hope in his eyes.

He looks at me with pity. "Let's just worry about getting you walking properly again, okay?"

"It's *Dad's* store." Loki's stressed voice shatters apart the memory of the day my dreams of dancing professionally vanished. "And he left it to me."

"He also left us to you, which seems like more of a burden than anything." I sink into a seat at the back and pinch the bridge of my nose.

"Don't say that." His voice cracks like glass. "You guys aren't a burden."

He's lying. Having four teenagers, one fourteen-year-old, two sixteen year-olds, and one seventeen-year-old would be a burden to most people.

I'm not exactly sure why my parents left guardianship to Loki, other than maybe they weren't expecting to die so soon. We don't have any living family other than my mom's sister, who lives in California and smokes a lot of pot. They both had friends, though, that were more equipped to raising four teenagers.

After the funeral, Loki said something about a note with the will that stated the reasons why my parents wanted him to raise us. He wouldn't let anyone read it. Not even Jessamine, who he used to be close to before the accident. Said it was solely for him.

"I think you should come home now. I can take you to

therapy and then go to the store. I don't like you walking around more than you have to. Plus, you're on probation."

"Yeah, that doesn't matter."

"You can't seriously believe it doesn't matter?" He leaves the statement hanging in the air, but I don't utter a damn word—can't—since I have no idea what I believe anymore. "Anna, you've been arrested twice in the last four months. And the police have brought you home two other times on top of that. You sneak out of the house, go to parties, steal, and those friends you hang out with are bringing you down. You skip out on school, and you're barely passing your classes. You won't go to your therapy sessions, and your leg's never going to get better if you keep it up . . . Don't you want to dance again?"

Dance? I'll never dance again. "I'll never dance again. You know that."

Silence stretches between us, and it's painful, aching, just like the scars on my leg and the hole in my heart put there the day my parents died—the day my life changed.

I'm just about to hang up when he says, "I really think we should start looking for a therapist, someone you can talk to since you won't talk to me."

"I don't need your help, or anyone else's." My knee literally twitches as the scars burn from underneath my pant leg. "I just need to be left alone."

"They're going to take you away from me if you keep it up," he says in a desperate attempt to get me to clean up my act. "You know they can do that, right?"

I smash my lips together, battling back the guilt and tears that cram their way up my throat. "Maybe it'd be better if they did."

"You don't mean that," he whispers. "I know you don't. You care about this family too much. You're just going through some stuff . . . because of the accident."

Maybe my brother and sisters don't deserve that, but I do —I deserve worse for lying to my dad, the man who was always there for me, who read me books, who took me on fishing trips, who was at every recital.

"I already got on the bus so you can't drive me to my appointment," I say, steadying my voice. "I'll call you when I get out of it, though."

"Don't hang up on me. I'm not done talking yet." He aims to sound firm, but he's only four years older than me, and I have a hard time taking him seriously. "I don't want you going off anywhere by yourself. We had a deal that you were going to stay away from your friends for a little while. Especially Miller."

Miller's the guy dads warn their daughters about, and even though Loki isn't my dad, he tries to take on the role. He hates Miller. Probably because he's been arrested many times, mostly for breaking and entering and drug possession. Or maybe it's because he doesn't have a job, likes to party, and has numerous tattoos and piercings.

Which are all the reasons why I like spending time with him.

"I'm not going to see my friends." Technically not a lie since I haven't decided where I'm going yet. I usually just wander around until I end up somewhere, because I can't figure out where to go or what to do with myself.

"You know, Cece came into the store the other day to pick up some books. She asked about you. Said she misses spending time with you. Your dance instructor even stopped by and said you could go hang out at the studio anytime you want. There's a ton of other stuff for you to do, Anna, other than get into trouble."

"I don't want to talk to Cece and the last thing I ever want to do is hang out at that studio." Just thinking about it makes my eyes water up. I suck in a deep breath. *I won't cry. I can't. Once I do, I won't be able to stop.* "You keep saying all these things to me, trying to get me to want stuff again. But all that stuff . . . Cece . . . dancing . . . that's not who I am anymore."

"It's okay to miss things, Anna." His voice softens. "And I get that you're not the same person, but you can still be happy—"

Alexis suddenly yells something in the background.

"What the hell was that!?" Loki shouts at her.

I hear Alexis blame Zhara for eating all her favorite cereal. Since the two of them could go on forever, and Loki always gets sucked into their fights, I hang up without saying goodbye. I sit back in the seat and stretch out my legs as the bus bumps down the road. My phone rings again, but not wanting another lecture from Loki, I don't answer. Everything he insists on reminding me, I already know, and hearing it over again isn't going to change my life. At the end of the day, I'll still be crippled with absolutely no idea what to do with my life. Or if I even want to do anything with my life. Maybe I'll just lay down next to my father's grave and stay there until my body gives up on me.

When my phone finally stops ringing, I decide I've been on the bus for too long and get off at the next stop. I should've paid more attention to where I was getting off, though, because I end up near the town cemetery.

It's not like I haven't visited my parents' graves since the funeral—Loki makes us go every other Sunday to take flowers—but without my brothers and sisters around, the silence in the area is maddening.

Their graves are side-by-side out by the farthest oak tree, and their headstones are engraved with "everlasting love." Every time I visit, it feels like I'm visiting a lie, where I thought my parents were happy, that my mother wasn't a liar —that I wasn't a liar. But that life was nothing more than an illusion, just like Alexis when she used to be a nice person. Or like Zhara, the now turned human robot who used to feel something other than overly fake happiness and positivity. Or like Loki, the philosopher turned parent. And Nikoli who barely talks anymore. Which parts of them were real and which parts were hiding under a mask?

After the bus drives away, I cross the street as quickly as my leg will allow me to, wanting to get as far away from away the iron gates as I can. I head north in the direction of the Victorian house. I don't know why, but I sometimes stand at the end of the dirt road that leads to the antique store. Rain, sunshine, cold, warm, I'll stay there for hours, just staring at the house. Occasionally, I deliberate whether or not I should march up to his door and knock, demand he tell me why my mom was there that day. But I can't march, can barely walk, and I'm honestly not sure I actually want to hear the truth.

Today, I grow tired fast. Five blocks later, I'm out of breath and exhausted. Making it to the Victorian house is impossible, so I take a break, leaning against the side of an apartment building. Minutes later, the cloudy sky fulfills its promise and starts to rain down on the world. The past crashes down on my shoulders—of dancing, birthdays, rain-storms, car crashes, and secrets. I don't want to feel any of it. The water. The pain. The loneliness. The confusion of my place in life and how nothing makes sense anymore.

I turn and head the opposite direction of the Victorian house and toward Miller's apartment. By the time I make it to the rundown two-story brick complex, my clothes are soaked, my hair is drenched, and my leg is so unsteady I can barely keep my foot underneath me.

I knock on his door a few times before walking in. Music is blasting and the stench of cigarette smoke and alcohol hits my nostrils. Crumpled beer cans are piled on the cracked coffee table along with an ashtray overflowing with cigarette butts and a mirror dusted with fragments of white powder. When I first met Miller, he wasn't into the heavier drugs, but about a month ago, he started experimenting with stuff stronger than pot.

"Hey." Miller grins at me from the small, dank living room.

He's playing a video game with one of his friends, who everyone calls Big Jay, and leans over the armrest to turn down the volume of the stereo. The singer, who had been screaming lyrics, silences. Part of me wishes Miller would turn it back up, let the screaming drown out my thoughts for a while.

Instead, he puts out his cigarette in the ashtray with his brows furrowed. "Why are you wet?"

I hitch a finger over my shoulder at the door. "It's raining outside."

His eyes sweep across my body, and his attention makes me feel numbly calm. "It's a good look for you," he says with a smirk as he sets the controller down on the frayed armrest. "You should rock it all the time."

"You think?" I pretend to be bored, pretend I fit in here.

"Definitely." His grin broadens as he gets to his feet.

Miller is tall and kind of gangly with spiky blue and black hair. He looks older, but he's only about a year and half a year older than me. I met him in a mall of all places, a little over a month after my parents' funeral. I was with Cece on one of the last shopping trips we ever made, using crutches that hurt my armpits. The entire three hours we spent there were awkward and exhausting. She kept talking about school, music, dancing, cheerleading, and Ben. She was stuck in the past, while I had been thrown into the future. Nothing made sense anymore, not even our friendship.

I ended up shoplifting a box of purple hair dye while I was listening to Cece drone on and on about how prom was coming up, and how she didn't know how on earth she was ever going to get a dress. Then she moved on to dancing and how I should really come with her and hang out at the studio, that everyone missed seeing me around.

I just wanted to feel again, something other than heartache, pain, loss, so while she was yammering on and on about her life, I snuck a box of purple hair dye in my jacket, thinking maybe I'd dye my hair. Perhaps it would go well with the new scars on my leg and help me get some sort of footing in this hellish life I felt like I was dying in.

Just stealing the box sent my adrenaline soaring. I'd never stolen anything ever—never wanted to. Rebellion had never been my thing, but maybe it could be.

Of course, the moment I got away with it, the excitement over stealing fizzled out, and I just felt guilty and lost again. Then Miller had strolled up to me, all pierced out and tattooed with his crazy blue hair, completely different from the guys I used to like.

Dangerous, I thought. *And nothing like Ben. Maybe this is what I need now.*

"A good girl like you could get a guy like me into a lot of trouble," was his lame pick up line.

"Oh, my god, does that ever work on anyone," Cece replied, staring him down with disgust.

I glanced back and forth from Cece to him. Known to unknown, past to . . . Well, I was still trying to figure out what lay ahead. "Maybe you're already in trouble." I have no idea where the courage came from. It was really unlike me, and maybe that was the point. I didn't know who I was anymore without my parents, the idolization of my mother, and without the dancer that used to breathe life inside me.

I had to be someone, though, and I could be anyone, even daring, bold, and blunt.

After my out of character move, Miller asked me to hang out with him, and against Cece's protest, I agreed. We snuck into see a movie then wandered around the streets, talking about nothing that had to do with my old life. For a moment, I felt alive again. Then he gave my first kiss, and I wondered if he could taste the guilt, anger, and confusion rotting inside me, because I sure as hell could.

"That was nice," he said when he pulled away.

I nodded, but it wasn't nice. It just . . . *was.* Like everything else. And I felt a twinge of sadness that I didn't get my first kiss with Ben on the night of my birthday party. But as quick as the thought came, I smothered it, knowing it was pointless to dream of anything. When I got home, I dyed my hair with the box of purple dye I stole.

"Come on, let's go to my room." Miller interrupts my thoughts, nodding toward the hallway.

His friend snickers, and Miller smacks him upside the head, laughing, then turns to me. "Your leg feeling okay?"

I gently place my palm on my thigh. "Yeah, I've just been walking on it too much."

"I still can't believe a horse fucked up your leg that much," he says, kicking clothes that litter the hallway out of the way. "That fall must have been killer wicked."

"Yep, hurt like a bitch." Not wanting to talk about my leg anymore, I crash my lips to his.

"What was that for?" he asks when I step back.

I nonchalantly shrug, being the cool version of myself. The one that doesn't give a shit about anything. "Does it really matter?"

Does anything really matter anymore?

He considers what I said with his head slanted to the side. "You're always so mysterious." A slow grin spreads across his face. "I like it."

Mysterious Annabella?

No more Open Book Annabella. No Sunshine-in-the-Rain or Chasing-Rainbows-and-Dreaming-of Glittery-Days Annabella. Is that who I've become now?

Dodging the dirty clothes, shoes, and empty bottles on the floor, I gingerly make my way to his bed while he rummages in his dresser for something. I flop down on the lumpy mattress, adjust my leg, but roll to my side when I feel something lumpy beneath me—Miller's favorite pipe. I set it on the floor then lie back down on the bed.

"So, what do you want to do tonight?" he asks, closing the dresser drawer.

"Anything that doesn't require being at home." I spread out my arms and stare up at the water-stained ceiling.

He chuckles as he scoots onto the bed beside me. "You better be careful giving me full rein to do whatever the hell I want." He leans in to kiss me, and I trap the air in my chest, mentally preparing myself for the numbness. "We could finally, you know, take this to the next level."

As deep as I am into this lie, I still haven't worked up enough courage to lose my virginity to him. "I told you I had a five month dating minimum before we did that."

"But it's been five months," he gripes. "Come on. I've been super patient."

"Fine," I agree, even though it makes me feel sick to my stomach. He grins, his gaze zeroing in on my lips. He leans in, but I place my hand over his mouth, stopping him. "Not right now, though . . . Later tonight."

He searches my eyes for a sign I'm lying, but I've become such a good liar that even I can't tell if I am or not.

When I lower my hand, he seals his mouth to mine.

Our kisses aren't magical, but I'm starting to believe kisses aren't supposed to be. They're just lips and move-ments, promising lies that mean nothing.

After several minutes of him kissing and rubbing his hips against me, Miller pulls his hand out of my shirt, looking high from the kiss. Knowing Miller, he might just be high. "You seem tense today. What's up?"

"I seem the same as I do every day." I stare past him, focusing on a jagged crack in the wall. Every time I look at it, it seems to have grown. One day, I swear the entire wall is going to crumble.

"No, it's something else . . . You seem out of it." He states it like he knows so much about me. But how could he when even I don't know anything about myself?

His endeavor to delve into my psyche makes me regret coming here. Miller is good for one thing—taking a break from being the Anna everyone scrutinizes and constantly worries about.

I push up on my elbows. "Maybe I should go."

He splays his fingers across my chest, pinning me down. "Don't get pissy. I was just pointing out you seem out of it." He squints at my face. "You aren't high, are ya?"

"No, I'm just . . ." I sigh. "Look, I don't want to talk about me, okay? I've had a shitty day, and I just want to relax and hang out like we usually do."

"Relax, huh? I think I might have something for that." He jumps off the bed and strides out of the room. When he returns, he has plastic cup in one hand and a small plastic bag in the other. "Pick a hand," he says, even though I can see what's in both. He's giving me a choice: temporarily escape reality and be left feeling tired and achy or plummet into an unknown world that I might never find my way out of. How fast and far do I want to fall? How hard do I want to crash?

I want to fall hard.

I want to fall fast.

I want to crash and burn and never feel anything ever again.

Past the pills I take sometimes to kill the pain inside. Past the alcohol. Past the scars I always have to carry with me.

But the faint memory of Dancing-Dreaming-Good-Girl Annabella clutches onto the ledge.

"I'll take the cup," I say, trying to figure out what my choice means. Am I good? Bad? What?

He seems mildly disappointed but still hands me the cup. "This'll take the edge off a little."

I inspect the brownish liquid that smells like gasoline. "What's in it? Just whiskey, right?"

"Just drink up and find out." He kicks the door shut and climbs back onto the bed, tossing the plastic bag on the mattress beside him. "I promise it'll blow your mind."

My parents' words of wisdom race through my head. *Don't do drugs. Don't drink. Don't give into peer pressure. You're such a good girl, Annabella.*

"You're wrong. I don't know who I am anymore," I say aloud to myself. Miller gives me a confused look, but I raise the rim of the glass to my lips. *This is why I come here. This is what I need.* "Goodbye, Anna. Goodbye, rainstorm."

FOUR
AS DESTRUCTIVE AS THE RAIN

After I down half the cup, Miller finishes the rest off, does a line, then goes to get a refill. As the alcohol flows through my veins, I sink onto the mattress and drift from reality. Not too much later, Miller joins me, and we lay side-by-side, floating in and out of meaningless conversation.

I can't see straight. Can hardly think. My body is so numb that I can't even feel my messed up leg.

"See, much better, right?" Miller asks as he stares up at the ceiling with his arm draped across his head.

"Yes . . . much . . ." *Is it really, though? Am I lying to myself?*

My phone rings, but I don't—can't—move to answer it.

"Good." Miller smiles lazily as he rolls on his side and props up on his elbow.

Minutes, maybe hours, pass before the effects of what-ever I drank begin to wear off. I become restless again. Start thinking too much. Regret drinking. Being here. Choosing to be this person. I don't like the feeling at all. Don't like that the old me still resides somewhere beneath the purple hair and goth clothing, the one who wants to dance, be good—the one who should have just died in the car accident. For once, I just want to forget who I was, who I've become, the anger I feel toward my mother, the guilt I feel for feeling the anger. The guilt I feel for not telling my dad. That's what I came here to do.

"Want to do something?" Miller asks, playing with the hem of my shirt.

I know what he wants from me, but I still can't seem to give it to him.

I bob my head up and down. "Yeah, let's go somewhere . . . Do something . . . Live a little . . ."

"But it's raining outside."

"So what?" I sit up and rub my eyes. "A little rain never hurt anyone."

Liar. Rain can do a lot of damage.

Miller unenthusiastically looks at the window. "Actually, if you're down for a little adventure, I might know of something we could do. You'd have to be up for anything, though. And I mean anything, Anna. None of that girly bullshit where you back out when things get sketchy. "

I've spent enough time with Miller to understand what the look in his eyes means. He wants to get into trouble, walk the line of danger. The old Anna, the good girl her parents raised, the one who worshipped her mother, would've run away.

Lightning zaps across the sky, thunder grumbles, and the rain suddenly picks up, as thick as the day of the accident. The day seemed so sunny, everything so crystal clear, until the rain came and washed that life away in an instant.

"Let's go then." Lightheaded and dizzy, I stagger to my feet.

Miller places a hand on my arm to steady me. "Wait. Don't you want to hear what we're doing?"

I weave around the dirty clothes on the floor. "I really don't care." All I know is that I want the fading numbness to return to my body, and I'll do just about anything to get it back.

He grins as he tosses me a hoodie. "All right. I like this side of you. Dangerous Anna," he ponders as he taps his finger against his lips. "It has a nice ring to it.

"It does?" I lean against the doorframe while I put the jacket on.

"Yeah, sure." He grins, meeting my gaze. "Let's go."

On our way out, Miller grabs his car keys from the coffee table and tells Big Jay we'll be back later. He offers me the rest of his drink before we head out, and even though I already feel woozy, I guzzle it down.

Outside, rain puddles the pavement, the sky is darker than it was when I walked here, and the temperature has plummeted. I draw my hoodie up and move as quickly as I can toward Miller's truck that has more rust than paint. He jogs ahead of me, his boots splashing through the puddles, and opens the door.

I heave myself inside, close the door, then watch the rain stream down the windshield. Memories surface—the sound of metal crushing, my parents' screams, my dad looking at me as if waiting for me to tell him the truth. My gut clenches. *I should have just told him.*

"You ready for this?" Miller asks as he slams the door.

I jerk from the memories, craving whatever escape lies ahead. "Yep. I'm ready for anything."

Miller chats on his phone with one of his buddies for half the drive, and I only pick up on fragments of his conversation. He keeps mentioning a house on Fairfield Lane, a street on the richer, more lavish side of town.

"So, you know the other day when Big Jay and I were talking about trying to find a way to get some extra cash," Miller says after he hangs up. "You remember Jeremy, right?" he asks, and I nod, even though I don't. "He found out about this house on Fairfield that's been vacant for, like, a month."

"So no one lives there?"

"No, someone lives there. They've just been gone for a month. And they don't even have an alarm system." He snickers. "What a bunch of stupid fucks. Seriously."

I scrape at my black fingernail polish, pretending to be more blasé that I really am. "Are you planning to break in or something?"

He flashes me a devious grin. "That's exactly what I plan on doing."

Even though I don't like that I do, I start to grow worried. I don't know how he got the information, but I do know is that Miller is currently on probation for breaking and entering.

Is that what's going to end up happening to me? Do I care? What do I care about anymore? I vibrate with anger. How am I supposed to be the Dangerous Annabella I'm pretending to be with all these thoughts in my head?

Shoving the thoughts from my head, I look out the window as Miller makes a turn down Fairfield Lane.

Extravagant two and three story homes border the quiet street lined with cherry blossom trees, and the grey sky casts shadows across the perfectly landscaped yards. The scene is almost too perfect. Like I know all too well, though, nothing is perfect, and I quickly spot the flaw—the murky streams flowing through the gutters.

I glance up at the cloudy sky as uneasiness seeps into my bones. "It's not even dark yet. People might see us."

"It'll look more suspicious if we show up at night," he replies as he turns into a paved driveway that leads to a brick mansion.

He parks in front of the garage and shuts off the engine. The rain has turned the yard and sidewalks into a giant puddle, completely ruining everything in its path.

Maybe that's where I'm headed. Perhaps I'm becoming as destructive as the rain, ruining my life, my family's life.

"Your truck kind of stands out," I say, anxiously glancing at all the expensive cars parked in the nearby driveways.

"As long as we pretend like we belong here, we'll be fine. Besides, it's raining so goddamn hard, you can barely see." He rotates in the seat, raking his fingers through his blue hair. "You don't have to do this if you don't want to. I know you said you were up for anything, but you always say that, and sometimes I can tell you don't really mean it."

His words piss me off. I don't like that he's right. That he can see that side of me. See the good girl I used to be.

I'm not her anymore! I can't be!

All riled up, I stretch my arm toward the door handle. Grinning, Miller hops out into the rain as the sky booms and the rain quickens. Ignoring my mother's voice inside my head, telling me this is wrong, I follow Miller up the driveway, staggering from left to right as the liquid concoction I drank earlier sloshes around in my brain.

Squeezing between the garage and the house, we sneak around to the back door. Miller jiggles the doorknob, but it's locked.

"Stand back," he says as he shucks off his jacket and wraps it around his fist.

I briefly contemplate running away, just disappearing into the rain. Push through the pain and run across the grass, keep going until my limbs ache and give out on me. But then Miller's fist slams through the window, and my chance at backing out shatters like the glass.

Shooting me an excited look from over his shoulder, he snakes his arm through the broken window, flips the lock, and pushes the door open. I hold my breath, waiting for an alarm to go off. When it doesn't, I'm disappointed, but fear backing out. If I backed out, what does that say about me? How would Miller see me? Would he still want to be with me? If I didn't have him to hang around with, then where would that leave me? With nowhere to escape to anymore.

We enter the house, stepping into a massive kitchen filled with stainless steel appliances and marble countertops. My head swirls with confusion as we wander into the home. I lose track of time the deeper we go, the alcohol I drank blurring my mind even more. I can't figure out who I am. How I got here. How to get out or if I even want to. It's not like I actually need to steal anything. Still, I pick up a crystal swan figurine off one of the shelves, stuff it into my pocket, then head through the foyer and up the winding staircase, like a lost little girl drifting through a meaningless life with no direction.

Hanging on the wall on the second floor is a large portrait of a family of four sitting on a beach, smiling in the sunshine. They all look so happy. There's a similar picture of my family back at my house. We appear happy. Do they realize life isn't all sunshine?

As some of the numbness evaporates from my body, anger ignites like thunder and lightning. Trembling with rage, I snatch the picture from the wall and chuck it as hard as I can at the bottom of the stairway. Glass shatters all over the marble floor like raindrops. I want to forget about all of it. The lies. The pain. The anger I always feel toward her. Why can't I just forget?

Miller runs back to the stairs, panting heavily and looking scared out of his damn mind. "What the hell was that?"

"A picture fell off the wall," I lie, gripping onto the banister as I battle to calm the fuck down.

Miller glances from me to the broken picture at bottom of the stairs and opens his mouth to say something. But the sound of sirens cuts him off.

"Shit. We have to go." He pushes by me, bumping me into the wall, and sprints down the stairway.

"I can't move that fast," I hiss in a panic, dragging my leg along with me like the useless limb it is.

By the time I've made it two steps down the stairway, he's already to the foyer.

He skids to a halt in front of the door, his gaze darting between the flashing lights out the window and me. "I'm sorry," he says in a panic, then takes off, leaving me to fend for myself.

I don't know why I'm surprised, but I am, as if I've

regressed back into that naïve girl who believed that pots of gold really are at the end of rainbows—that all people are good. That danced around her room and dreamt of kissing her crush at her birthday party.

Having no other choice, I pick up the pace, but by the time I make it to the bottom of the stairs, the front door swings opens.

With the wind howling behind him, an officer barrels inside with a gun in his hand and his eyes locked on me. "Put your hands up," he orders.

I do what he says and put my hands in the air. I wait to be cuffed, knowing I should be afraid—that that's how I'm supposed to feel. But with the alcohol still swimming in my veins, I can't feel the fear.

Can't feel anything at all.

FIVE

NO MORE TEARS

MILLER GOT CAUGHT, ANYWAY, AND WE BOTH END UP BEING hauled down the driveway by officers.

Hands cuffed behind his back and jeans covered in mud, he's forced toward one of the three police cars parked out front. Neighbors have gathered to watch the scene. I wonder if any of them know me, if they've ever seen me in town at holiday gatherings in the park.

"I'm so sorry, Anna. I just didn't know what to do," Miller pleads with me as an officer guides him into the backseat.

I concentrate on the raindrops streaming down the glass until the officer drives toward town. I know I'm in a ton of trouble, way more than I ever have been.

I spend the next two hours trying to figure out how I feel about what happened. I want to feel indifferent, but under the sea of numbness, I still care that I'm ruining what's left of my life and putting more stress on Loki. He's always been a great big brother and like my father, he doesn't deserve to

64

be treated like crap.

When Loki shows up at the police station to pick me up, he's wavering between disappointment and anger. He hardly says more than three words during the drive home and only acknowledges my existence when he parks the truck and shuts the headlights off.

His jaw is set tight as he strangles the steering wheel. "I have no idea what the heck to say to you," he says quietly.

"Me either," I mumble as I stare up at the stars. Oddly enough, after all the rain, the night sky is crystal clear, the calm after the storm.

If only that were true in life.

He scowls at me. "Do you realize how much trouble you're in? God, you're going to have to go to court, and since this isn't you're first time getting into trouble, they're not going to go easy on you." He shakes his head, puffing out a frustrated breath. "You're grounded."

"Okay." My simple response seems to rile him up more, which wasn't my intention.

"I'm serious. No going out unless it's to therapy. And no more hanging out with Miller." He grits his teeth. "I know he played a huge part in this, even if you won't admit it."

I bite my tongue until I taste blood, but my refusal to say anything has nothing to do with Miller. I'm not even sure how I feel about him now. Never really did. He was supposed to be an escape from my life, the opposite of the kind, caring boys that I used to want to spend time with. I knew who he was when I met him, that chivalry wasn't his thing. When he bailed on me to save his own ass, he was only being himself, which is more than I can say about me.

"Did you hear anything I just said?" Loki asks, growing

even more frustrated when my lips remained fused. I want to say something, but I can't figure out what the right thing is. Right and wrong? Do I even know the difference anymore? "Goddammit. I can't take this anymore." Jerking the keys out of the ignition, he shoves open the door.

I feel bad for upsetting him, but I also feel so hollow. Empty. Dead inside, rotting like corpse.

I silently wait for him to get out of the car. Knowing Loki, he'll storm into the house and lock himself in his room until he cools off. Maybe by tomorrow, I can figure out something to say.

But he pauses before getting out, throwing me for a loop.

"I hate to say this, because I know how much it hurts you when I bring up Mom and Dad," he mutters with his back to me, "but they'd be so disappointed in you." His final words before he storms into the house.

Sorrow, rage, remorse, and so much more chips through my shield of numbness, and pain engulfs me. He's right. If my parents were alive, they'd be so disappointed in me, and as much as I hate that it does, their opinion matters a lot—even my mom's.

No longer wanting to feel the aching sadness, I punch the side of my leg until the muscles are sore, until the physical pain overpowers the emotional pain. Then I get out of the car and drag my leg behind me as I head up the driveway.

As I near the back door, a muffled voice catches my attention. It's past midnight and the rest of the neighborhood is fast asleep. More curious than I want to be, I grip onto the railing and crane my neck to peer into the new neighbor's yard.

Someone is sitting on the porch beneath the deck light,

talking on the phone. The voice is low, baritone, and doesn't belong to Tammy or Luca.

"Look, you can't call here anymore," he says in a low tone. "I know. I know. But that was the deal—that's why we moved here." He presses his fingers to the bridge of his nose and lowers his head. "Fine. I'll send you more money, but I have to go now. Please don't call here anymore."

He hangs up and stares at the road with his phone clutched in his hands. Moments later, his body starts to shake as he sobs.

About two months ago, I caught Loki doing something similar. It was late at night, and I was trying to sneak out of the house when I saw Loki crying on the back deck. He didn't know I was standing in the shadows, spying on him. I haven't really cried since the accident and seeing Loki so openly emotional like that made me uncomfortable, more with myself than anything, because I can't seem to cry anymore, let myself feel the pain. It's been so long since I let it all out that I wonder if maybe my tears are broken.

I figured he was crying over our parents, but I found out the next morning that his girlfriend of three years dumped him, said she couldn't handle his new, complicated life.

"What a bitch," Alexis growled when Loki told us Camila would no longer be coming around.

"I'm so sorry." Zhara gave him a big hug.

Even Nikoli offered a few words. "I didn't like her that much, anyway."

Even though I witnessed his pain, I said nothing. I felt bad for him, and the old Anna would have opened her heart and tried to console him. But this Anna, the one rotting away in her life with one good leg and a bunch of lies, couldn't figure out how to do that without falling apart, too.

When the neighbor's crying fades, I go inside, forcing myself to forget what I heard and saw.

SIX
INVISIBLE GIRL

Ever since the accident, whenever I wake up, I can't remember anything I dreamt. Sometimes I wonder where my mind goes when my eyelids lower, especially because Zhara insists that I scream almost every night. Sometimes I wonder if I relive the accident or maybe I dream of perfect first kisses and dancing onstage, stuff that no longer holds a spot in my life anymore.

I spend the next two days and nights lounging in bed, stirring in my own filth and dreaming of nothing. I reek of dirty sweat, my hair is matted to my forehead, and my leg hurts more than it usually does.

On Tuesday, Loki forces me to get out of bed and go to school. Not bothering to take a shower, I brush my hair into a messy bun, pull on a hoodie, and go out to the kitchen where I pop two pain pills before heading to the truck where the rest of the Baker clan is waiting impatiently for me.

"Headed to school?" Luca appears seemingly out of

nowhere. He charms me with that lopsided grin as he strolls up to the fence.

My heart betrays me, missing a beat, and I glimpse from left to right, praying he's talking to someone else, but no one else is around.

"Um, yeah." I sling the strap of my backpack over my shoulder. "Aren't you?"

He glances down at the plaid pajama bottoms and faded grey t-shirt he's wearing. "Since there's only, like, a week left until Christmas break, my mom's letting me start in January."

"Lucky you. I'd kill to be able to sit around in my pajamas all day."

"It has its downfalls."

"Like what?"

A flirty smile rises on his lips, and I immediately fear where the conversation is going. "Like it's making me a slob. I mean, look at me. A few days of freedom from school, and I've already gotten so lazy that I'm standing here talking to a pretty girl in my pajamas."

I miss a beat and end up standing there, staring at him like an idiot. But no one, not even Miller, has called me pretty before. And how I look now, dressed in wrinkled clothes, smudged makeup, and messy hair, there's no way Luca could think I look pretty.

He has to be lying. I'm not the kind of girl someone thinks is pretty.

Unable to find my voice, I turn to bolt for the truck.

"Hey, Anna," he says before I can make my escape.

I pause, my adrenaline racing. "Yeah?"

"I was being serious yesterday." Nervousness edges his voice. "It'd be cool if you could show me around town."

I glance back at him, my gaze sweeping up and down his body. I try to convince myself that I'm not checking him out, that I'm just reading his vibe. That's all. But I've become such a good liar that I even lie to myself now.

"I can't right now . . . I'm grounded."

His eyes sparkle with interest as he rests his arms on top of the fence. "What'd you do?"

"Something terrible," I say evasively. "Look, Luca, you seem nice. But you don't want to be friends with me." *And I can't be friends with you. Like Cece, you remind me too much of the past with your lopsided smiles that turn me into that dreamy girl.*

"You must be really unperceptive," he teases. "Because that's exactly what I want to do."

"You don't even know me, though."

"But isn't that the point of becoming someone's friend? The whole getting-to-know-the-other person. In fact, it's one of my favorite parts."

I elevate by brows, questioning his words. "Really? I think that part sucks. I mean, it's such an awkward phase."

"Awkward can be fun." His smile grows when I frown in doubt. "Don't try to tell me that you've never been entertained by someone acting awkward."

I open my mouth to tell him no, I haven't, but then I remember the days of laughing at lost tourists, looking so out of place in our town. In fact, I was doing it the day of the accident.

"Nope. Never," I lie for at least the tenth time today.

"Liar, I can tell by the look on your face that you totally do," he calls me out on my bullshit, just like that, and it throws me off.

Hardly anyone ever puts me in my place or tells me like

it is. Even when I'm acting like a brat, everyone that knows me looks at me with pity, carefully choosing their words.

"I have to go." Opening the truck door, I prop my foot onto the running board.

"See you around, Anna. Can't wait to get started on our awkward friends phase." He uses my nickname even though I didn't even give him permission to.

I hate that he just does it so causal, like he's supposed to be using it. Most of all, I hate how much I like hearing him use my old name.

Shaking my head in disbelief, I hoist myself into the backseat with Nikoli and Zhara.

"Was that one of our new neighbors?" Loki asks as I close the door.

I unzip my backpack to get a stick of gum. "Yeah, I guess."

"He seems nice," Loki says, lacking any form of subtly. "Is he your age?"

"He's in my grade, but he's definitely not anyone I'll hang out with," I tell him, needing to get that thought out of his head now.

The last thing I want is for Loki to push me into being friends with the sweet, nice guy next door who, back in the day, I could have easily had a crush on. I can't go back to that place in my life. I don't belong there anymore—don't deserve to belong there anymore.

"Do they have any other kids?" Zhara asks, aligning the row of blue and grey beaded bracelets that match the cheerleading uniform she's wearing.

I pop a piece of gum into my mouth and look out the window. "Beats me. I didn't ask."

"So, then you've talked to them?" Loki asks as he backs out onto the street.

"No, they talked to me." I drop my bag onto the floor. "The mom came strolling up to me yesterday and chatted my ear off."

He shoots me a stern look from over his shoulder. "I hope you weren't rude."

Alexis snorts a laugh as she props her unlaced sneakers on the dash. "When isn't she rude?"

"You're one to talk," I retort. "You know people at school call you an evil bitch? Everyone's afraid of you now."

She shrugs nonchalantly. "So what? It's better than being called Freaky Gimp Girl."

Even though I know they already do, her words sting.

"Alexis," Loki warns. "Don't even go there."

"Why? She started it," Alexis gripes. "You always take her side because you feel sorry for her, and it's turning her into a spoiled brat."

"Alexis, be nice to Anna. She's been through a lot." Zhara chimes in, trying to play the role of our mom again.

"We've all been through a lot," Alexis snaps, her hair whipping around as she aims a death glare at Zhara. "And coddling Anna isn't going to help anyone."

I've somehow turned into Invisible Girl, and I seize the opportunity and keep my lips zipped, wishing I could vanish, even if only for a day or two. If no one noticed me then maybe I wouldn't have to be anyone at all. I could just blend into the walls and vanish from this world.

"Oh, my god, I can't stand this anymore." Nikoli tugs his red baseball cap lower as he slouches in the seat. "All you guys do is argue. When Mom and Dad died, you all lost your freaking minds."

No one speaks for the rest of the drive. When Loki pulls up to the drop off area, Alexis bails out before the truck even comes to a complete stop. It takes me a couple of minutes to gather my things, and by the time I get out, my sisters have already made it to the entrance of the school.

Nikoli goes to the middle school, so he stays in the backseat but doesn't wave goodbye to me.

"I'll pick you up at exactly three ten," Loki hollers at me as I close the door. "And, Anna, you better be here. I'm serious. If you wander off and I have to track you down, I'm going to be super pissed."

I nod and shut the door.

Honeyton's weather has its up and downs, but mainly there are a lot of ups. We don't really have a winter, but we do get occasional sporadic rainstorms and bursts of heat. Even though it's December, a heat wave has rolled in over town. The campus yard is packed with students lounging on the grass, soaking up the sun.

Enough time has passed since I've taken the pills, and I feel sublimely sedated as I push through the growing crowd toward the school with my chin tucked down. But I can feel people's eyes on me, which is normal these days. Occasionally, someone dares to bring up the accident, like I actually want to talk about my parents' deaths.

"Hey, Anna." Cece coyly waves to me as I pass her locker.

It's odd seeing her act so reserved toward me when she's such a spunky, outgoing person. But what's really mind-boggling is that I used to fit in with her smiles and giggles, pretty hair and outfits. I'd get all cleaned up to impress guys and acted silly over first kisses. That's who I was.

Was.

I look down at my leg that doesn't bend right as I walk.

Another time. Another life, Anna.

I fix my attention on the dinged up lockers until I reach my own, but unfortunately, Cece follows me.

"I need to talk to you about something," she says, glancing around the nearly vacant hallway. "Maybe in private."

Like Zhara, she's wearing a cheerleading uniform and a perky smile; she's all positivity and rainbows, and I can't even bring myself to look her in the eye, so I focus on spinning the combination to my locker because it's easier than facing reality.

"This isn't fair, Anna. I don't even know what I did. One minute we were best friends, and now you won't even look me in the eye." She combs her fingers through her long blonde hair, tapping her foot against the linoleum. "I know it's because of Miller. Ever since you started dating him, you won't talk to me."

"I'm not dating Miller. We just hang out." I open my locker and exchange my backpack for my books.

"I saw you at that party the other night." Her cold tone implies she isn't happy about whatever I was doing. "But I doubt you'd remember. You were so out of it."

Slamming my locker, I swing around her and limp down the hallway.

"This isn't fair," she yells after me. "I didn't do anything."

I slow to a stop in the middle of the hallway. "You're

right. You didn't do anything. All this . . ." I gesture between us, "is my fault." Hope flashes in her eyes, but I squash it. "But I can't be friends with you anymore, Cece. It's just too . . . hard."

Tears flood her eyes as she spins around and races off toward the girl's bathroom.

I go to class early, sinking further into my guilt and wishing I had more painkillers to take, wishing I wasn't such a shitty person, wishing she'd just let me go. I meant what I said. We can't be friends because the Anna Cece used to know died and all that's left is a hollow shell of a person who can't figure out what to do with herself.

It's hard to avoid Cece, though, especially when she's in my first period class. She enters about five minutes after I sit down and looks like she's about to burst into tears again when she sees me. Still, she waves shyly at me as she takes a seat. I know her well enough that I can tell she's nervous.

About a minute later, Ben, the six-foot, brown haired football player I once had a crush on, saunters into the class-room. He drops his binder on the desk right next to Cece's and grins as he sits down and says something to her. Cece, who was the biggest flirt even before we started high school, smiles, coiling a strand of her hair around her finger. He soaks her attention up like she's the sun and dazzles her with one of his infamous dimpled smiles. She returns his smile, but grows apprehensive as she casts a wary glance at me.

Jealously briefly burns inside me. *Are they going out?*

The feeling fizzles out as I train my gaze on the tattered cover of my notebook. *It doesn't matter.*

My phone bounces on my desk as it vibrates, and I swipe my finger over the screen to read the message.

Cece: I don't care what u say. We've been friends since we were in kindergarten and I'm not going to let you just throw it away. Please, just talk to me. After school maybe?

I can't even figure out a reply, so I shut my phone off. Cece catches my gaze, and her eyes water, as if she's about to cry. I feel like crying, too, but like the last six months, my eyes remain dry.

I cower in my chair and study the cracks in the desk until I can no longer feel Cece staring at me. When I peek over at her again, she's laughing at something with Ben and Cadence, who's taken the position of Cece's best friend.

I observe how she laughs, how happy she looks. I long for the days when I'd be right by her side, looking just as happy, which only makes me want to swallow more pills.

Cece doesn't look at me or text me during class. When the bell rings, she rushes past me with her head down.

I'm sorry, I almost say, but bite down on my tongue and bury the grief down, allowing the pain pills to suffocate my emotions.

SEVEN

A HOUSE INFESTED WITH GLITTER

THE WEEK FEELS LONG, MOSTLY BECAUSE ALMOST EVERYONE at school got word of my arrest. Gossip flutters up and down the hallways, and people gawk at me more than usual.

Friday, Mr. Dalcebee, the school guidance counselor who likes to wear a lot of smiley face ties, calls me in for a visit to chat about my grades and try to pry into my life, something he does once a month.

"You're barely passing your classes," he says. "This isn't good, Anna."

"I know," I reply, picking at the chips in the wooden armrests of the chair I'm sitting in.

He grows annoyed with me with each question he asks. "I know you can do better than this. You used to be a straight A student."

"I don't know what the big deal is," I say. "I'm not failing any of my classes."

"The big deal is that you have the potential to be a great student, and right now, I'm not seeing that potential. Look, I know things have been difficult for you, but I really would like to see you focus on school again and maybe apply to some different colleges, maybe ones you haven't looked into yet."

I know where the conversation is heading, and my back stiffens.

One of the many downfalls of living in a small town is everyone knows everyone. Mr. Dalcebee has known me since I was four. His wife used to attend the same book club as my mom, and they'd go shopping and wine tasting on the weekends while he and my dad would hang out in their man cave, aka the basement.

I hate that he thinks he knows my story because he occasionally drank beer and played pool with my dad. He doesn't know anything. No one really does when it comes to my family, not even my family. My brothers and sisters, they don't know the truth about everything. Sometimes I get so angry that I'm the only one that knows about my mom, which only makes me hate myself even more for becoming this cruel person that wants other people to suffer with me.

"Can I go?" I rise from the chair. "I don't want to be late for math or my grade's going to drop even more."

Those seem to be the magic words.

"Fine, we'll talk later," he says, stuffing my folder back into the file cabinet. "And, Anna. If you need anything, you can always come to me. Even if it's just to talk about your parents."

"Yeah, sure." My skin dampens as I grasp the doorknob.

When I exit his office, I lean back, my head banging against the wooden door. "Goddammit, this sucks."

Miss Manerton, the receptionist, glares at me from

behind her wire-framed spectacles. "Watch your language, Annabella, or I'll write you up."

I utter an apology then limp out into the crammed hallway. The whispers instantly funnel around me, like gnats. The calm, drug-induced haze from the pill I popped this morning is wearing off, so snubbing the gossipers takes more effort. Deciding to cut out early, I sneak out the back doors and head home. It's only a three-mile walk, but it takes me forever, and my leg feels like it's been cut open all over again. But that's okay. Pain is easier. Pain is simple. It's everything else that sucks.

When I make it to my house, I go straight up to my room, crawl into bed, and pass out, sleeping all the way into the next morning.

Thankfully its Saturday so no school and no stares. I consider not getting up, just lying in bed until the sun goes down and falling right back into a dreamless sleep again. But someone knocks on my door, and the idea dries up like the rain.

"Are you awake?" Loki sounds calmer than he was the past few days. "I need to talk to you about skipping out on the last half of school yesterday." When I don't answer, he gently shakes my shoulder. "I know you're not asleep."

I open my eyes and scowl at him. "I was until you woke me up."

"Don't act like that." He yanks the blankets off me. "Get up. You're coming to the store with me."

Shaking my head, I crawl my way up to the pillow. "No way. I'm not going there."

"Yes, you are. In fact, you're going to start coming with me every weekend. And you might as well prepare yourself to spend a hell of a lot of time at the store, because that's where you're going to spend every evening. And when Christmas break starts, you can count on spending the days there, too."

I cover my head with the pillow. "I can't do it, Loki. Don't make me do it."

He snatches the pillow, tosses it on the floor, then flips on the lights and tugs open the blinds, blinding me with sunlight. "I've been talking to Laretta, and we both kind of agree that I've been too easy on you. You need discipline and something to focus on, and the store's a great place to start. It'll keep you busy and hopefully keep you out of trouble until you can figure out what you want to do with your life."

What I want to do with my life? I used to have some answers. Dancing. Being happy. Going to college. Eventually getting married. When I looked into my future, I saw so much happiness and sunlight. Now all I can see is an empty path that leads to nothing.

I glare at him. "Why were you talking to the neighbors about me?"

"Because I need someone to talk to." He looks so lonely, so very unlike the old Loki I used to know. We've all changed so much. Does everyone else see an empty path like I do now? Or are they stronger than me? "And Laretta's nice. Plus, she used to be really good friends with Mom. Besides, she went through something similar with her son." He rounds the foot of the bed. "You remember Steve, right?"

"Vaguely," I say through a yawn, stretching my arms above my head. "But I'm not like him."

"You're going to be if you keep going down the road you're headed on."

"You're overreacting." But really, Loki could be right. I could be like Steve. I don't know myself enough to validly argue that point, but I still try because I really, really can't go to my dad's store. "I'm not even close to being like Steve yet. So what if I got busted for breaking and entering. I haven't done anything major yet, so chill out."

"Haven't done anything major yet?" He laughs sharply. "You were arrested for the third time the other night, and you're only seventeen. You have your second court hearing on Thursday." He shakes his head in bafflement. "Take a look around you. You're ruining your life."

My guilt builds, vining and gnawing inside my stomach. No matter how hard I fight it, I can't seem to make it vanish. "It could be worse. I could be doing drugs."

"Could be worse?" He throws his hands into the air exasperatedly. "No one can even recognize you anymore. I wouldn't even be surprised if you are doing drugs." He pauses, waiting for me to protest. I should just lie to him—I do it all the time—but the words won't come out of my mouth. His shoulders sag. "You're going to the store with me, and you're going to start going to physical therapy again. I'm not going to let you waste your life away, so get your ass up and get dressed in something that won't scare the customers away." He storms out of my room.

Anger, guilt, and frustration explode to the surface. I haven't been to my father's store since the accident. Too many memories live in the shelves and books that fill the building, and if I relive them, I might lose it. All that guilt I fight to feel —everything I fight to feel—might become too much.

I pound my fist into the pillow until I compose myself.

Dragging my butt out of bed, I hobble over to the window and peer down at the grass and sidewalk below. How bad would it hurt if I tried to jump out? Probably not as bad as when my leg was crushed by the car.

I unlatch the window, glide it open, and stick my head out.

"What are you doing?" someone asks.

I raise my gaze and find Luca standing on the strip of grass behind the fence line. He's sporting a plaid shirt, jeans, and his glasses, and looks adorable in that cute, nerdy sort of way.

I remember when I used to dream about a cute guy showing up below my window and tossing pebbles at the glass. I'd sneak down and kiss him, and we'd keep kissing all the way until the sun rose. But like my dreams of dancing onstage, that dream was shelved six months ago.

"Looking out the window." I sit down on the windowsill. "What does it look like I'm doing?"

He crosses his arms on top of the fence. "It looked like you were thinking about jumping."

"That'd be a pretty stupid thing to do since the fall would probably break my leg." I pretend the idea is appalling, when only moments ago I was contemplating it.

"I don't know . . . It depends on why you were jumping. I mean, if it was for a good reason, like say to escape something, then yeah, I'd say that was totally justifiable. Everybody needs to escape sometimes, right? And the fall isn't that far. You might fuck up your ankle or something, but nothing too major."

I don't like that he's looking at me with insinuation, as if he understands me. Whether he's found out about the accident or not, he doesn't get me.

"I'm not trying to escape anything," I feel the need to say.

"I never said you were." His knowing smile bugs me.

"Why are you watching me?" I ask indignantly.

"I wasn't watching you," he replies, unfazed by my feistiness. "I was actually just talking to your sister and was about to head in when I saw you staring at the ground, thinking about jumping." He smiles when I glare at him. "I'm just kidding. I promise I don't think you're going to jump. I just have a weird sense of humor."

I don't know what to make of him, know I shouldn't make anything of him at all, but I find myself asking, "Which of my sisters were you talking to?"

"I have no idea. She never said her name, but she did look a lot like you. You seem really happy in comparison to her."

I wrestle back a grin, sucking my bottom lip between my teeth. "That was probably Alexis."

"Well, she seemed lovely," he says flatly. "Especially when she told me she'd rather stab out her eye than talk to me."

My mouth pleads to smile. But smiling seems so . . . wrong in the shambles of my life. No one else seems to smile, other than Zhara, but hers are fake. And my dad, the last smile he ever had was when he got in that car that rainy day, thinking his life was so perfect.

"Don't take it personally," I say to Luca. "She's not much of a talker."

"Yeah, I kind of got that." He thoughtfully muses over something with his head tipped to the side, strands of his hair dangling in his eyes. "But you didn't seem like much of a talker when I first met you, either, and look at us now, sitting here, talking to each other like we're almost friends."

Another smile creeps up on me at his utter adorableness. Damn him. "We're not talking because we're almost friends. I just got distracted."

"By what exactly? My good looks or my awesome personality?"

I bite down on my lip hard. *No laughing, Annabella.* "Are you like this all the time?"

He taps his finger against his lip. "You'll have to be more specific. I've been told I'm a lot of things all the time."

I flick my wrist, waving my hand in his direction. "All arrogant and sure of yourself."

His mouth opens as he feigns shock. "You make me sound like a cocky douche bag."

"Are you?"

"That all depends."

"On what?"

"If you're into cocky douche bags," he says with a clever grin. I almost lose it, right then and there, as a smile creeps up on my lips. Thankfully, for my sake, he ruins it. "I'm guessing no, though, since you don't really look like the kind of girl who would be."

Is that how he sees me? As some girl who's into nice, sweet guys like him? That's not who I am anymore. Or am I? I mean, I am sitting here talking to him, on the verge of smiling.

Panicking, I duck back inside my room. "I have to go." And I slide the window shut before he can say anything else.

Desperate to run away from my thoughts, I crank up

some music. "Habits (Stay High)" by Tove Lo comes on, but I immediately shut it off as the urge to dance pulsates through me. I crank up some From Autumn to Ashes and dig through my closet until I find the perfect outfit; a baggy black sweater, skin-tight black jeans, and black boots that lace up to my knees. I top off the outfit with a leather jacket and kohl eyeliner. I leave my hair the way it is, letting it run down my back in a tangled mess. I figure my appearance might be just enough over the top that it'll get me out of going to the store on weekends.

The kitchen smells like a combo of vanilla air freshener and old trash, and I find myself longing for the days of burnt bacon and eggs.

Loki glances up from the toaster, takes one look at me, and jabs a finger in the direction the stairs. "No way. You're not going into Dad's store dressed like that."

"Then I guess I'll just have to stay home." I get a Pop-Tart from the pantry.

"It's supposed to get warm today. You're going to sweat to death."

"I'm sure I'll live. I always do," I say, and he freezes, his expression plummeting, and I feel like an asshole. "Can we just get going? If I sweat, then I sweat, okay? It'll be my problem."

He grabs the car keys off the wall hook as he stuffs his wallet into his pocket. "Meet me in the car. I have to get a box out of the garage."

One foot in front of the other. You can do this. You've made it through everything else. Sort of.

Like when I walked to the Victorian house, my legs have other ideas, and my feet remain glued to the floor. I think about the last time I was at my father's store, and moving seems even more out of the question. My heart squeezes, and my leg begins to shake as my father's face flashes through my mind. *He always seemed so happy. He couldn't have possibly known about the affair.*

I yank open the cupboard above the sink, fumble for the bottle of pain pills I was prescribed for my leg, and pop two in my mouth. I swallow them down then hobble to the living room, trying to catch my breath. As I'm stepping over the threshold, my leg buckles. I stumble and fall face first onto the floor.

Pain throbs through my body as I start to push back to my feet, but something silver and sparkly catches my attention. Leaning in to get a better look, the pain in my leg abruptly vanishes, and the ache in my heart takes over.

Remnants from the glitter rainstorm are embedded into the cracks of the floorboards. Panicking, I try to dig them out, but my fingers won't fit into the cracks. Tears sting my eyes.

Don't cry. Don't cry. Once you do, you won't be able to stop.

I press my cheek to the cool hardwood floor, squeeze my eyes shut, and take a few measured breaths. The foggy memory of faint giggles surrounds me, and I can almost feel glitter showering across my skin.

The last perfect day, where everything seemed possible. . .

"Did you steal my shirt!" Alexis shouts at Zhara from upstairs, sounding as angry as she has for the last six months. "Seriously!"

My eyes snap open as the memories of happier days fizzle out.

"Why would I steal your shirt?" Zhara asks. "We don't even have the same taste. And I would never just take your clothes without asking."

"Oh, yes, because you're perfect." Alexis snorts a condescending laugh.

"Would you two knock it off!" Nikoli shouts. "I'm trying to watch the game."

Loki's worn sneakers appear in my line of vision. "Shit, did you fall?"

"No." I grip onto the end table for support as I get my balance.

"Then what happened?" He inspects me over from head to toe.

I dust a few fragments of glitter off my hands and they float back to the floor. "I just felt like laying down and stretching my legs out."

He sighs heavily. "I have to tell Zhara we're leaving. Go get in the car." He trudges up the stairs, looking more defeated than normal.

I open my mouth to apologize, but I hesitate for too long, and before I know it, he's disappeared upstairs. Turning away, I head outside. With each step, the medication slowly settles through my body.

By the time I make it to the car, I've slipped into a state of numbness, so far gone, I can barely feel anything anymore.

EIGHT

MEMORIES HAUNTING EVERY PAGE

THE PILLS HELP AT FIRST. I MANAGE TO GET OUT OF THE CAR and into the store without too much procrastination. When Loki puts me in charge of stocking the shelves, I worry the shield will crack. But the medication keeps my anxiety subdued. I feel pretty okay as I sit down on the floor and sort through books with the scent of fresh new pages lingering in the air. I almost want to crack each book open and inhale the scent, just like I used to do when I worked for my dad. I stop myself, though, knowing I'll be opening pages to a past that never really existed in the first place.

Eventually customers wander in from outside. Behind the antique cash register, Loki grows tense and keeps casting panicked glances in my direction. He pretty much shits a brick when a little boy points at me and starts crying.

"Go work back in the office," Loki says, striding down the aisle toward me.

I glance up from the stack of books. "Why?"

"Because people are complaining about you. Did you

89

know that little boy thought you were a ghost?" He crouches down in front of me and lowers his voice. "You can't dress like this. Not while you're here. It's too unprofessional."

I eye his faded grey t-shirt and dark jeans. "You're not dressed any better, though."

"This isn't how I usually dress. I just forgot to do the laundry last night," he says. "And it's still better than what you have on. You look like those kids who are always hanging out back, smoking all the time, like they don't have anything else better to do with their lives."

"I *am* one of those kids who hang out back smoking."

"You *smoke?*" His expression teeters between rage and shock.

"No, I was speaking metaphorically, Loki." Gripping onto the lower shelf, I lift myself to my feet. "If I embarrass you, then I can just go home."

He stares warily at my injured leg. "You're not supposed to be walking on your leg that much, especially when you haven't been to physical therapy in over three weeks. If you keep it up, you're never going to get better."

"We both know I'm never really going to get better," I say, then smash my lips together, wanting to retract my statement.

The tension in his eyes eases a notch. "Anna, I know things have been hard for you, and I'm sure it doesn't help that I'm always on your case about stuff, but physical therapy is important. If you don't build up strength in your leg, then you might end up walking with a cane or something, and I know you don't want that."

"It doesn't matter to me," I say, my fingers stabbing into the wooden shelf as I struggle to breathe evenly. "Just like your online classes. Sure you take them because you feel like you have to, but it doesn't replace what you lost, right?"

It takes him a beat to answer. "Things might not be the same as they used to be and they probably won't ever be again, but I'm not just going to give up on all of my dreams. I still want to do things with my life eventually. Maybe my future plans aren't the same and I have to work twice as hard to get things done, but sometimes that's just life." He shakes his head, his eyes flooding with pity. "There's so much more out there than you even realize right now. Beyond Honeyton. Even beyond dancing."

It's like he's knocked the wind out of me. I can barely breathe. "I need some air." I start down the aisle, but he snags the sleeve of my shirt.

He tows me back to him before letting me go, then he rakes his fingers through his hair. "Sorry, but after the shit you've been pulling, I'm not letting you out of my sight. Just go in the office and take a breather, okay?"

"There's nothing to do in there." I gripe, mainly because the idea of going into my dad's office makes me feel like I'm going to vomit.

"You can hang out. Eat lunch. Stare out the window. I don't really care, just as long as you stay where I can keep an eye on you." Worry lines crease his face. "And no going out back," he warns, then returns to the register.

I glare at him as I weave through the shelves, past the lounge chair shaped like a bookshelf, and duck into the room in the back section of the store, which used to be my father's office.

The small, cluttered space causes memories of the last few times I spent here to tumble over me. My airway constricts, but I don't gasp for air and bottle up the sadness. I trace my fingers over a framed picture on his desk of my dad and me in front of the store. He has his arm around me and we're laughing about something. He looks so happy, and so do I.

I miss that. Miss him.

I sink down in the chair and let my eyelids drift shut. It'd be easier if I could just go to sleep or pass out, but with all the memories floating around the room, even with the pills I took, make it impossible.

Growing restless, I open my eyes and move over to a short bookshelf in the corner where my dad kept a collection of older books that he was too in love with to sell. I lower myself to the floor and skim my fingers along the titles on the bottom row. Most of the titles I don't recognize—my dad had an oddly unique taste in books—but there are a few that I know by heart because he took the time to read them to me. Stories of princesses and magical kingdoms. He was such a good dad, and how did I repay him? By lying to him in his final moments in life.

I'm so sorry, Dad.

I draw in a breath and clumsily get to my feet, but a thick, leather book with no title or author catches my attention. I slide it out and open it on my lap. My breath catches in my throat. The pages are covered with my father's handwriting.

"He kept a journal," I say aloud to myself. But as I fan through the pages, I realize my father's journal endeavor was short lived because he only managed to fill up three pages.

I thrum my fingers against the page, wondering what to

do with book. I want to read it. I want to burn it. I want to hug it and never let it go.

With trembling hands, I slam the book shut and hoist myself to my feet. I write Loki a note on a post-it, stick it on the office entryway where he can find it, and sneak out the back door with the book. I hike across the gravel parking lot toward the street. A cloud of smoke circles around me as I pass by the drearily dressed group that always seems to be smoking near the garbage cans. When I reach the sidewalk, something catches my attention in my peripheral vision.

Just down the street, Cece is leaning against Ben's red lifted truck, twisting a strand of her blonde hair around her finger. She's wearing a pair of yoga pants over her leotard, which means she just got out of ballet class. She has her flirty smile on and keeps biting her lip.

Guess they really are together.

I feel the slightest sting in my heart, but don't react, won't become that girl. Cece can do whatever she wants and so can Ben.

Ripping my gaze off them, I veer left toward the block my house is on. I have to move slowly; otherwise, my leg won't make the four mile walk home. Back when I helped my dad at the store, I'd sometimes pop in my earbuds and dance my way home. Yeah, people looked at me strangely, but I was too wrapped up in my own world to care. There was something freeing about dancing around in a world that was packed with so many people just walking around. It was probably the most abnormal thing I've ever done, and the toes on my good leg ache to relive those days of being so free, so at peace with who I was. But the toes on my bad leg are numb and my leg can barely handle walking anymore.

I don't make it very far down the sidewalk before my muscles start spasming. Sometimes this happens and between the ache and the sweater and leather jacket I'm wearing, I grow exhausted quickly.

Sinking down onto the curb, I lay my head on my lap. I'm so sweaty that my clothes are sticking to my skin. How wonderful would it be if the world opened up and swallowed me whole?

"Annabella?"

I tilt my head and my eyelashes flutter against the sunlight.

Tammy, the new neighbor, is staring down at me with concern. "Oh, honey, are you all right? You look sick."

She's wearing a red sleeveless dress that matches her lipstick and black boots and hoop earrings. Again, she reminds me so much of my mom that my heart skips a beat. But beneath the fashionable outfit, is she really like my mom? Does she lie to her husband? Does she have Luca lie for her?

"I'm fine," I reply, hugging the book against my chest.

Her brows knit. "Honey, why are you sitting on the curb? Are you hurt?"

Sighing, I raise my head. "I was just walking home and needed to take a break. I'm good, though. Totally refreshed and ready to go."

Refusing to set the book down, I attempt to stand without using my hands, but end up falling right back down on my ass.

"Oh, my goodness." She flails her hand around, waving at someone in the parking lot. "Luca, come help me get Annabella up."

Oh, my god, no way is that about to happen. Walking with a limp is bad enough.

Gritting through the pain, I shift forward, and putting way too much weight on my bad leg, trip to my feet. Searing pain clenches in my muscles and tears sting at my eyes, but I'm standing and that's all that matters.

Tammy looks back at me with pity in her eyes. "Let me give you a ride home, okay." Her gaze falls to my leg.

She knows what happened to me.

"It's only a couple more miles." I lift my foot to walk away, but the blinding pain shifts to full-on, knock-my-breath-out-of me throbbing. My jaw clenches, and I end up biting my tongue. The foul taste of rust fills my mouth, and my eyes water.

Gripping onto the post of a street sign, I inhale deeply and force the waterworks to stay put. When Tammy answers her phone, I breathe in relief. Now's my chance to get away.

"Here, let me help you." Luca steps in front of me and blocks my escape. He isn't wearing his glasses, and his hair is sticking up all over the place. Again, I have the silly urge to run my fingers through it and fix it back into place.

I shuffle away from him. "I said I'm fine. Yeah, I have a messed up leg, but I know how to walk."

He freezes, his hands suspended in midair. "I was actually going to offer to carry the book for you."

I try to decipher if he's for real or not. "What is this? 1950? Guys don't carry books for girls anymore."

His lips tug into a lopsided grin. "This guy does."

I bite down on my lip, fighting back a smile. "That was really lame."

He chuckles, his cheeks tinting pink. "I know. Sorry. I'm

blaming it on the move here. It's thrown me off my game."

I tuck the book underneath my arm. "Sounds like an excuse to me. Maybe you never really had any game to begin with." I internally cringe at the playful edge in my voice.

"Maybe you're right." He massages the back of his neck as he stares at the ground. "Now everything's suddenly making sense. No wonder every girl I tried to talk to ran off." A smile rises as his hands drop to his sides. "Just like you did earlier."

I remember how he called me pretty. How he assumed that I like sweet, nice guys. "I wasn't running away from you. Just something you said." I instantly regret my words. Why am I being so honest?

"It was the cocky, douche bag remark, wasn't it?"

"Kind of."

"I'm really not a douche bag. I promise."

"But you're cocky," I speculate.

He wavers, pulling a reluctant face. "I have my moments sometimes, but I also have my un-cocky moments, too."

"What kind of word is un-cocky?"

"The super cool kind."

"So, let me get this straight. You're a sometimes cocky, sometimes un-cocky, book carrying, awkward phase loving kind of guy that makes up his own words."

He points a finger at me. "You've been paying attention."

"No, you've made me pay attention by refusing to leave me alone." I aim to sound annoyed but come off more amused than anything.

"I know. It's kind of a defense mechanism when I get really nervous," he says with a sigh. A pucker forms at his brows. "Usually, it doesn't work, though, and people end up running in the other direction." He glances over my shoulder at something. "Like that girl over there. I tried to charm her with my awesome social skills, but either she's blind or she was pretending to be."

I scratch my nose to keep from grinning. "Don't take it personally. Cece's just that way. If you really want her, keep trying. It's what she wants."

"Are you friends with her?"

"I used to be." I clamp my jaw down, realizing how true my words are. That we're not friends anymore, because I chose to run away from her, too. How many things can I run from before I won't have anything at all? Shaking the thought from my head, I move to step around him. "Sorry, but I need to go."

"No, wait." Luca looks over at his mom then back to me. "Okay, I'm going to give you a head's up. She's not going to give up until you accept the ride, so you might as well just let us take you home. And if you try to walk off right now, she's just going to chase you down. And trust me, as funny as that sounds, it's kind of embarrassing."

I drag my teeth over my lip, suffocating a laugh. "She's done that to you before?"

"Oh, yeah. Many, many times."

"What were you doing that she needed to chase you?"

He cracks his knuckles, shifting his weight. "Let's just say I used to like to run away a lot."

Run away like I do, or does he mean something else by that?

I eye him over, trying to read him. "It's really not that big of a deal. I'm not really running away. Just trying to get home, and it's only a couple of miles away."

"Yeah, but she'll still chase you down, so you might as well just get in the car, save yourself the embarrassment, and enjoy the free air conditioning." He takes in my outfit with a slow, deliberate gaze. "So, is the sweater and leather jacket some rebellious family uniform? Because I'm pretty sure your sister was wearing one yesterday, and it was equally warm outside."

"No, I just like sweaters and leather jackets." I glance over his scuffed boots, dark denim jeans, and plaid shirt. "And like your outfit's any better. Long-sleeve plaid. Yeah, that screams warm weather."

"Hey, I have my sleeves pushed up. And besides, the weather is freakishly weird around here, something I didn't realize until now. I mean, one minute it's raining. The next it's seventy-five degrees. It doesn't make any sense." He waves his hands around, talking animatedly, and I have to bite back another giggle because he looks so cute doing it. "Either be warm or cold, but not back and forth. It's confusing and makes me miss LA." He sighs, his arms falling to the side. "And just so you know, I don't always dress like this. I just had a meeting I needed to dress up for."

I peer down the street lined with quaint secondhand shops, a cozy café, and a travel agency. Thankfully, Cece and Ben are gone. "What kind of meeting?"

He scratches at his arm and frowns. "One with my dad. It was a job interview actually."

I remember the other night how I saw the man crying on the porch and wonder if that was his dad. "Where does your dad work?"

"He bought the hobby store on the corner and is fixing it up. The grand opening is in a few days. I had an," he makes air quotes, "interview so he could make sure I'm qualified to work there."

"Your dad made you interview for a job . . . That's kind of harsh. My dad never made me interview when I decided to work at his store." My heart tightens in my chest at the mention of my dad and how nice of a guy he was.

"Yeah, it sucks, but that's just how he is, and honestly, we've never really gotten along. I wouldn't even bother working at his store, but I need the money for college and stuff," he says, unwinding a bit. "As much as I love my parents, I can't wait to be out on my own. And not in Honeyton. No offense, but this town's a little strange."

"None taken." I used to be okay living in this town at one time in my life, but now, too many people know my family's story. Whenever we walk around or attend town events anymore, I feel like I'm in the hallways at school, like everyone is staring at us. "My sister went to college overseas . . ." I have no idea why I'm telling him this—telling him anything at all. It's like my lips have taken on a life of their own and have taken freedom in telling everything they know to the guy who knows nothing about my history.

"That's really freaking cool," he says. "What's she studying?"

"Cooking. She wants to be a chef one day. She's really good at it, too. She used to bake wedding cakes for people around town before she left."

"What about you?" he asks. "Are you going to college?"

Am I going to college? A seemingly simple question and one I used to have an answer to.

But now, all I know is that I want to get away from this town and everyone who knows me. The easiest route would be just to go to some random college. My parents set up a fund for each of us, but the plan to major in dance and then perform with a company is no longer an option, no matter how much my mom and dad tried to help me make that dream come true.

I remember when I got a call from the administrator at the university about two weeks after the funeral. She had called to reschedule because we had missed our appointment.

"What was the date of the appointment?" I had asked, strangling the phone to death.

"Let me check." The sound of keys clicking flowed through the receiver. "June sixth."

June sixth. The day of my birthday. My surprise.

"So, do you want to reschedule?" she asked. "Are you still there?"

"Yeah . . . And no, I can't attend anymore." I dropped the phone and sank to the floor, unable to breathe as I stared down at the hideous scars on my leg.

I'm never going to be able to dance again.

"Anna, are you okay?" Luca waves his hand in front of my face.

I jerk back, realizing my eyes have watered up. "I'm fine. I just have allergies." I wipe my eyes with my sleeves. "Were you saying something?"

"Nothing important." He studies me for a moment or two with his brows knit. "I was just asking you what was up with that giant bronze gnome in the center of the park. I thought it was really creepy and wondered why the hell they put it there."

I have no idea how we went from talking about college to

talking about a gnome, and almost wonder if he's intentionally giving me a subject change, letting me off the hook with his question about the future. "That's not a gnome. That's a statue of Theodore Tessingture. He was, like, the first mayor of Honeyton or something . . . There's a plaque that explains his story. Go read it if you want to know."

"Wait. That was a *person*? His body was seriously disproportionate compared to his legs and arms."

"He's just a little stumpy."

His eyes round. "Stumpy is an overstatement. I seriously thought it was an enlarged gnome or maybe even an Oompa Loompa."

A laugh escapes my lips, and my eyes snap wide open as I slap my hand over my mouth.

"What's wrong?" he asks, looking confused and a little curious.

"Nothing." My clipped tone causes him to wince. But I can't help my rudeness. He made me laugh, and I think I might hate him for it. "I have to go." I turn to leave, ready to run back to my house, pop a few more pills, and plunge further into my guilt.

I don't deserve to be here laughing.

His fingers fold around my arm and a shiver courses through me. "Just get in the car, okay? I'm with my mom. It's way too hot for you to be walking on your . . ."

I look back at him with my eyes narrowed, and he promptly releases my arm. I open my mouth to ask him just how much he knows about my leg, about me. Has he heard the story of the girl who breathed dancing and the accident that forever stole her air away? The girl who now wanders around, gasping for a simple breath of air.

"Just get in the car, please." He uses that adorable half smile on me again. "You'll be doing us a favor if you do."

My lips part to refuse his request. No matter how cute he is, I won't accept a ride—won't accept that I need one. "Luca, I—"

"Ready to go?" Tammy interrupts, dropping her phone into her purse. "My car's parked out back of your family's store, Annabella."

For the hundredth time since the accident, I wish I could literally run. I took it for granted. Moving quickly. Having an easy escape.

"Fine," I agree reluctantly.

She smiles cheerfully as we make our way back toward the parking lot. "So, how long has your family lived in Honeyton?" she asks me.

"Since before I was born," I say, wiping my sweaty forehead with the back of my hand.

"It's such a lovely town," she remarks, taking in all the old fashion stores and secondhand shops around us. "Although, I do miss some of the perks of a L.A., like being able to find any store you want, or takeout. God, I miss takeout."

"Why'd you move here, then?" I ask. "I mean, it sounds like you liked L.A. a lot."

Silence settles between us as Tammy stares out at the road and Luca massages the back of his neck. Our shoes crunch against the gravel and fill up the quiet. But the hourly town bell tolls, overlapping the stillness.

"We just needed a change of scenery," Tammy says after the bells chime twelve times. She strains a smile as she glances at me. "My husband and I actually drove through

Honeyton during one of these crazy road trips we used to take when we were first married. And we sometimes came out here during the summers and rented a place for a couple of weeks." She dazes off into empty space then quickly blinks. "But anyway, I've always loved how secluded it was, and it seemed like the perfect place to live and raise kids."

"How many kids do you have?" I ask as we stop beside a red Honda Civic.

She hastily shakes her head, digging through her purse. "Oh, no . . . Luca's an only child . . . but I still think of him as my little boy sometimes." Her voice is off-pitch.

Avoiding eye contact with me, Luca scratches at his arm, seeming as nervous as his mom.

Strange. And somehow, the moment kind of reminds me of when my mom got into the car that day.

"Okay, let's get you out of the sun." Tammy presses the key fob and the locks click.

Fully agreeing with her, I climb into the backseat and close the door. The air is more stifling inside the car, and I fan my hand in front of my face as Tammy turns on the ignition and cranks up the air conditioning. I breathe in the coolness, hugging the book to my chest, but stiffen when Luca slides into the backseat with me, bringing in with him the smell of his cologne and that half smile that I can't seem to stop staring at.

I drop the book to my lap, slide as close to the door as possible, and reach over my shoulder for the seatbelt. "What're you doing?"

The corners of his mouth tease upward as he buckles up without taking his eyes off me, giving me his undivided attention. "Sitting here in the car. What're you doing?"

"But why are you sitting in the back?" The lock clicks into place and I suddenly feel so . . . trapped. He smells so good and he keeps looking at me like he thinks I'm pretty and like he wants to get to know me. All I want to do is dive out of the car, run from how my body's urge to slide closer, my fingers craving to tousle his hair into place, and my lips need to tell him stuff I don't want to. "I mean, don't you want to sit in the front? It's probably cooler up there"

"Seems as good of a place to sit as anywhere else." He relaxes back in the seat with his hands tucked behind his head. "Besides, it's not everyday that I get to sit this close to someone so pretty."

I blink at him then shake my head. "You're so weird. Seriously, what's with all the pretty comments?"

"What? I'm just being truthful."

I roll my eyes, but wince when I feel my cheeks flush. "I think you might be as blind as Cece. Seriously. Because there's no way you could possibly think hey, there's a girl with purple hair, sitting in sweaty, oversized clothes, and, man, does she look pretty."

"Why not?" he challenges. When I stutter for a response, he grins. "Besides, there's more to you than just your looks, even if you don't want me to think so."

His question makes me pause, and I mean *really* pause, to the point where I overthink my whole entire existence.

Looking really pleased with himself, he wrestles his arms out from the sleeves of his plaid shirt. Underneath it, he's wearing Pink Floyd t-shirt.

The shirt reminds me of my dad, and knots ravel in my chest. He used to listen to them all the time. In fact, I was listening to them the day of the accident, right before my mom drove out to the antique store.

Luca tracks my gaze to his shirt. "You ever listen to them?"

I slowly shake my head. "No. Never."

He cocks a brow, giving me a skeptical look.

"I swear haven't." I feel the need to make him believe my lie, because it makes it easier to lie to myself.

"Okay, you haven't then. But it'd be cool if you had. It's a really cool band." He still sounds doubtful that I haven't heard of the band, and the accusation in his tone flusters me.

I want to look away from him, but I can't bring myself to. It's creeping me out because I swear it's like he knows the old me . . .

"So, what do you like to do for fun, Annabella?" Tammy interrupts our moment as she drives onto the road, slipping on a pair of aviator sunglasses. "Or do you go by Anna? I think I heard your brother call you that."

"When did you talk to my brother?" I ask her, still staring at Luca who's staring at me with curiosity in his eyes.

"For a little bit yesterday evening, and also this morning. He's a very lovely young man. That's how I knew your family owned the bookstore." She adjusts the rearview mirror, angling it right at me.

Mascara and eyeliner are melting down my face, and my skin looks pallid. Oh, my god, I feel so mortified. I want to wipe the mess away with my fingertips, but force myself to place my hands on my lap. I can't be that girl who cares if a guy sees her looking like a mess. If I'm her, then I'll be the girl who loves glitter. Who dreams. Who worships her mother. Who was a dancer . . .

Tears threaten to seep out, and I start counting my breaths, crossing my fingers we'll get home soon where my pills will be waiting for me.

Deep breaths. Deep breaths. Don't cry.

"Your brother also told me you like to dance," Tammy says, and I just about lose it, right there in the car. Start sobbing like a freak. "I think that's great," she continues, oblivious to my meltdown. "I used to dance myself. That was quite a while ago, though. I'm not even sure I could do it anymore—it's been so long."

The sunlight burns against my eyes as I stare unblinkingly out the window. "I *used* to dance but not anymore." I pinch the side of my leg, stab my nails into the fabric of my jeans, bite down on my tongue, seeking pain strong enough to erase the agony stirring inside me.

"Oh. I'm sorry if I upset you."

I don't utter a word. Can't. Can barely breathe.

"Hey, Mom. Weren't you supposed to call Dad when we were heading back to the house," Luca says, and if I didn't know any better, I'd guess he was giving me a break from her questioning.

"Shit, I forgot." She grabs her phone from her purse and dials a number.

While she's chatting with Luca's dad, Luca inches closer to me in the seat. "Hey, are you okay?"

I bob my head up and down. "If I knew she was going to ask all these question, I would've just walked home."

"Yeah, sorry about that," he says in a low, quiet tone. "She's really bad at sensing when people don't want to talk about stuff."

"I think I would've been better off getting chased down

the street," I admit, picking at my fingernails with my head tipped down.

"You say that now, but until you've lived the full experience, you don't get how embarrassing it can be." He pauses, taking a breath or two. "You want to talk about what's bothering you?"

I give him an are-you-insane look. "Why would I? I don't even know you."

"I know, and I honestly don't really expect you to open up to me," he says, offering me a timid smile. "But since we're at that awkward new friends phase, I figure I could ask."

"You're seriously the strangest person I've ever met."

"Now I know that's not true. Not when you've met my mom."

"She doesn't seem that—" I say, but he holds up a hand, silencing me.

"Just give it a minute," he tells me, looking at his mom who's still talking on the phone.

"Of course I want you to have an opinion," she says. "It's your store, too, sweetie." She pauses, and Luca spreads his hands apart in front of him, as if signaling a grand finale. "But wouldn't it be really amazing if we all dressed up like puppets and did a life size puppet show. Luca could be part of it, too, and I could make our outfits out of those matching doll Halloween costumes we wore a couple of years ago." She smacks her hand against the steering wheel, getting even more excited. "I could even bedazzle them up, put some rhinestones and sparkles on them."

Luca eases back in the seat, propping his foot onto his knee. "And there you go."

"She's not that bad," I say, but deep down, I want to laugh at her excitement over doll costumes, rhinestones, and puppet shows.

"Not that bad." He gapes at me. "Anna, she's going to make me wear a doll costume."

"So." I find this conversation way too amusing. "There's guy dolls, too, you know."

"With rhinestones," he adds, staring at me disbelief. "And sparkles."

"Rhinestones and sparkles can be cool," I say. "In their own glittery way."

He examines me with suspicion in his eyes. "You're speaking from experience. I can tell." He wags a finger at me. "Admit it, you secretly like rhinestones and sparkly things."

"I so do not," I say in horror. "I hate stuff like that."

"I bet you even secretly like all that stuff," he continues on, ignoring me. "I bet late at night, when you think everyone is asleep, you trade your boots and leather jacket for pink, glittery dresses."

"No, I don't." My nerves are so frazzled I can't think straight. "Luca, I'm not like that anymore."

"*Anymore?*" he questions, and waits for me to answer.

But I simply shake my head and fix my attention on the ranch-style houses, the trees outside, the people wandering around the streets. Everything is buzzing with life. I miss that feeling.

Luca must sense that he's struck a nerve because he remains quiet.

By the time we reach our neighborhood, a cringe-worthy silence has built between the three of us. I'm so relieved to be home that I bail out of the car a little too eagerly, roll my ankle, and fall down on the concrete.

"Oh, my goodness, are you okay?" Tammy rushes over, fussing over me.

"I'm fine." I motion at her to get away as I stumble to my feet. "Thanks for the ride." I don't look at either of them as I round the fence between our properties.

"Hey, Anna." Luca jogs after me, and I want to run from him, but have no choice but to stop. "I'm sorry if I upset you in the car. I didn't mean to."

"I'm fine." I swallow hard at the lie. "Look, I have to go. I need to check up on my brother and sisters." Another lie. So many are piling up that I wonder if I'll be able to discern fact from fiction.

"Okay." He seems a little upset, but waves at me before heading back down the driveway.

I have the craziest urge to chase after him, beg him to joke around with me more, let myself have what I used to want. But instead I turn for door and walk away.

By the time I make it inside, blood has soaked through the knee of my jeans, and my skin is on fire.

Not bothering to clean up the wound, I climb the stairs, fishing out my phone from inside my pocket. I have three missed texts. One from Miller, one from Cece, and one from Jessamine, my older sister. Every once in a while she tries to check in, but I never reply because I don't really have anything to say to her.

I read Miller's first, knowing it'll be easier to handle.

Miller: Hey, it's me. Just seein' if u wanna come over and hang. I know things were intense yesterday so I thought we could just chill and take it

easy for the night. Maybe go c that movie you've been wanting to c. That one about that guy and girl who go on that trip. I could even pick u up.

I have no idea what movie he's talking about since we've never discussed my likes and dislikes. More than likely he's getting me mixed up with someone else, probably another girl.

Mentally preparing myself, I switch to Cece's message.

Cece: Hey, I was looking through this old box of photos for my mom and found one of you and me that we took that the party last June. Remember how much fun we had that night dancing? I really miss that . . . But anyway, I just wanted to say hi. I know things have been really awkward and u say u don't want to talk, but I really think we should, especially after the other day. I saw the look on your face in class when I was talking to Ben. This thing with him isn't what u think. We're just friends. I promise I won't do that to u . . . Please, just call me okay. Maybe we can get together over Xmas break or something!

My heart squeezes at the exclamation point at the end. Totally a Cece thing to do, and it makes me sad, makes me miss things I don't want to miss.

With unsteady fingers, I move to the final one.

Jessamine: Hey, it's me. I haven't heard from u in a while. Loki texted me the other day and said there was a lot of stuff going on and wanted me to talk to u. Call me, Anna. U never pick up when I call. Pleaz. I want to help.

"No, you don't. Trust me," I mutter to the screen.

"You're better off away in London—far, far away from this mess I've created."

I don't reply to any of the texts. Ignoring the yelling coming from the family room, I go straight up to my bedroom. I flop down on my bed with the book and fan through the pages again but stop at the inside back cover. An envelope is taped to it with *Dennis* scribbled across the front. I gulp. Dennis who? I want to find out the answer, yet I hesitate. The handwriting resembles my mother's. My mom the liar. The cheater. Dead in her grave, buried with her secrets, only she left some of them here with me.

What the hell is wrong with me? I'm filled with so much hate all the time.

"God, I hate myself." Tears threaten to pour out, and I chuck the book across the room and bury my face into a pillow, smothering a scream until the anger is locked back inside me again. But no matter how hard I fight back the rage, this time I can't seem to get myself under control. I need to get out of here. Get away from a house haunted by memories and glitter. Where my dreams of dancing started. Where I used to be a happy person, used to be so much more than what I am now.

I open Miller's message and my fingers hover over the keypad.

Me: Yeah, come pick me up.

Miller: Sweet. What's your address?

Giving him my address means handing over a real piece of my life. That's not what Miller's for, but I really want to leave and my leg aches way too much to be walking around.

Sucking in a breath, I text him my address, then change my clothes, preparing to run away again.

NINE
SHARDS OF BROKEN GLASS

On my way outside to meet Miller, Zhara comes barreling out of the family room. "Where are you going?"

"Out." I dodge to the right to swing around her but she sidesteps me and blocks my path. Without directly looking at her, I grab onto the banister. "Zhara, move out of my way."

She shakes her head. "I . . . I can't do that."

"Yeah, you can. Now move." I move to step around her again, but she sidesteps me, getting in my way again. Frustration bursts inside me because she's blocking my escape to freedom. "Zhara, seriously. Get out of my way before I make you move."

Her cat eyes widen. "Loki texted me and told me not to let you go anywhere . . . I don't want to get in trouble if you leave."

"You won't get into trouble." I push her aside to squeeze by.

"Anna! Please don't leave! I don't want to get into trouble," she says, chasing after me.

"Take a look around you." I motion at the empty house. "No one here cares what we do."

"That's not true!" She sniffles. "Mom and Dad used to. And Loki cares now. And so do I."

"Yeah, well, Loki's not here." I start down the stairs, my focus on one thing—the bottle of pills in the cupboard.

"How can you be so mean and uncaring all the time?" she asks, looking at me like she has no clue who I am anymore. "You used to be so nice."

I descend the stairway, gripping onto the railing to keep weight off my scarred leg. "I used to be a lot of things."

"You can still be those things," she says, shuffling after me. "I know some things are different, but you still have me, Loki, and Nik who want to help you get through this. Even Alexis would probably help."

"I don't need help from anyone." I leave her close to tears and duck into the kitchen to pop a couple of pills. Then I sit on the porch to wait for Miller.

Right as the pills are kicking in, I spot his truck bumping up the street.

The exhaust backfires when he pulls up to the garage, and Mrs. Fefferson from across the street shakes her head in dismay. I head down the driveway, but stop when I notice Luca watching me from his front yard. I don't like how he's looking at me, as if he's worried and . . . Well, disappointed.

"Why are you looking at me like that?" I ask, unsettlingly offended by his look.

"I wasn't looking at you. Not the whole time anyway." He squints against the fading sunlight as he crosses the strip of grass to the fence. "I was actually heading over to invite your family to dinner. My mom's cooking a roast, and despite her crazy fetish with doll costumes and rhinestones, she's actually a really great cook." He smiles, but it doesn't quite reach his eyes as he casts a glance at Miller's truck.

"You can knock on the door and ask my brother and sisters, but I already have plans." I practically jump out of my skin when Miller honks the horn.

"Hurry up and get in!" Miller shouts out the window, clearly in a pissy mood over something. "I have to pick up Big Jay before we head to the party!"

I shoot a dirty look at Luca when he elevates his brows and mouths, *wow*. "Stop looking at me like that," I say, mostly because the look makes me feel ashamed that I'm going with Miller.

"I already told you, I'm not looking at you like anything." He glances at Miller's truck. "Him, on the other hand . . ."

Trying to shove Luca's judgment aside, I turn to face the truck, but I'm super aware of him studying me intently, as if he's trying to unscrew a bolt to my thoughts. "I thought we were going to the movies?" I ask Miller.

"Change of plans," he snaps as he smashes his phone to his ear. "Now get in the truck."

"Who the hell is that guy?" Luca mutters. "He seems like an asshole."

"He's not like this all the time. He's just in a . . . bad mood." I am only being half truthful. Normally Miller isn't rude unless he's strung out or one of his friends has done something to piss him off. "Stop judging me, okay?"

"I'm not judging you. I'm judging him." But the judgment in Luca's eyes suggests otherwise.

I no longer feel ashamed that I'm going with Miller, but I am ashamed of who I am now—of who I've chosen to become. *What would Mom and Dad think of me if they saw me now?*

But who else am I supposed to be?

I jostle the thought from my mind, letting the pills take over. "I have to go," I say to Luca. "I'll see you later, maybe." Bracing my hand on the hood of the truck, I reach for the passenger door.

"Wait a sec." Luca bounds over the fence and fishes a pen from his shirt pocket. His warm fingers fold around my wrist, and my stomach flutters stupidly, something it hasn't done for months.

"What are you doing?" I ask, jerking back in a panic.

He scribbles something on my palm before I can pull my hand away. "Call me if you need anything, okay?" He casts a distrustful glance at Miller who's yelling at someone on the phone. "Like if you need a ride or something."

I run my thumb along the ink on my palm. "Why are you being so nice to me?"

"Because I'm a nice guy, something you're clearly not used to." He gives another pressing glance in Miller's direction.

Again, I feel ashamed, but let the pill smother out the feeling like rain does to fire.

"So, you tried to carry my book and wrote your phone number on my hand. You are seriously old school, aren't you?" I say. "Let me guess. This number is to your home phone."

"Ha, ha," he replies sarcastically, then flashes me a grin that causes my heart to beat like crazy. "No, it's my cell, you goof."

I don't like how he's making me feel inside, like I'm . . .

Anna. Not Mysterious Annabella. Not Freaky Gimp Girl. Just plain, ordinary, sometimes good Anna who gets butterflies in her stomach.

"Thanks, but I promise I'm not going to need anything." Before he can say anything else, I haul my ass into the truck.

"I don't fucking care what's going on," Miller growls into the phone as he thrusts the shifter into reverse. "It's not my problem. It's your problem. That's what you get paid for."

Luca eyeballs the truck as Miller backs down the driveway, and part of me wants to bail out of the truck, keep talking to him, feel what it's like to be that girl again. Instead, I stay put and Luca turns for my front door as Miller drives toward the intersection at the end of the block. We make a right, and just like that, Luca and my need to be that old, silly girl vanishes out of sight.

I concentrate on the road while Miller continues to yammer on the phone, driving toward the highway on the opposite side of town. I wonder where we're going, but don't ask because it doesn't really matter, as long as I get to escape my house and my thoughts.

As we near the site of the accident, I rest my forehead against the cool glass. Sunlight glistens across my face as I close my eyes and silently count to twenty. When I open my eyelids again, we're smack dab in the middle of the road where the semi sideswiped my parents' car. The mile marker is still bent from the crash and tiny metallic fragments still speckle in the grass on the side of the road.

The faint echo of metal crunching fills my head . . . The slam of the impact . . . The scream . . . The deafening silence . . .

He chucks his phone onto the dashboard, jolting me from the memory. "So, this fucking sucks."

I tear my eyes away from the window. "What does?"

He fiddles with his eyebrow ring, hooking the tip of his pinkie through it. "The home owners are probably going to press charges."

"How do you know that?"

"That was my lawyer on the phone. I mean, it's not official or anything, but he said there's a good chance they're going to."

"You have a lawyer?"

"Don't you?"

I prop my clunky boots onto the dash, shrugging, being intentionally evasive, because Miller doesn't need to know any more about me than he already does—it's not what he's for. I do have a lawyer, though. Jane's a friend of the family and knows way more about me than she should.

"Well, you should, especially if you're going to be hanging out with me a lot." He shoots me an artful grin. "I have a bad habit of getting nice girls into trouble."

My lip curls in annoyance as I remember how he abandoned me at that house. "I'm not a nice girl, Miller." Which might be the most truthful thing I've said. I used to be, but now I'm just the girl who stresses out her brother, makes her sweet sister cry, and who ignores her younger brother. Alexis is the only one I'm not a bitch to, but that's because she doesn't care enough to even try to talk to me anymore.

"Yeah, you kinda are." He continues to grin smugly, and it probably irks me more than it should. He sighs. "Look, I know why you're really upset. I get it. I was kind of an ass for bailing on you like that." He splays his fingers across my thigh and strokes my knee, and like always, I feel nothing from his touch, no shivers, no sparks.

It sends that familiar numbing feeling through my body, which is why I'm here, right? Usually, I can answer myself with an easy yes, but today I pause, remembering how I briefly contemplated going back to the house.

"But I'm already on probation, and I just . . . I don't know. I panicked," Miller continues on, withdrawing his hand and tugging his fingers through his blue hair. "If the owners do press charges, I'm in deep shit. I might even get jail time."

I want to feel bad for him, but he brought it on himself. Just like I brought all of this on myself. If I would've been stronger and opened my mouth when my dad got in the car that day, then maybe it would've put an end to the trip. Then we would've never been on the highway, never been in the accident, and Loki wouldn't have had to give up his college life to become both a mom and dad to the four of us. Zhara would be really happy instead of trying to fake it all the time. Alexis would be the silly, caring person who loved art and making other people smile. Nikoli would say more than three sentences to me in an entire week. And me, I'd be that dancer who would probably have a huge crush on the sweet, cute guy next door who didn't honk his horn and yell at me to get into the car.

God, the what ifs. Just thinking about them is too overwhelming.

"Don't worry. I'm sure they'll go easy on *you*," Miller rambles, his voice conveying a drop of bitterness. "You're not on probation, and I'm guessing those rich parents of yours will help out."

"Rich parents . . . What are you talking about?"

"You know exactly what I'm talking about. And I'm kinda pissed you never told me you were rich. I would've had us steal shit from your house."

"I'm not rich," I argue. "Not even close."

"Could've fooled me with that fancy fucking house you live in," he says snidely. "It's ridiculous you've been living like that the whole time, and we've had to hang out at the dump I live in."

"I don't live in *that* nice of a house."

"Whatever. Keep fucking lying to me."

Not knowing what else to say except for the truth, I seal my lips and refuse to say anything else.

"Who was that guy you were with when I pulled up?" The gears grind as he downshifts.

I scrape at my nail polish. "Just a neighbor."

His gaze cuts to me. "You sure about that?"

I feel like banging my head against the window. This is a new side of Miller, and I don't like it at all. I want the numbness back instead of this icky, frustrated feeling festering inside me.

"Yeah, I'm sure," I say quietly.

"Whatever." He slips on his sunglasses. "I know we aren't, like, a super close couple or anything, but I've always been really honest with you. You know how shitty my parents are, and you know how messed up my past is. I've been really open with you, more than I have with anyone. I thought we were on the same page, but clearly we're not. Which really sucks, because I like you. I just hate being lied to."

I want to argue that I'm not a liar, but I'd only be defending a lie with a lie. Everything Miller said is right, except for him implying that something is going on with Luca and me. What's shocking, though, is how upset he is.

"You said you liked that I was mysterious," I remind him. "And now you're saying you don't. It's confusing."

"There's a difference between being mysterious and being a liar," he snaps, a vein in his neck bulging.

I think he might be strung out, which puts me on edge. I've seen him like this a couple of times before, and he can get really angry, but, typically he takes it out on Big Jay or another one of his buddies. Not me.

He parks in front of a tiny cabin located in the middle of nowhere. Broken vehicles cover the yard and there's an outhouse in the back. Just diagonal from the property is the junkyard, but I can't see a house, business, or person sight, except for the roof of the antique shop just up over the hill.

"Look, I'm sorry I'm being a jerk. I'm just a little hungover, okay?" Miller hops out of the truck and glances back at me with his bloodshot eyes. "You coming in?"

I shake my head, and he kicks the door shut, cursing.

I try to figure out what to do, where to go, but the answer leads me to a thousand paths I'm not sure I'm ready to take.

I stay in the truck as the sun sets behind the hills and the sky shifts from a bright orange pink to a dusky grey. The moon and stars wake up. Around seven, someone starts texting me, but I ignore each one, not ready to face what's in them.

The effects of the pill I took earlier slowly fade away with each passing hour. Around eight or so, a tall, gangly guy wanders out of the house. The guy is at least Loki's age, if not older, but looks way rougher around the edges. He's on the thin side with overly long hair and yellow teeth, and for the first time in a while, I grow uneasy.

Standing under the porch light, he pops a cigarette into his mouth and lights up. His eyes lock on the truck as he exhales a cloud of smoke, and I don't like how nervous his look makes me or how aware I am that no one else is around.

I try to force the numbness into my body, pretend I don't give a shit, but out here, all alone, almost fully sober, my uneasiness shifts to full-on panic. I push the lock on the door then scoot toward the driver's side as the guy hops off the steps and heads in the direction of the truck. He beats me to the door, jerks it open, and the interior light clicks on.

"Hey, what are you doing out here all alone?" he asks with a smirk.

I inch toward the passenger side. "Nothing. Just waiting for Miller."

His wolfish grin broadens. "Hate to break it to ya, but Miller ain't comin' out for a while." He glances at the house then his eyes lock on me again. "Why don't ya come inside and find him."

I stick my hand into my pocket to get my phone. "No, thanks. I'm good where I am."

His eyes scroll over me from head to toe, then he nods at the cabin. "It's not really a question. I was just being polite. You're makin' people nervous, and you need to come inside." A look of warning flashes across his face. "Come on. I don't bite."

"Fine." I plant my feet on the ground and stumble out into the dirt.

Grinning, the guy bumps the door shut, and he remains way too close to me as we head to the front door.

The first thing I notice inside the cabin is the stench, like musk and mold mixed with too many people crammed into too small of a room. Music is booming and people are dancing, drinking, and smoking. I've been to parties before, but this one is more intense. Everyone looks older than me and seems comfortable with all the drugs and drinking.

"There's your boy right there." The guy points to Miller who's sitting on a bright orange couch, smoking and chatting with a girl.

She's wearing a short black dress and boots, has a red streak in her strawberry blonde hair, and multiple facial piercings. Her style is similar to mine, but I have a feeling we're not even close to being the same. Her look screams *notice me* while mine begs *hide me*.

Miller spots me through the crowd, and his expression lights up. Clearly, he isn't as pissed off as he was earlier, and I'm betting the dazed look in his eyes has something to do with that.

He staggers to his feet and stumbles past people, making his way to me. "Hey, I was just wondering where you were."

He hands me the cup he's holding, and I chug half of it down, trying to burn away my uneasiness with alcohol.

"In the car, where you left me." When he juts out his lip in a pout, I sip the rest of the drink down to hide my eye roll. "Look, I just came in to see if you could give me a ride home. I just got a call from my parents, and they want me home."

He chuckles, rubbing his bloodshot eyes with his fists. "Yeah, there's no way I'm leaving right now. After what happened last night, I need a break from reality." He removes the cup from my hand, sets it down on the cracked linoleum, and then laces his fingers through mine. "You should stay. You look like you could use a break, too, and this place is awesome for that."

A break from my life is the reason I came with him tonight—is the sole reason I spend time with him at all. But he's been getting on my nerves tonight, and my thoughts are all jumbled over whether or not I really want to be here.

Miller hauls me toward a group of people dancing. "Come on, Anna, dance with me." He roughly grinds his hips against mine while gripping my wrist and moving our linked arms above my head to spin me.

I dig my heels into the carpet. "I don't dance. Ever."

"Yeah, ya do," he says, grinding against me again. "Remember that one time a couple of weeks ago when we were hanging out at Big Jay's?"

"That wasn't me," I holler over the music.

"Yes, it was." His head tips back, and he stares at the ceiling. "You were wearing that blue dress I love."

"I don't wear dresses, ever." Partly because of the scars but mostly because I burned most of my dresses after the accident.

Loki walked outside and caught me when I did it and about had a breakdown. "What are you doing?" He ran to get the hose to put the fire out. "You can't just burn your clothes."

"I already did." I left the yard and went inside, convincing myself I felt better that all my old clothes were gone, and that I'd somehow managed to burn away the person I once was.

But even the fire hadn't been able to kill off the old me completely. Deep down, I wanted the dresses back.

"Oh, I must have been thinking of someone else, then." Miller stares at me with a drunken grin on his face. "Guess we'll just have to do it now."

He elevates my hand above my head and gives my arm a tug, attempting to spin me around.

My knee twists, and I trip over my feet. "I said I don't dance," I say through gritted teeth. Jerking away from him, I shove my way toward the kitchen to get another drink.

I pour a cup of juice mixed with vodka and sip the eye-watering liquid as I watch the crowd, my thoughts of dancing and dresses gradually fading away after taking a few hits off a joint someone hands to me. I sit back and focus on the people around me. Usually at parties, there's at least one person I know from school, but everyone is older here, and even with a cloudy head, I feel oddly out of place. It doesn't really make sense, considering I'm not chatty, anyway. And anyone that *really* knows me—*really* knows my family— always wants the juicy tidbits of what happened. So, I should be grateful that I'm surrounded by unfamiliar people, yet I feel lonely, like an outcast, out of place.

I don't belong anywhere.

I frown at the drink in my hand. My escape from myself tonight has turned into a disaster.

"What's with the pouty face?" Miller appears in front of me, his eyes so bleary he's barely able to focus.

I discard my cup in the trash. "I think I'm ready to go."

"No way. Not yet." He entwines our fingers together, pressing his clammy palm against mine. "Let's go somewhere and talk."

Talking is the last thing I want to do, but before I can respond, he steers me out of the kitchen and down a dimly lit hall. The alcohol seeps through my veins, and I stumble into a dizzy spell. The stained brown walls and faded orange carpet grow blurry. My body feels detached from my mind, as if I'm floating, and I have no choice but to grip onto Miller; otherwise, I'll fall down.

The deeper we go into the cabin, the danker the air becomes, and the more I plummet into a state of vertigo where I can't tell what's up or down, if I'm supposed to be here—if I want to be here.

I'm so confused all the time.

When he leads me into a bedroom and slowly closes the door, a chill slithers up my spine.

Something doesn't feel right.

The lock clicks.

Does anything anymore?

I collapse onto a bed and my heavy body bounces against the hard mattress as I gaze at the ceiling beams. After I get my bearings, I prop up on my elbows and focus dazedly on Miller.

He grins, and I hate it. Hate him. Hate myself so much I can barely stand it.

I just wish I could call my mom and dad, ask them to come get me and bring me home. I could curl up in a ball and forget the last six months ever existed. Wish this wasn't my life. Wish I hadn't messed everything up.

Tears burn my eyes.

Goddammit! Stop thinking so much.

Just be Mysterious Annabella and relax . . .

Maybe it's the pungent scent of the air or how heavy my

body feels, or Miller's gaze boring into me, but I can't seem to chill out. Even the alcohol swishing around inside me is doing nothing to calm my nerves.

"I'm thinking we should pick things up from where we left off the other day," Millers murmurs with his arms crossed over his chest. His bloodshot eyes deliberately drink me in as he bites his bottom lip. "Yeah, I'm definitely thinkin' that's what we should do."

My stomach drops. The other day? The other day when I promised him we could have sex? I try to relax, ask myself, why not? Just get it over with it, it doesn't matter. *Nothing does. Nothing you thought existed ever did.*

The way I pictured my first time creeps up on me. I was always with someone I loved and who loved me just as much, and I was definitely sober since Delusional, Naïvely-Believed-In-Happily-Ever-After's Annabella never felt the urge to drink or get high. No matter how angry I get with myself, no matter how lost I feel, I still want that moment to be how I once dreamed it would be. That's the thing with dreams. I can run away from them, try to shove them aside, but deep down, I still *want* everything I dreamt of—that life I created in my head.

Blood roars in my eardrums. "I'm not sure I want to do that anymore."

His eyes flare with rage. "Why not?"

I feed him a lie. "Because you ran off and left me."

He grimaces. "I apologized for that."

"Yeah, you did." I roll off the bed and stare out the window, trying to disregard his withering stare. "But I'm not in the mood right now."

"Why did your brother pick you up from the police

station?" he asks. "It's been bothering me for the last few days because it doesn't make any sense. You're under eighteen, right? Why weren't your parents there?"

I feel so drowsy, so disconnected from my body. "My parents sometimes work the night shift."

The floorboards creak under his weight as he stalks closer. "Where?"

"What do you mean where?"

"Where. Do. Your. Parents. Work?" He stops just behind me and firmly grasps me by the hips.

"At a place," I reply as his body heat suffocates me. My feet hold my weight but unsteadily, and I regret getting so trashed I can barely grasp onto reality.

"Stop bullshitting me, Anna." He yanks on my shoulders and forces me to face him. "Tell me the truth," he demands, no longer looking happy high, but angry high. When I say nothing, he shoves me into the wall. "You know, I'm starting to wonder if everything you've said is one big fucking lie. If you're one big fucking lie." When I say nothing, he shakes his head, fuming mad. "I should've known this was how you were going to be when I first met you. You were so desperate to be someone else. Figures you were just another rich girl trying to escape her perfect life."

"That's what this is about? You're pissed off because you think I'm rich?" My semi-intoxicated mind can barely make sense of what he's saying.

"No, I'm pissed off because you're a little rich brat who's going to get off because mommy and daddy can pay for the best lawyers while my ass is going to rot in jail." His face reddens as he reaches for me.

I skitter out of the way, but put too much weight onto my

bad leg. The room spins as my knee buckles, and my hip bashes against the windowsill. I cry out in pain, and Miller grinds to a halt. The pain is good. The pain thins the fog in my head, helps me clutch onto reality more.

"And that's another thing," he continues, getting more riled up. "What the hell is wrong with your leg? The whole time I've known you, you've walked around with a limp. You said it was from a horse, but there's this guy I know that said you were in some sort of car accident."

I rub my hand over my face, knowing that the solitude I had with Miller is gone. The angry guy standing in front of me is too demanding and needy to be my escape anymore, even if he is high.

Putting most of my weight on my good leg, I step forward. He doesn't budge, and my shoulder bumps into his chest.

"Move out of my way." My voice wobbles, my cracks showing, the old Anna slipping through, and I loathe it— loathe her for being so weak.

His gaze lingers on my chest. "This is such bull," he says, snatching hold of my arm. "Five months and I didn't even get laid. What. A. Waste." He shakes his head in disgust.

"You're hurting me," I cry out, bending my arm to try and pull away.

He looks down at his hand on my arm, and for a moment, his fingers tighten. When I wince, he pushes me down on the bed.

I shut down, let a door slam shut in my mind, as he covers my body with his and starts kissing my neck. I tell myself I can do this—that I won't panic—but when his hands dip down my pants, anger, hurt, and shame obliterate the numbness.

"Stop! I fucking said no!" I press my hand to his face and shove him back.

He glares down at me as I breathe raggedly then slides off me. "Get the hell out of here. I'm too strung out to deal with your drama."

Fixing my shirt, I squeeze by him and out of the room, only breathing again when I make it to the kitchen. I grab a beer and fumble to pop off the cap. The fresh air somewhat helps clear my foggy mind. I start down the driveway, taking a few swallows, trying to compose myself. But reality is seeping in as I realize just how bad the situation could have been if Miller hadn't stopped. Goosebumps dot my arms, even though I'm wearing a jacket, and tears pool in my eyes, threatening to pour out. But I suck them back, pull my shit together, and wander deeper into the night, trying to figure out how I'm going to get home. I could call Loki or maybe try getting home on foot. More than likely, the second choice will end with me on the side of the road in unbearable pain. Still, out of the two, the latter seems the most enticing—calling Loki means facing stuff I can't face, especially after what just happened.

Cece would probably come get me, but calling her means talking during the drive home. Right now, I just need a ride, without complications or potential meltdowns.

My boots scuff against the dirt as I glance down at the palm of my hand. It's too dark to see the number so I use the flashlight app on my phone. Luca doesn't know me that well, so hopefully he won't drill me with questions.

It takes me a few tries to punch in his digits correctly, but

I finally dial his number. My finger hovers over the talk button for a minute or two before I actually push it. It's only ten o'clock, but when the phone rings four times, I wonder if maybe he's in bed.

He answers right as I'm about to hang up. "Hello?"

"Um . . . Hey."

"A . . . hey, too, whoever you are."

I sit down on a large rock at the end of the driveway, set the barely touched beer down, and stretch out my legs. "Oh, yeah. This is Anna . . . from next door."

"Oh, hey." He goes from confused to upbeat. "Wow, I'm really surprised you called."

"That makes two of us." I squeeze my eyes shut, feeling queasy. "Did you really mean what you said? About calling if I needed anything?"

"I never would've given you my number if I didn't mean it," he tells me with a trace of amusement in his tone.

"Good. Because I need you to come pick me up."

"Like, right now?"

I open my eyes as headlights shine on me, and I tense, worried it might be Miller. "Yeah, like right now."

He pauses, and I hear a door close. "Where are you?"

I trap my breath in my chest as the car zooms by, kicking up a cloud of dirt. My gaze travels toward the silhouette on the hillside. The roof of the house isn't visible anymore, but it's there, hiding in the dark. "I'm out by the junkyard about a mile past an antique shop. There's a sign, so you should be able to find it."

"*Wait?* Why are you at a junkyard?"

"I'm not at the junkyard. I'm sitting out on a rock in front of a cabin *near* the junkyard."

"Are you okay?"

"I'm fine . . ." *Am I, though?* "I just need a ride home."

"All right, I'll be there in, like, thirty minutes," he says easily. "Are you going to be okay until I get there?"

"Of course I'll be okay." I self-consciously touch my leg. "Why wouldn't I be?"

"You tell me. You're the one calling me in the middle of the night asking for me to drive out to a junkyard." Silence fills the line. He sighs. "Okay, I'm on my way."

I yawn, wishing I were home so I could pass out. "Okay, see you in a bit, I guess."

"Okay, Anna, see you in a bit." Humor touches his tone as if he finds my attitude funny.

I hang up and lie down on the rock with my phone clutched in my hand. My heart rate calms as I gaze up at the stars, listening to crickets chirp, and trying to ignore the foul odor drifting from the junkyard.

Memories of my family camping under the night sky sneak up on me. My dad would tell us stories of ghosts, monsters, and aliens—he always had a crazy imagination. My mom used to tell me that I shared my dad's crazy imagination and that one day it would take me somewhere amazing. I used to believe her, but now I can't figure out what the truth is or ever was, just like I can't figure out who I'm supposed to be.

Growing restless, I slide off the rock and dust off the dirt from the back of my jeans. I pace the end of the driveway, biting on my fingernails. Tonight could have been worse. How did I end up here? How did I become this person? Why do I feel so confused? So *empty*?

My gaze flicks to the hillside. *It all started there.*

I want to know what lies inside—what happened that day—but at the same time, I don't want to know. I want to run toward the house, but I can't. I want. I can't. Want. Can't.

Too many questions flood my mind as I wander down the side of the desolate road, taking lazy steps. As the cabin —and Miller—grows further away, I quicken my pace, and my leg muscles groan in protest. But I keep moving until I'm at the end of the dirt driveway that leads to the two-story house by the antique shop. The lights are off, and in the darkness, it looks so harmless, just a house and store.

The air is still except for the crunching of the gravel beneath my boots as I stagger over a few potholes and trip over a couple of rocks. I make it to the front porch steps, farther than I've ever gotten before. My gaze bores a hole in the door. What's on the other side of it? Who was that man? What did my mom really do while she was here on my birthday? Was she really having an affair?

I inch up the rickety stairs until I'm standing on the wrap around porch. I cup my hands around my eyes and press my face to the window. I can't see anything other than the outline of furniture, but I'm filled consuming rage.

It all started here. The lies. The secrets. The destruction.

Anger erupts through me, like hot lava about to explode. Backing down the stairs, I scoop up a rock and chuck it as hard as I can at the window with so much hatred inside me it's terrifying. Shards of broken glass fly everywhere, and I feel myself shatter right along with it.

TEN

GUESSING GAMES, OLD SCHOOL ROCK, AND LIFE-SAVING INK

I STAND THERE, STUNNED AT THE DAMAGE I'VE CAUSED. THEN a dog starts howling from inside the house and an upstairs light flips on. My phone rings, breaking my shock into smithereens.

Fumbling to shut off the ringer, I hurry away from the house. My leg muscles kink as I dive behind a tree right as the front foot door swings open and light beams across the yard.

"Who's out there?" a man hollers. "Whoever you are, you're in deep shit."

I align my back to the trunk of the tree and hold my breath. Shoes scuff against the dirt, growing closer to me. I almost walk out from my hiding spot, just to see if he is the man from that day.

"I'm calling the police!" he shouts, then slams the door.

Balling my hands into fists, I stab my nails into my palms and take off through the dry field toward the road. When I reach the road, I travel the path along the fence line just in case the cops show up.

My leg just about gives out several times as I trip through the dark, unsure of where to go. I have the heartbreaking urge to be home, curled up in a ball, like I used to do when I got sick. My mom would bring me soup and have a romance movie marathon with me. I felt so loved and taken care of . . .

I hunch over and dry heave until all the alcohol I drank earlier comes back up. As I'm wiping my mouth clean with the back of my hand, my phone rings again, and I dig it out of my pocket.

"Yeah," I answer with a cough.

"Hey, where are you? I'm parked in front of the cabin near the junkyard, but I can't see you anywhere . . . You aren't inside, are you?" Luca asks with apprehension.

"No, I'm walking on the side of the road . . . near the antique shop about a mile back." I press my hand to my damp forehead and breathe in and out through my nose as my stomach gurgles again.

"Okay . . ." He sounds perplexed, but doesn't ask questions. It makes me like him just a tiny bit more. "I'm headed there now." I move to hang up when he adds, "Stay on the phone with me until I get there."

"Why? You're not that far away."

"Yeah, but you seem like a wanderer."

"I'm not." The dry grass kisses my legs as I start hiking down the side of the road again.

"All right. I guess you'd know better than I would," he says over the humming of an engine.

"Yeah, I would." But I'm not sure I'm right.

Music gently flows through the receiver.

"Are you listening to the classic rock station?" I ask, unable to help myself.

"Of course. I'm old school, remember? What else would I listen to?"

My dad used to listen to that station all the time when he was at the store. He was always humming tunes by singers and bands like Journey, Lynyrd Skynyrd, and even Johnny Cash. Sometimes, when I shut my eyes, I can still hear him humming . . .

"You still there?" he asks a minute later. "Or did I lose you?"

"Are you still there?" I retort, opening my eyes.

He chuckles. "Yeah, I'm still here, Anna. Where else would I go?"

"I don't know . . . Home? In fact, it might be wise . . . I'm a mess right now," I babble as a spout of wooziness overcomes me again.

"That's okay . . . I'm used to that kind of stuff." He gives an elongated pause, hesitating over something.

"You're used to dealing with people who're a mess?" Exhausted, I kneel down in the gravel on the side of the road.

"Kind of . . . You're okay, though, right?" His concern unsettles me because I don't deserve it. Don't need it. Don't want it.

I kind of do, though.

"Why wouldn't I be?" I ask through a yawn.

"I don't know." His tone drips with sarcasm. "Maybe 'cause you called me up in the middle of the night to pick you up near a junkyard out in the middle of nowhere. Plus, that cabin . . . It seemed sketchy."

"It is sketchy," I agree, hugging my knees to my chest. I feel sick and beaten down and super freaking tired. I think I went overboard tonight. Too much alcohol or something. Or maybe what happened with Miller is twisting up my gut.

Miller. Tonight. His hands all over me.

I shift to my hands and knees, the phone falling to the ground as I dry heave again. By the time I'm finished, the ground feels like it's an out of control merry-go-round.

"God, I just want to go to sleep," I mutter.

"Anna, are you there?" Luca's voice comes from somewhere on the ground.

I feel around until I find my phone. "Yeah, I'm still here," I say, sitting back in the dirt.

"I thought I lost you for a moment," he says, sounding worried.

Poor guy. I kind of feel sorry for him and the mess he's about to walk into.

I'm just about to let him off the hook, tell him to turn around and go home, that I'll find another ride, when I spot a pair of lights shining through the darkness.

Relief washes over me. *I just want to go home.* "I think I can see your headlights."

"Okay . . . where are you? I don't see you anywhere."

"Sitting on the ground near . . ." I squint through the dark. "Mile marker six."

The car screeches to a stop a few feet away from me. Hanging up, I trip to my feet, but frown at the height between the ground and the door.

The door opens on its own, and Luca is leaning over the

console. "Are you going to get in or just stand there?" he asks in a playful tone. He's not wearing his glasses again and is sporting a grey knitted cap. That cute, nerdy look he had going on the other day would be gone except for the goofy grin he has on his face.

"Where's your car?" I ask, grasping onto the door.

"That's my mom's. The Jeep's actually my dad's." His mouth sinks at the mention of his dad.

Clearly, Luca doesn't have a fantastic relationship with his dad—I could tell that when he told me about the interview. But what I don't get is why his dad was crying out on the porch.

I massage the side of my leg before reaching up and grabbing the top of the seat. Putting all of my weight on my uninjured leg, I bounce up and down on my toes.

"Shit. Do you need help getting in?" he asks, reaching for door handle to get out.

"I got it." To prove it, I drag myself up into the leather seat. Pain surges through my leg, but my teeth clamp down on my lip, stifling the cry clawing up my throat.

"Are you sure you're okay?" he asks worriedly. "You look like you're in pain."

I close the door and the interior light clicks off. "I promise I'm okay. Always okay." *Liar. Liar. You're anything but okay right now.*

"Because you could tell me if something happened," Luca says cautiously. "That guy you drove off with . . . He seemed really intense."

"He is." I rest my head against the cool glass. "But I swear, nothing happened." Nothing I'm ready to talk about right now, anyway.

He studies me for a moment before driving down the road. Thankfully, he has the music turned low; otherwise, my crumbling night would end up in a pile of dust on the floor. Of course, the silence between us is extremely uncomfortable.

As the miles stream by, my nausea declines to drowsiness, and I almost pass out, my thoughts promptly drifting back to what almost happened. I can still feel where Miller's fingertips pressed into my skin, hard enough to leave bruises. I feel like getting drunk until I pass out, getting so high until I can't think straight, kissing someone until I'm so numb I feel dead inside . . .

My stomach muscles clench and vomit burns at the back of my throat again. Tears sting my eyes as I choke it back, refusing to hurl all over Luca's car.

"So, are you going to bite my head off if I ask what you were doing all the way out here?" Luca asks as we near the city limits, where the fields turn to closed shops, the grocery store, and the bank.

Inhaling and exhaling, I struggle to keep my tone even. "I was at a party." I hunker down in the seat when a cop car zooms down the street toward us.

"Must have been quite the party for you to want to leave early." His gaze flicks from me to the road. "What're you doing?"

"Nothing." I only breathe freely again when the cop car flies by us.

"Is there something I should know about? Like, am I harboring a fugitive?"

"I'm only a fugitive if you let me get caught. So really,

the ball's in your court. You can either turn around and hand me over or just let it go."

He searches my eyes for something. "I guess that all depends on what you did."

"That doesn't really matter." I drape my arm over my tender stomach. "It wasn't anything major."

"I think I should be the judge of that."

"How do you figure?"

"Because you seem to overlook really intense stuff."

"Like what?" Sitting up in the seat, I feel defensive all over again, like I did in the driveway.

"Like when you were roasting out in the sun, wanting to walk home like it was no big deal." He counts down on his fingers. "Or when your boyfriend was yelling at you in the driveway and you just shrugged it off."

"He's not my boyfriend," I say, suppressing a moan as my gut churns. "And even if he were, he isn't anymore. Not after tonight."

"He did something to you, didn't he?" His knuckles whiten as he strangles the wheel.

"No, he didn't," I say, surprised by his intense reaction. "Seriously, Luca. Nothing happened, so chill out."

He turns his head and looks at me, still holding a death grip on the wheel. "But something almost happened." It's not a question, but a statement.

"Almost isn't something you need to get all worked up about."

"Yeah, I do. If he almost did something to you, then that means he tried." He flexes his fingers and tilts his neck from side to side. "I seriously want to go back and kick his ass."

"You don't seem like the kind of guy that'd be very good

at ass kicking," I say. "And trust me. It's not worth the risk of getting your ass kicked."

He shoots me a dirty look. "Hey, I can hold my own."

"You seem too nice to hold your own in a fight."

"I can be mean when I want to," he says sternly, but I can tell he's struggling not to smile. "If you want, I can turn around, drive back to that cabin, and prove it to you."

On the brink of smiling, I casually cover my mouth with my hand. "Fine, I totally believe that you can be a mean asshole when you want."

"Then why are you almost laughing?"

"I'm not." Collecting myself, I lower my hand to prove it. "And I don't even know why we're having this conversation. I never said anything happened, and even if it did, it was probably partly my fault." I swallow hard as tears flood my eyes.

"Anna, whatever happened back there, it wasn't your fault." He places a hand on my knee, and I suck in a breath.

Breathe. Air in. Air out. "You don't know me well enough to make that assumption, and trust me, a lot of the shit I do is my fault."

"Not what happened tonight, though."

"You don't even know what happened." *Inhale. Exhale.* My belly aches. "Can we please talk about something else?"

He opens his mouth to say something else, but snaps his jaw shut. He flips on the high beams with his gaze fastened on me, his eyes meticulously scanning me over. "So, fess up. What'd you do?"

I'm so relieved he dropped the Miller subject that I end up answering his question without thinking. "You know the antique shop a couple miles back?" I ask through a yawn, and he nods. "I . . . threw a rock through the window."

"Just before I picked you up?" His expression is unreadable.

"Yeah, it's why I was walking down the road. And that's probably where that cop was heading."

"Interesting." Musing over something, he turns up the volume of the stereo and drums his finger on top of the wheel to the faint sound of "Last Kiss" by Pearl Jam.

"Interesting?" I sit up straight in the seat, suddenly feeling very awake. But his nonchalant attitude isn't what I was expecting. "That's all you have to say, after what I just told you?"

He lifts his shoulders, shrugging while watching the road. "What do you want me to say?"

"How about 'get out of the car.' Or 'I'm never talking to you again.'?"

"Why would I say that?" He seems to get his kicks and giggles off making me uneasy.

"Because you seem like a good guy who doesn't get into trouble," I say with a shrug. "And trust me, I'm trouble, even when I don't mean to be."

He presses his hand to his chest, feigning to be appalled. "How dare you accuse me of being a good guy? I thought we already established that I could be mean and that I know how to kick ass."

"Yeah, that was more you saying that than me," I say. "And I'm not joking. I really threw a rock through the window. Go back and look if you don't believe me." Why am I so dead set on him believing me?

"I totally believe you, but it's not that big of a deal, and I don't really think you're trouble, even if you think you are. Although, I'm really curious why you threw the rock." He watches me, testing my reaction.

My eyes narrow into slits. "Because I can't stand the guy who lives there." I bite down on my tongue as soon as I say it. What am I doing? Pouring out my secrets to him? Is this who I am now? Blabbering, Semi-drunk Annabella.

His curiosity piques. "Why can't you stand him?"

"No reason. Forget I said that." When he doesn't say anything, I flop back in the seat. "Can we talk about something besides my anger issues?"

"Sure, but FYI, this is the second subject change I've given you, so you owe me," he says with a straight face, so I can't tell if he's kidding or not. "What do you want to talk about?"

I sweep my hair out of my eyes. "Anything, just as long as it has nothing to do with me."

"Hmmm . . ." He taps his finger against his lip. "Did you know that Pearl Jam had five different drummers?"

"I actually did," I say, confused by his choice of subject, but in the best way possible.

"Ah ha! I knew it." He points at me, grinning from ear to ear.

I jolt in the seat, glancing around, startled. "Knew what?"

"That you liked classic rock. That the emo rock you were listening to earlier was just a cover up, like the purple hair." He rests his hands on the steering wheel, smiling proudly.

"You're so far from being right it's not even funny," I say, but it feels like a whopping lie.

"No, I'm so close to being right it's frightening." He winks at me, and I have to catch my breath.

We stare each other down, and then he busts up laughing, his eyes crinkling around the corners. His laughter is contagious, and I find myself plagued by it. A laugh tickles at the back of my throat, begging to come out, and I bite down on my lip, desperate for a subject change. I could try to kiss him as a distraction, but considering how madly my pulse beats just contemplating the idea of our lips pressed together, I don't think it's a wise idea. Luca clearly isn't Miller and isn't going to give me that same numbing sensation I seek when I kiss him.

"Why'd you guys really move here?" I sputter suddenly.

His laughter vanishes in a heartbeat. "My mom already told you why."

I fiddle with a frayed hole in the knee of my jeans. "But it kind of seemed like maybe there was another reason."

"Like what? We're really criminals on the run?" he jokes flatly. "You really want to know, because I'm not really supposed to tell anyone."

I hesitate. Do I really want to know more secrets? "I'm not sure."

The conversation screeches to a halt when three more squad cars fly by, red and blue lights flashing. Luca curiously looks at me again, but doesn't ask questions. I wouldn't have answers even if he did. I'm as clueless as he is as to why on earth there'd be that many cops responding to a broken window.

"If you're not sure, I think I'll keep it to myself." He focuses on the road. "So, how cool is it to own a bookstore? I think it'd be pretty freakin' cool. Well, unless you don't like to read. But in that case, I think I'd have to kick you out of my car."

And the conversation spins right back to me again. "Fine, I really want to know why your family moved here."

"Are you sure you're sure? Because I got a whole bunch of fun music facts I could share with you." He stares at me with hope in his eyes.

I'm twistedly glad that he's the uncomfortable one now. "Nope. Fess up. What's the real reason?"

He cracks his knuckles against the steering wheel. "Fine, but just for the record, I'm only doing this because it's pretty clear you don't want to talk about yourself, and since I've pretty much got you all figured out, I know I'm making you really uncomfortable."

I open my mouth to protest, but shut my trap when I realize arguing is exactly how he wants me to react. "You're clever, but I'm not going to fall for your subject-changing tricks this time."

"Dammit, I'm going to have to come up with new tricks now." He massages the back of his neck, sighing. "My mom wasn't lying. She really did want a change of scenery."

"But there was more to it than that," I guess, sticking my hand into my pocket to silence my phone as it vibrates.

"A lot more. And most of it has to do with my sister."

"But I thought you were an only child?"

"That's the story my mother's been feeding everyone, but my dad found out this morning and got super pissed, so now she's switched it to she does have a daughter who's away at college."

"I'm guessing she isn't in college, though?" My phone

rings again, and I shut it off, knowing it's probably Loki calling to scold me.

Luca laughs, but the hollow noise sends goosebumps sprouting across my flesh. "Not even close."

I start to ask where she is, but trail off as he turns into the only twenty-four hour gas station in Honeyton. "What're you doing?"

He parks in a vacant spot close to the entrance and flips off the headlights. "I need a caffeine and sugar run."

I squint at the red, slightly burry numbers on the dash. "Right now? It's almost midnight? Don't you need to get home?" I say, because it feels like we're hanging out now. If I wanted to do that, I would've called Cece.

He grips the door handle to get out. "Says the girl wandering down a dirt road just thirty minutes ago."

I slouch back in the seat. "But I really need to get home."

"I'll only be, like, five minutes." He hops out and glances back into the cab. "You can come in if you want or sit out here, but I'm not bringing you anything." A challenge dances in his eyes as he closes the door.

I stubbornly stay in the seat. But my stomach grumbles, reminding me that about an hour ago, I emptied its contents into the grass. I'm starving and candy sounds so good right now. And maybe a soda to wash the bitter taste out of my mouth.

Blowing out an exasperated breath, I climb out and limp into the store. The florescent lighting stings my eyes as I pass the cash register and stroll down the candy aisle. The cashier, a girl who's around my age, watches me like a hawk, and I avoid eye contact with her, praying to god that I don't know her.

Luca strolls up to me as I'm assessing the candy options, my attention bouncing back and forth between M&M's and Snickers, two of my favorite candies. In fact, I used to eat them together all the time, taking a bite of chocolate and chasing it with a handful of M&Ms.

"So, what's your poison?" Luca asks. He has a fountain drink in his hand, and as usual, he's grinning. "No wait. Never mind. I know what it is."

"Are we talking drinks or what? I ask with an arch of my brow.

"Don't pretend like you're a bad girl," he says. "You're not, and you knew I was talking about candy."

His bluntness makes me lose my footing, and between that and the fact that I'm still a little drunk, I can't think of a comeback.

My gaze slides to him. "There's no way you could know what my favorite candy is."

He grins goofily at me. "Yet, somehow, I magically know exactly what you're about to pick." He nudges my shoulder. "Guess I'm just super perceptive."

I cross my arms and stare him down. "Alight, Mister Perceptive. What was I about to pick?"

He slurps his soda, staring at me. "What do I win if I get it right?"

"Anything you want." I play along since there's no way he's going to get it right.

"Okay, you're on." He reaches for my hair and tugs on a strand. "You were about to pick Skittles." Before I can shake my head, he says, "I'm just kidding." When I roll my eyes, he adds, "Sorry, but I couldn't help it. I'm going to be serious now."

I widen my eyes and gasp in mock shock. "You know how to do that?"

"I do actually," he quips, handing me his soda. He cracks his knuckles then he rubs his hands together as he carefully assesses the candy choices. With a dramatic flair, he lifts his hand and swirls it around in a circle above the candies before scooping up a bag of M&M's.

"Dammit." I don't mean to say it aloud. "How the heck did you get that right?"

He holds up a finger. "Just a sec." He also grabs a Snickers. "I think these were what you wanted, right?" He presents the candies to me in the palms of his hand, like he's giving me prizes.

I grunt as I grab them. "Okay. Fess up. How'd you know?"

A cocky grin spreads across his face as he takes his soda from my hand. "Because I'm a mind reader, obviously."

"Well, obviously." Sarcasm drips from my voice, thick like honey. "No, seriously, how'd you know?"

He grabs a pack of gum. "No way. I'm not telling you my secret."

I lean against the shelf as my leg starts killing me. "That's not fair."

"It's completely fair. And it'll drive you just crazy enough that you'll want to hang out with me to find out how I'm so clever." He picks up a Twix and turns it over in his hand.

"I highly doubt you're that hard up for friends. And if you are, go hang out at the football field during lunchtime. That's where almost everyone our age hangs out, even during break."

"See, that's why I need you to be my friend." He snatches

up a bag of Skittles, winking at me. "You know all the ins and outs of this town."

"They're not that hard to learn." I rub my eyes with my free hand as another spurt of dizziness hits me like a bag of bricks. "There's probably a total of three."

He selects a few more snacks. "Yeah, but this place is kind of intimidating."

"You lived in L.A. How the hell could Honeyton be intimidating?"

"Because everyone knows everyone here, which makes it hard to find people wanting new friends." He glances at the stash of candy in his hand then skims the shelf again.

I gape at him. "Are you seriously getting more?"

He gives me an innocent look as he reaches for a bag of chips. "What? I'm a guy. I get hungry."

I eyeball all the junk food he's holding. "Dude, even someone with the worst case of the munchies wouldn't eat all that crap at once."

"Speaking of munchies. Your eyes look super bloodshot right now."

"I'm just tired." I blink a few times to hydrate my eyes.

He brushes by me and heads for the register. "It's okay if you're high. I'm not judging you. I just thought I'd let you know so you don't get in trouble when you get home."

"I'm not high," I protest, trailing after him.

"Okay," he says simply.

"I'm being serious." I feel the need to argue, something that seems to be a growing trait around him. "And how would you even know if I was?"

He shrugs, growing tense. "It was just a guess."

He's lying, but why? Maybe he gets high? He doesn't seem like the kind of person that does, though. Then again, six months ago people would've said the same thing about me.

He drops all the candy on the counter then sets his soda down, smiling at the cashier when she gapes at his teeth-rotting collection of sugar. "Half of it's hers," he says, nodding his head at me, shooting me a devious grin.

I scoot enough candy to hold me over until Halloween toward the register. "No. It's all his. I'm not taking credit for your crazy-ass sugar eating habits."

He steals the candy from my hand and adds it to the pile. "Now it is."

"I can pay for my own," I reach to snatch my candy back.

He swats my hand away. "No way. You're not paying on our first date."

"Aw, it's your first date." Cashier Girl swoons with a flutter of her eyelashes and a clasp of her hands.

"It's not a date," I say, glaring at Luca.

"Ignore her," he tells Cashier Girl as he retrieves his wallet from the back pocket of his jeans. "Anna has this thing with calling the best night of her life a date."

He's gotten way too comfortable, winking at me, teasing me, calling me Anna. "You know my name's Annabella, right?"

"Yeah, but you prefer Anna," he says. "Even if you won't admit it."

I scrunch my nose at him, and he smirks.

"Wait . . . Annabella Baker? Oh, my god." Cashier Girl stares at me as if I've suddenly sprouted a third eye in the center of my forehead. "Jesus, I hardly recognized you. You look so . . . different."

It takes me a second to figure out who she is. Charlotte Levingson, Cece's cousin.

"That's an interesting choice of hair color," she says when I don't utter a word.

I touch a strand of my hair. "It's just purple."

"Yeah, but you don't see a lot of purple hair around here." She begins ringing up the candy bars. "Not that it's a bad thing or anything. It's just a little out of the norm." The register beeps as she scans the bar codes.

"Which is why I did it," I lie, letting my hair go.

"That's cool." She smacks her gum as she discretely checks Luca out.

Luca has his attention fixed on me and doesn't seem to notice her. "That's why you did it? Wow, I'm kind of disappointed."

"Why? Isn't that why everyone does crazy things like dye their hair and pierce their body—to stand out?" I ask, propping my elbow on the countertop, staring back at him.

He shakes his head. "When I got my tattoo, I got it to represent something major that happened in my life."

My brows shoot up in surprise. "You have a tattoo?"

"It's not that big a deal. My mom and dad took me to get it done one day for . . . certain reasons," he explains cryptically as he rolls up his sleeve, showing a tattoo on his forearm.

It's small, about the size of a quarter, with a few horizontal lines that connect to form the bottom of a heart.

"Wow, that's so awesome." Charlotte grazes her finger across his arm. "What does it mean?"

"Strength," he replies, tugging his sleeve down.

"That's really cool. I'm thinking about getting a tattoo soon." She scans the last item and presses the tally button. "Probably when I head to college here in a couple of months so my parents can't get all pissy at me when I do it."

He smiles at her as he hands her a twenty. "Just make sure you get something that means something to you, or at least something that you won't hate in a couple of years."

They chat a little bit more about tattoos while I peel open the Snickers and munch on it.

As Charlotte gives Luca his change, she asks, "So, you're new around here, right? I'm pretty sure I haven't seen you around."

Luca nods as he puts away his wallet. "I just moved here a week ago."

"Cool. There's a bonfire down at the docks this Friday. You should come." She glances at me. "You should come, too. Cece should be there."

I stuff my mouth full of chocolate. "I already have plans, but thanks." There's no way I'm going someplace where I'll be surrounded by stares and ridicule. Besides, after tonight, I'm not that eager to go to another party.

But then what the hell am I going to do with myself?

"Well, think about it," she says. "I know she's been worried about you ever since your parents died. It really sucks what happened to them. They were such good people—"

I walk away before she can finish, push out the door, and step out under the stars. The crisp air burns my dry throat and reminds me that I forgot to get a drink. But I'm not about to go back inside to get one.

I wrap my arms around myself as my body begins to shiver. I try to convince myself it's from the cold, but I know that's not the reason. Charlotte struck a nerve, reminded me of their deaths, that stupid fucking day that ripped my life out from underneath me. Usually I can choke down what I feel, but after such an emotional night, I'm struggling.

The door dings as it swings open, and Luca steps out. "Are you okay?"

I stare at the vacant street in front of me. "Yep, perfect. I forgot to get a drink, though."

He moves up beside me and offers me his soda. "Drink up."

I eye the cup then him. "You really want me to drink from yours?"

"I promise I don't have cooties," he says, urging me to take the soda.

I take a few long gulps, washing down the bitter taste in my mouth before I hand it back to him. We get into the car without saying anything else, which I'm super thankful for. Although, he's grinning idiotically about something.

"What're you smiling about?" I ask as he slides the key in the ignition.

"It's nothing." His grin widens as he backs out of the parking space. "I just find you amusing. That's all." He twists a knob on the stereo, surfing for a station, still amused by something.

"But I didn't do anything."

"That's not true." Clearly he thinks I'm entertaining, and it's starting to drive me crazy that he won't share why.

After he selects the same station he started out on, he places his hands back on the steering wheel and drums his fingers to the beat of the song. The sleeve of his shirt has ridden up and the bottom of his tattoo peeks out.

"You don't seem like someone who would have a tattoo," I say as I tear open the bag of M&Ms.

"That doesn't really seem like a fair statement," he replies, giving me a curious sidelong glance. "That'd be like me saying that you seem like the kind of person who should have a tattoo."

"Maybe I do have one."

"Do you?"

I shake my head. "No."

He smiles, but it's a mask with sadness hidden behind it. I want to ask him why he looks sad, but since he didn't push me to talk at the gas station, I return the favor to him and remain quiet.

About halfway home, though, all that chocolate suddenly wants to come back up.

"Shit. Pull over," I sputter, covering my mouth to fight back the vomit.

Luca slams on the brakes, and I fall out of the car before it even comes to a complete stop. When I land on my hands and knees, the gravel scrapes at my skin through my clothes. I puke my guts out on the side of the road. My eyes water, and my stomach feels like its tearing open with each gag. Somewhere in the midst of gagging and moaning, Luca crouches down beside me and holds my hair out of my face. I want to tell him to go away, that he shouldn't have to witness what I deserve, but I'm too exhausted to get the words out.

By the time I've emptied my stomach, my legs are too

weak to budge. I lie down in the dirt, fully prepared to go to sleep.

"No, don't go to sleep. You need to get up." Luca slips his hands under my arms.

"I'm fine. Just go home," I mutter, resting my cheek against the rocks.

Ignoring me, he pulls me to my feet and steadies me as I sway. "Don't be silly. I'm not leaving you on the side of the road." He guides me to the car with his hand around my back, supporting most of my weight.

I bury my face into his chest, murmuring. "You smell so good. So much better than I do."

He chuckles, his chest vibrating as he smoothes his hand over the back of my head. "Yeah, let's get you home."

He practically has to lift me in the seat, and instead of protesting like I usually do when someone helps me, I let him and feel the smallest bit of gratitude when he draws the seatbelt over my shoulder and buckles me in.

He gets into the car, and I focus on the stars in the sky to keep my stomach under control. Before I know it, we're pulling up in his driveway. The lights are on upstairs in his house, but my home is dark. My bet is that my family is out looking for me and that all the missed calls and texts I have are from Loki trying to track me down.

"Thanks for the ride." I unfasten my seatbelt. *And holding my hair back while I hurled.*

He offers me a soft, but concerned smile. "Anytime."

Holding onto the door, I gradually lower my feet to the ground.

"Anna, I can help you out," he says, rushing to get out.

"I'm good. I swear, I'm feeling a ton better." As I put

weight onto my legs, the muscles clench up. One side of my jeans feels super tight, probably from inflammation, which means not only will I have to spend the next few days lying around with my leg elevated, but Loki's going to be riding my case even more about going to physical therapy.

He meets me around the side of the car. "You want me to walk you to the door?"

"Luca, it's right next door. I swear I'm fine now."

He peers warily at my dark house. "Are you sure you're going to be okay being alone?"

"Positive." I move around him, wanting nothing more than to be in my bed. Maybe sleep will help me forget this night ever happened.

"Hey, Anna," Luca says as I limp down the driveway.

I pause at the fence line, tensing. After everything that happened tonight, and everything I told him, I have no idea what he's about to say and that makes me uneasy.

"I was thinking, as a favor for picking you up tonight and winning our little candy bet, you could show me around town." His voice is surprisingly light, and if I wasn't already feeling grateful toward him, I definitely would be now. "It sucks moving here during break. I've seriously spent the last week binging on Xbox and episodes of *Ridiculousness*. It's starting to drive me crazy."

"What about Charlotte?" I say without looking at him. "I'm sure she'd be happy to show you around."

"If I didn't know any better, I'd say you were jealous."

"Don't be weird. I don't even know you well enough to be jealous." Am I, though? It's hard to tell anymore what I am or aren't.

"Yeah, but if you hang out with me, that'll change. And

maybe we can get past this awkward friends phase," he teases.

I resist a smile. "Is that what we are?"

"Yeah, and considering I just saw you puke your guts out on the side of the road, I think our friend status might have been bumped up to the sharing-embarrassing-moments phase."

I cast a glance over my shoulder. "That's not true. I haven't seen you do anything embarrassing yet."

"Oh, give it time. Trust me, embarrassing myself is one of my many talents." He stuffs his hands into the pockets of his jeans. "So, what do you say? Will you show me around town? Be my awesome tour guide?"

"How do you know I'll be awesome," I say. "Maybe I'm super annoying and give lame and super annoying tours."

"Yeah, I have a hunch that's not true. Just like I have a hunch that we are going to end up in the super-close-friends phase. And I'm never wrong when it comes to my hunches." He sounds so much like the old me, all hopeful—*delusional.*

I picture myself showing him around town, waving my arms around as I show him all the cool hangouts and the very uncool hangouts as well. We'd make jokes about the frumpy statue in the park while eating slushies. I'd wear one of my dresses just like I used to, and maybe we'd even hold hands. It'd be a perfect first date that would end with an amazing kiss. I can see it so vividly it's terrifying, and the idea of acting on it is so heavy and unbearable, I feel like I'm suffocating.

I start to tell him no, crush his hope, but after what he did for me tonight, I can't bring myself to do it. "So you're a *Ridiculousness* fan, huh?" I avoid answering him.

"I guess you could say I have a weird sense of humor," he says, sounding nervous for my answer. When I don't reply right away, he adds, "If you want, I'll get down on my knees and beg you to show me around. In fact, it could count as my embarrassing moment."

I pretend to be repulsed by his offer, when secretly I think I might like it. "Please don't do that. And besides, that's not as embarrassing as puking on the side of the road." My phone rings in my pocket, and I sigh. "Look, I'll show you around *if* Loki will let me out of the house. But don't get too excited. He's pretty pissed off at me right now."

"I have a feeling he's going to make an exception for me," he says, and I can hear the smile in his voice.

"I doubt that, but I'll ask." I drag my foot with me as I hobble toward my back door.

"See you tomorrow, tour guide girl!" Luca hollers. "And don't pretend like you're not looking forward to spending more time with me. I can see you smiling all the way from over here."

I bite down on my tongue to keep from doing exactly what he just accused me of. For the first time since the accident, I think I might actually be looking forward to getting grounded. The last thing I need is to be hanging around with Luca and his joking, flirty, contagious smiling, rescuing me from the side of the road, and holding my hair back while I puke myself. He's way too nice and way too much of what the old me would want. If I let him in, then what? I'm just supposed to be that person again? Only I won't be able to dance—be able to do anything that I used to love. Could I be okay with being that person?

I blink my burry eyes as I stumble into the kitchen. My

phone hums for the umpteenth time as I turn on the lights. Deciding it's time to face the music, I open my texts.

Miller: Hey, where r u? The cabin is getting raided and I can't find my truck keys.

I reread the message at least ten more times and then check the time stamp. The text was sent pretty close to when Luca picked me up.

A crushing weight settles on my chest as I listen to my voicemail. Five messages from Loki, all of him yelling at me for leaving with Miller. Not wanting to hear him yell at me, I text him that I'm home, then shut off my phone, go upstairs to my room, and flop down on my bed.

I don't want to admit it, but just like the time when Miller first pulled up to rob that house, I can't deny the truth that's right in front of me—that part of me really doesn't want to get into trouble. I've spent the last six months pretending I'm some sort of rebel who doesn't give a shit about anything, but when it all comes down to it, I still care more than I want to. This rebellious thing I'm trying to pull off is as unfitting as me trying to dance with my useless leg.

Where does that leave me? Back to square one with no clue as to what to do in this world anymore?

The only real thing I'm sure of is that if Luca hadn't rescued me from the side of the road, I would've been wandering around the area when the arrests were made. I could've gotten picked up, maybe even for breaking the window. And only days after getting arrested.

Yep, the stupid ink saved my ass tonight.

I was saved from a lot tonight, though. So much that it's overwhelming.

I look at my reflection in the mirror. Big eyes traced with

so much eyeliner, I can hardly recognize myself anymore. But they're still the same eyes I had before the accident—I'm still me underneath the heavy makeup and hair dye.

My body shakes as the night crashes over me and yanks me down.

No, I'm not Anna.

I'm Annabella.

I'm mysterious.

I'm rebellious.

I don't care about anything.

Don't want to care.

I'm so lost.

I miss my dad and mom.

I curl up in a ball and hold my breath until I feel like my lungs are going to explode. Then I roll over, bury my face into the pillow, and scream until I have nothing left inside me.

ELEVEN

RUN ALL YOU WANT, BUT THE PAST WILL ALWAYS CATCH UP TO YOU

THE NEXT MORNING I HAVE ONE OF THOSE MOMENTS WHERE I wake up and can't remember a damn thing about the night before. This is a growing habit in my life, and I know in a minute or two, I'll remember some tidbits.

As I'm getting out of bed, memories of Miller hurting me, drinking too much, and Luca saving my ass rush back to me.

"Oh, my god, I puked in front of him." I don't know why, but I feel really mortified.

Embarrassed Anna? Guess I really am back to square one.

When I go down to get some breakfast, Loki informs me that I'm grounded over Christmas break for taking off from the store, which also means no visitors, including adorably nerdy neighbor guys. So, Luca was wrong, and I was right. I'm more sickly gratified by it than I should be.

Sunday morning, I pop a pill to numb the pain in my leg

and in my soul. Without Miller around, I realize that in order to obtain the numbness, I'm more than likely going to have to take more pills.

As part of my ongoing punishment, I go to the store with Loki, which ends up being less intense than the first time, but that might be because I'm exhausted. When we come home that evening, I head straight up to my room to elevate my leg. I spend most of night watching television and skimming over Miller's texts.

Miller: This is so screwed up. U should have warned me they were coming. Big Jay said he saw u sitting out in front of the cabin so I know u saw the cops before they got there.

Miller: Was it because of what happened in the bedroom?

Miller: I know u r mad, but I thought u wanted it til u flipped out. It's not my fucking fault I didn't know. U r so hard to read.

Miller: Seriously, u can text me back. I'm probably going to jail.

Miller: We're over.

Miller: Come on. Answer a goddamn text. I need a favor.

And there it is, the reason why he's so dead set on getting ahold of me. Whatever the favor is, I'm betting it either has to do with money or drugs. If he knew the truth about that night, that I might have been the cause behind the police raid, he might be more pissed off than he already is.

Apparently, the cop that busted the party was initially headed out to another call but spotted a bunch of people hanging out at the cabin and made a pit stop there because the owner of the house was on probation for drugs. The officer investigated, and yeah, I knew what kind of drugs created the musty, dank, sweaty-body smell in the air because it was the same kind of drug Miller's been smoking more frequently. My bet is the cop was originally headed to the antique shop to check out a call about a broken window.

Over the next couple of days, I distract myself with school, the store, and trying to ignore Luca the best I can. He makes it difficult, though, and deep down, I know shutting him out is wrong. After what he did for me, he deserves better. But I'm not ready to give anyone better, including myself.

When I leave for school Monday morning, Luca just happens to be outside, though, eating his cereal and messing around with the garage door.

"Holy shit, you do still live here. I was beginning to worry you might have ran away just to avoid me," he jokes lightheartedly, but there's a nervous gleam in his eyes.

"Wow, you think pretty highly of yourself, if you think I'd move just because of you," I retort, unable to stop the words coming out of my mouth.

"Yeah, you're right. But you were hiding out because of me. Admit it." He waggles his eyebrows at me then grins.

I shake my head. This is so getting out of control. "I wasn't hiding from you. I've been grounded.

He shovels a spoonful of cereal into his mouth as the garage door lowers to the ground. "For how long?"

"Indefinitely." I squirm in my own skin, hyperaware of the Baker clan eyeballing us from the truck.

"Did you ask Loki if you could at least spend a couple of hours showing your awesome new best friend around?" he asks, wiping a dribble of milk from his chin.

I snort back a laugh. "Awesome new best friend? Is that the title you've given yourself now?"

"What? It's the perfect title. Just like yours."

"Which is?"

"My awesome-friend-who-loves-trying-to-sleep-on-the-side-of-the-road. I have to say, I've never had one of those before."

I don't even know why I bothered asking. It only leads me into danger of laughing and smiling, and with my siblings right there watching me, it just doesn't seem right. Not when any of them laugh anymore.

"Well, awesome new best friend," I refrain an eye roll, "hate to break it to you, but I asked Loki and he said no exceptions, even for you."

"You could tell him it's for charity," he suggests, balancing the bowl on top of the fence. "You could tell him it's for the Luca is Super Lonely and Needs to Get out of His House and Away from His Crazy Mom Charity."

"Yeah, I don't think he'd buy that."

He sighs dejectedly. "Fine, I guess I'll just have to come up with something more clever."

I shift my weight to my good leg. "You could always try stunning him with you candy mind-reading tricks."

Picking up his bowl, he backs toward the front door. "That's actually not a bad idea. I'm going to go practice."

"I wasn't being serious," I shout after him, but he's already jogging inside the house.

My creative mind conjures up all sorts of possibilities about what he's rushing to do. Practicing telepathy? His Jedi-mind skills?

I smack my forehead with the heel of my hand. *Seriously, Anna. Get a grip.*

Shaking my head at my absurdity, I turn to get into the truck.

Loki watches me inquisitively as I scoot into the backseat.

"Why are you looking at me like that?" I ask, combing my fingers through the snarled locks of my hair.

He trades a grin with Zhara then looks back at me. "No reason."

"Would someone please tell me what's going on?" I demand, tossing my bag onto the floor. They goofily smile at each other again, and it floors me. "Seriously, guys, what's going on?"

"They're just acting like idiots because you were smiling like a dork while you were talking to the dorky neighbor guy," Alexis sneers. "Jesus, I swear everyone's losing their damn minds. I mean, who gets excited over a smile?"

"But she never smiles," Zhara says, flinching when I scowl at her.

"I wasn't smiling." I touch my fingers to my lips. Was I? No. There's no way. But the possibility that I could've been plagues me to the point until I feel sick to my stomach again, just like last night. How can I be happy when no one else is? "We weren't even talking. Luca was just being weird and asking me all these questions, and I listened to be polite."

"Polite's more than we get," Zhara points out, dusting a few crumbs off her pants.

I start to protest, but no noise comes out except a sputter. Agitated, I face the window and keep my lips sealed.

The next morning, I move as slow as humanly possible while getting ready for school to avoid running into Luca.

But Loki grows really impatient with me and honks the horn repeatedly.

I throw open my window. "I'll be down in a minute!" I yell down at the truck, but tense when I see Luca bouncing a basketball around in his driveway, sweaty, wearing nothing but a pair of basketball shorts. He's not ripped or anything, but he's definitely in shape, and I can't help but gawk.

"Oh, Anna. Oh, Anna," he singsongs as the ball swishes the through net, breaking me from my trance. "Let down your purple hair."

I stab my teeth into my lip to avoid any and all potential smiles. "That was really lame."

He shrugs as he bends over and scoops up the ball. "So what. It almost got you to smile."

"No it didn't." But it *almost* did, and that scares the shit out of me. Happiness isn't supposed to be what I'm feeling. Sad, sure. Guilty, yes. But all smiley and gooey inside, no.

With my pulse soaring, I slam the window shut.

I manage to make it into the house that evening without crossing paths with Luca. But later the next night, I hear muttering coming from the house. I toss and turn, then bury my head under my pillow, trying to ignore it. But eventually, my curiosity gets the best of me, and I climb out of bed, pad over to the window, and peer outside.

Darkness blankets the neighborhood except for a few lampposts and porch lights. Next door, a man is sitting on the steps with the phone pressed to his ear. His head's bowed down, and the sound of his sobbing cover up whatever he's saying. I swallow hard as pity clogs my throat. Whatever's going on is causing him a lot of pain, just like Loki, Zhara, Niki, Jessamine, and Alexis went through right after my parents died. I feel sorry for him. For all of them. I even kind of feel sorry for me.

No, I don't deserve pity, even from myself.

Jerking the cord, I yank down the blinds, pop my headphones in and crank up the most earsplitting music I can find, then stretch my leg out onto a pillow. I have boxer shorts on so my scars are visible. I trace the rough edges of the uneven skin, remembering how smooth it used to be. Remembering what it felt like to circle my leg around, toes pointed as I lifted my weight. My body was stable and supported my graceful movements, let me dance to the rhythm, get lost in the music . . .

"I need a pill," I mutter to myself, rolling out of bed.

Zhara, Loki, and Nikoli have gone out to see a movie, leaving Alexis and me with the house to ourselves. The place is quiet except for the neighbor talking on the phone again.

I wander downstairs to grab the prescription bottle from the cupboard, but when I walk into the kitchen, Alexis is there.

"Your roots are showing," Alexis says with a fake smile.

"Your nose piercing looks infected." I open the fridge, pretending I came down here for a snack.

"Yeah, it happens sometimes." She collects a plate of pasta from the beeping microwave. "And just so you know, I saw Loki searching your room yesterday while you were in the shower."

I pick up a bowl of what looks like mac and cheese. "Why?"

She shrugs indifferently as she gets a fork from the drawer. "I'm guessing it has something to do with the conversation he had with that nosy bitch Laretta about the signs someone's on drugs."

"Like Loki doesn't already know the signs. He used to get high all the time during his senior year. Remember that time we caught him in the garage? He said it helped clear his head and figure out the meaning of life. Like that was a legit excuse."

She chokes on a laugh, spitting out pasta all over the countertop. "Oh, my god, I totally forgot about that." She reaches for a paper towel to clean up the mess. "But I don't think that's the kind of drug he's worried you're doing, and he decided to take extreme precautions." Her gaze travels to the cabinet above the sink.

Even though I'm desperate to look and see if the pills are still there, I calmly lift the plastic off the mac and cheese. "He can look all he wants, but he's not going to find anything."

"He knows Miller got busted for possession," she says, balling up the paper towel and chucking it into the trash. "Just in case you don't already know, he's a total loser. You should really stop seeing him."

"Why do you even care?"

She diverts her attention to her food. "I don't. I'm just sick of hearing Loki whine about it all the time. It's starting to get annoying."

I think there's something she's not telling me. "How'd

Loki find out about Miller getting busted for drug possession?"

"Probably through town gossip." She throws me a wave over her shoulder as she heads for the doorway. "Well, it's been great talking to ya, but I have way better shit I could be doing, and I'm sure you want me to get the hell out so you can raid the cupboard and look for those pills you came down here for."

"I didn't come down here for pills," I say, feeling way too transparent. Am I really that obvious?

"Sure you weren't."

"I wasn't, Alexis, so stop assuming things." Noting the splatters of neon paint on the back of her grey t-shit and holey jeans, I shift the focus onto her. "Wait. Are you painting again?"

She scrapes her fingernail across one of the pink paint spots on her shirt. "Nope, these are from last night."

"You're still in your clothes from last night . . . What, were you, like, at a rave or something?"

"That's none of your damn business." Shoving a forkful of pasta into her mouth, she strides out of the room.

Moments later, her bedroom door bangs shut and music booms through the house.

I rush to the cupboard to check for my pain meds and immediately flip out. They're gone. "Shit." I slam the cupboard and massage my temples.

I don't need them. I'll be fine.

But my skin clams up just thinking about it, and as I head for the stairs, my body feels so weighted, heavy, like I have absolutely no energy at all, yet my mind is the opposite, wired, needy, begging me to feed the hunger inside. I swear

I'm going to die if I don't find a way to get some more pills. I just about break down and text Miller to buy me some and bring them over, but then I picture the last time I saw him, how his fingers marked my skin, how he held me down. My stomach burns just thinking about it, and I know I'm not ready to go to Miller for anything yet.

When I shut my eyes that night, the last dose of the pill I took is pretty much out of my system. I'm shaky and out of it and tumble into a dream for the first time since the accident.

I'm in the rain in the middle of the road wearing tattered ballet shoes too small for my feet. I know I'm supposed to be somewhere, but I can't get my legs to move, as if the flesh of my feet has melted to the asphalt, and the pain is so unbearable, I nearly pass out.

When I wake up, I don't really understand the point of it, but the fact that I dreamed at all doesn't sit well with me. I end up getting my father's journal and stare at the envelope.

Dennis, who are you?

Drenched in sweat, I almost open it. But half an hour later, I put the book away without looking inside. I spend the rest of the night streaming episodes of *Buffy the Vampire Slayer* on Netflix and then turn on *Halloween*. Back in the day, I would've watched something cheery, like a romantic comedy, but mushiness is the last thing I think I can endure at the moment.

After a night of horror movie marathon, with hardly any sleep, Loki barges into my room, looking stiff and awkward in the button down shirt and slacks he's wearing. His shoes are shinier than lip-gloss, and even his hair is combed to the side. Only a year ago, when he came home from college last summer, he'd been sporting scraggily hair, a scruffy beard, and lots and lots of plaid shirts and torn jeans.

He takes one look at the blood and gore on the screen and frowns. "You used to hate this kind of stuff. In fact, you'd almost pass out if you so much as got a paper cut."

My gaze remains locked on the television screen. If I look at him while I'm sober, I'm going to crack apart. "Things change after seeing your leg flayed open and your parents bleeding out next to you."

He studies me from the foot of the bed, then leans over to catch my gaze. "I've been thinking and talking to some people, and I really think it might be a good idea for you to see a therapist."

"No, thanks. I already spend way too much time with the school counselor."

"This isn't the same kind of counselor. He specializes in cases like yours."

"I don't have a case. My parents died, and I changed. That's it." My voice is too high—too revealing. I quickly focus on the television screen.

"You can't keep running from the past like this. It's unhealthy, and one day it'll all catch up to you." When I remain silent, he turns off the television. "You're going to talk to a therapist. End. Of. Discussion. I'll set up an appointment on the same days as your physical therapy, which you're going to begin tomorrow. I have an appointment scheduled, and I took off the morning so I can personally drive you there." He smiles an ah-ha-now-let's-see-you-get-out-of-it smile.

"I'm not going to physical therapy. It's just a waste of time." I pick up the remote and flip the television back on

"And, FYI, you really need to stop getting information from Laretta. She may *think* she can relate to you because she *thinks* Steve is like me, but she's not a twenty-one-year-old parent to four teenagers, so her opinion's pretty irrelevant. Plus, Steve's been in jail more times than I can count."

"Don't be so unsympathetic. Laretta's a single parent." He grows even more frustrated when I don't react. "God, don't you even feel the slightest bit bad for her? For *anyone*?"

"I feel bad for you that you have to talk to her." *I feel bad for you for having to take care of me. I feel bad because you don't know the truth. I feel bad because I do. Yes, Loki, I feel bad, but I worry if I tell you, I'll tell you about everything. The pain. The secrets. The lies. The confusion. Everything I've done over the last six months. Tell you about the horrible person I've become.*

He steals the remote from me, clicks off the movie, and sinks down on the edge of the bed. "I didn't come in here to argue with you." He tugs his fingers through his hair, causing a few strands to go askew. "I came to tell you that I have some good news and bad news." He rolls one sleeve of his shirt up then starts on the other. "The good news is the owners of the home you broke into have dropped the charges. I guess they know what happened to Mom and Dad and took pity on you."

"I don't want anyone's pity . . . I'm not a charity case."

"You should be damn grateful they do. Do you know how much shit you would have been in if it went to trial . . . You already have shoplifting charges pending against you that we have to go take care of later today."

I reach for a bowl of stale popcorn on my nightstand and shovel a handful into my mouth. My head is pounding from this conversation and my ears feel super sensitive to noise. "I thought that was next week."

"I reminded you yesterday morning and the morning before that." He snatches the bowl from me. "Get up and get dressed so we can go. I want to get there early and try to look like I have some clue about what I'm doing. If you care about this family at all, you'll at least try to clean up a little." He leaves my room, slamming the door behind him.

I sift through the clusterfuck of emotions coursing through me. Who do I go as? This version of me, whoever I am today? Do I get dressed in something appropriate? Who's going to court? *Me*? I glance at the mirror. *Her*? Black liner rings my eyes, and my purple hair is a tangled mess.

I really start missing the pills the more I think about it—the more I think period.

I get out of bed and go into my closet to find something to wear. As I'm rummaging for a hoodie, my phone buzzes from my nightstand. Backtracking to my unmade bed, I pick it up. Even though I didn't add him to my contacts, I recognize Luca's number.

Luca: Word on the street is the bad girl next door might be going to jail today.

An audio file is attached to the message. I consider deleting it, but curiosity gets the better of me, and I push play. "Folsom Prison Blues" by Johnny Cash turns on. I roll my eyes, but I'm on the verge of grinning as another text comes through.

Luca: Or we can go more emo, if that's what you're digging today.

Another audio file is attached, and with hesitancy, I click on it. "Prison Song" by System of a Down screams at me through the speaker of my phone. My fingers dance around the screen as I reply back.

Me: I'm glad you find my messed up life so entertaining.

Luca: I don't find it entertaining. I'm just trying to cheer you up.

Me: Well, it didn't work. Not at all.

Luca: Yeah, right. I bet you're smiling right now.

I brush my fingers across my mouth and find my lips turned upward.

Me: Whatever. I so am not.

Luca: Your short response means I totally win.

My eyes shoot invisible daggers at the phone.

Me: I'm trying to figure out what ur deal is . . . Why u r so persistent on making me smile and talking to me and wanting to hang out and be my 'new best friend.' It doesn't make sense when clearly you've heard rumors about me. And u have eyes. Plus, u witnessed me in fine Anna form the other night while I was hurling on the side of the road. That wasn't an act. I really am messed up.

Luca: I already told u I'm okay being around messed up people. And besides, u NEED to smile more.

Luca: P.S. U totally lost me at the eyes thing. Please explain your weirdo-ness.

Me: I meant you can c me, right? Ur not blind. U know what I look like.

Luca: Um, yeah. I probably c u more than u want me to.

His response makes me uncomfortable.

Me: So how does your mom feel about u wanting to make me smile? Because I'm guessing u learned about my court date from her.

Luca: My mom doesn't really care about that. She tries to see the good in everyone, maybe too much sometimes.

I wonder if that remark has to do with his sister or maybe even his dad who seems to spend so much time crying on the porch.

Me: That doesn't matter since I have no good in me. I'm all wicked, my friend. Trust me.

Luca: Trying to scare me away with your wickedness? Because it's not going to work. Plus, u called me your friend so u lose.

I shake my head. How can he be so positive all the time?

Me: I'm just trying to warn u that I'm a terrible person who does bad things and lies to good people.

Luca: I'm not going to take your word on that. U have a messed up self-perception.

Me: No, I don't. I'm just saying stuff how it is. U won't find anything good within ten feet of me no matter how hard u look.

Luca: I bet you a date that ur wrong.

Me: No way. I'm not betting u anything ever again.

Luca: Too scared I'm right, huh?

Me: No . . . U know what . . . consider it a bet. But ur not going to win.

Luca: Trust me. I'll totally win.

"Anna! Come on! We have to go!" Loki yells up the stairway.

Me: Good luck with that. I have to go before my brother loses more of his marbles.

Luca: K. I just wanted to wish u luck. Cheer up and don't let the man get ya down :)

By the time I put the phone away, I'm grinning again. I try to get it under control, but it's impossible. As I head for the closet, I purposely twist my knee, just to erase the happiness from my face. As my muscles wind into tight, painful knots, I realize how seriously fucked up I am, preferring pain over happiness.

Is this how I'm going to be for the rest of my life?

As I'm slipping on a studded leather jacket over my baggy shirt, someone knocks on the door.

"I'm coming!" I shout. "I'm just getting my shoes on."

The door creaks open and Nikoli pokes his head in. "Hey. Can I come in for a minute?"

"Oh, I thought you were Loki coming to bug me to hurry up," I say, reaching for my clunky boots that are caked in about two pounds of mud.

He tentatively enters my room, instantly noting my bare walls. "What happened to all your posters and pictures you had hanging up?"

"I took them down a long time ago." Six months ago to be exact. Stuffed them away with my ballet shoes and leotards and hid them in the back of my closet where they're now collecting dust.

He ruffles his messy brown hair into place as he faces me. "You should put some of them back up when you're ready. Your room's kind of creepy without anything on the walls, like a tomb or something."

"Tomb? That's an interesting choice of word. Are you reading ghost stories again?

He shrugs, stuffing his hands into his pockets. "It was the first thing I could think of when I looked at your room.

"Did Loki send you up here to make me hurry up?" I ask, picking up a hairbrush from my dresser.

He shakes his head, staring out the window. "Nah, I came up here on my own. I wanted to talk to you about something . . . I want to ask you for a favor."

I roughly comb the brush through my tangled locks. "You know I'm not good at favors."

He meets my gaze. "You used to be."

For a faltering moment, I see my younger brother standing in front of me, the one I used to get along with and talk with all the time. The one I pushed in the swing when we were kids, stole cookies from the cookie jar with, played hide-and-go seek with.

"We all used to be a lot of things," I say quietly, dropping the brush onto the dresser as I swallow hard.

"I know. And I know things have changed, and no one's the same, but I really don't want to end up living in some weirdo's house, so I'd really appreciate it if you'd at least pretend for the day that you care about someone other than yourself and impress this judge dude."

"No one's going to take us away, Niki." I feel so bad that he thinks that, and knowing Nik, he probably worries about it more than he lets on. "Loki just says that sometimes to get us to behave."

"He used to, but I overheard him talking to someone on the phone the other day, and he was muttering all these things about not taking us away and that he could handle it."

He scuffs the tip of his sneaker against the carpet. "Please, just do this, okay? Do it for Mom and Dad because they wouldn't want us living with someone else. And you owe them. They were good parents."

I feel sorry for him for being in the dark about the truth, but at the same time, I envy him. It'd be so much easier to change my clothes and comb my hair—make myself presentable—if I could still hold onto those Fourth of July days filled with warm sunshine, showering fireworks, and the scent of apple pie. Now, every memory is tainted with thunder and lightning, and it's hard to see clearly through the downpour.

"But anyway, that's all I have to say. Thanks for listening." He rolls his eyes and leaves my room, as if he's already convinced I'm not going to give him what he asked for.

I don't want to do it. I want to wear my tattered clothes and smudge on more eyeliner, cover myself up, and sedate my body and mind by swallowing a couple pills. Walking into a courtroom as the shy, timid, fully aware of the consequences of her actions Anna will be a hell of a lot difficult. Doesn't-Gives-a-Shit Annabella can deal with life so much better. Can deal with death. Getting into trouble. Knowing that she really doesn't have a future anymore.

No, I need to be Doesn't-Gives-a-Shit Annabella.

But, as I reach for the eyeliner, a tsunami of guilt crashes over me, pierces my heart, strikes my darkened soul.

I attempt to ignore it as I slip on numerous leather bracelets, but as soon as I reach for the doorknob to leave, I hesitate. An invisible rope is tied to my waist, secured there by a guilt woven so thickly, I can't break it.

Letting out a sequence of curses, I shuck off my jacket,

kick my boots aside, and wipe off my eyeliner. I dab on some lip-gloss, braid my hair, and change into a clean purple, button down shirt. The fabric has been untouched for so long a layer of dust covers it. I brush it off, change my holey jeans for a pair of black slacks, and slip on a pair of ballet flats.

Ignoring my reflection, I limp down the stairs to the kitchen.

Loki's eyes widen at the sight of me. "Wow, you look—"

"If you say anything, I'll go upstairs and change," I tell him, grabbing a bottle of water from the fridge.

He elevates his hands in front of him. "I didn't say a word."

I unscrew the lid off the bottle. "But you were thinking it."

"I was thinking a lot of things."

"I don't care just as long as you keep them to yourself." Otherwise, I won't be able to handle this. I move toward the door, but halt when he doesn't follow. "Why are you just standing there? I thought we were on a time crunch or something."

He lingers near the kitchen island. "We are, but it's just . . ." He shakes his head, then brushes by me on his way to the front door. "Nothing. Never mind. Let's go."

"This doesn't mean I'm going to permanently change," I call out as he hurries out the door. By the time I get to his truck, I'm out of breath and all worked up. "This is only temporary. And I only did it because Nik said he overheard you talking to someone about us getting taken away." I wait for him to unlock the door. "Is that true, Loki? Is someone going to take us away?"

"No." He pats his pocket for the keys. "I mean, yeah, Family Services has been checking up on things, but no one's going to take you away."

I can't tell if he's lying or not, but the idea that it's possible—that I might end up being the cause of our family breaking apart—scares me to death.

What if we get taken away? What if I never see them again? What if? What if? What if?

What if I would've just told Dad?

After we climb into the truck, Loki shuts the door and his gaze fastens on me. "Anna, I promise I'm not going to let anything happen to this family. I made a promise to Mom and Dad that I'd take care of you, and I'm going to do that, even if it kills me."

I clench my hands into fists. "Not everything's in your power."

"I know, but some things are, like making this family what is was. That I can do. It'll take some time, but I'm going to fucking make it happen." He taps his foot on the gas, revving up engine.

"You're wrong. Sometimes you can make all the smart choices and do everything right, but one rainstorm can come along and rip your entire life away, leaving you left with nothing. You can't fix what we were. That life died with Mom and Dad, it doesn't exist anymore, no matter how bad you want it."

He turns in his seat, gaping at me. "You seriously don't believe that you were left with nothing. Please tell me you don't think that."

"None of us were. We're all different and not for the better. No one's happy anymore. Everyone just seems confused and . . . drifting." I fix my attention on a hydrangea bush near the fence, my eyelashes fluttering as I fight back the tears.

When my mom planted the shrub, she said it was because she loved the purple flowers that grew and that it added life to the lawn. Now, the bush sits out in the yard, haunting it with memories of her.

"We're not drifting," he tries to reassure me. "Yeah, stuff's changed and we're all confused, but give it some time. Eventually, we'll figure out how to walk in the world again."

The engine grumbles for another minute before Loki gives up and backs onto the road. A few tears roll down my cheeks, and I swiftly wipe them away, hoping he doesn't see them.

The entire car ride to the courthouse is made in silence. Loki keeps messing with the stations then just turns off the stereo. Once the truck is parked, we hop out and make our way up to the rotating glass doors. We empty our pockets and get whisked through security. We've been through the process so many times we're on a first name basis with the security guards.

We silently ride the elevator to the third floor, and when doors ding as they glide open, Loki pats my shoulder.

"Everything's going to be okay. Amilia's going to make this go away and then we can go home and finish what we were talking about. I'm not going to let you keep drifting. We're going to fix this."

I'm not sure if I believe him, if he really has that kind of power, but now's not the time to argue.

My gaze flits to the twin oak doors at the end of the

corridor where a thirty-something-year-old woman wearing a white pantsuit is waving at us. "Who's Amilia?"

"Your lawyer."

"What happened to Jane?"

"She moved. But don't worry. I've heard good things about Amilia."

We meet Amilia at the doors, and she gives us a brief summary of how she predicts the trial is going to go down.

"I really want to work the angle that Annabella is going through a tough time due to the recent loss of your parents," she says, running her hands along the fabric of her jacket to smooth out the wrinkles.

"But won't that make me look bad?" Loki asks, worry written all over his face.

"It should be fine. The real concern right now is to make sure Annabella gets the bare minimum sentence," she explains, sorting through the papers she has with her. She drops a few of them and bends down to collect them. When she stands up, she offers us a smile as she yanks open one of the oak doors. "Don't worry. Everything's going to be okay."

Loki smiles with hope.

I frown with doubt.

Thirty minutes later, my doubt is justified.

The judge, a man who's around my dad's age and who used to come to the bookstore a lot, doesn't take pity on me. "I had the pleasure of knowing your mother and father. They were good people in the community." He shifts in his chair, overlapping his hands on his desk. "Having said that, this isn't the first time you've been in trouble like this, and letting you off with probation doesn't seem to be helping. I'm sorry, but I'm going to have to hand out a more severe punishment. Hopefully, this time you'll be able to learn from your mistakes."

Loki squeezes my hand as reality piles down on my shoulders.

I may have been trying to run away from my life—from my past—but not only did it catch up with me, it knocked me down hard.

TWELVE
PINKIE PROMISES, BUTTERFLIES, AND ANKLE BRACELETS

THE ANKLE BRACELET I HAVE TO WEAR OVER CHRISTMAS, and all the way into the new year, itches like a bitch. It's almost as bad as having a cast on. Plus, they put it on my injured leg, and it feels like another scar has been added to my limb. In a sick way, though, I guess the torturous punishment is fitting.

"You do realize how much trouble you'll be in if you set it off," Loki warns for the millionth time this morning. He's headed to the store for a few hours and is hardcore nervous about leaving me home alone. "You can't mess up anymore. You heard the judge. There won't be another chance. Next time you'll get jail time."

"Yeah, I got it." I stir the barely touched bowl of cereal in front of me.

Without any pills, alcohol, or Miller to distract me, the last few days have been difficult. I've spent a lot of time confused and way too emotional, on the verge of bursting into tears at any given moment. I feel out of place in my own shoes, like I'm walking in someone else's life, only it's my own life, the life I have now, and I have no clue how to deal with living it. During the day, I feel sluggish, like I'm sinking into a sinkhole. At night, I sleep restlessly, dreaming of dancing onstage, of my mom backstage encouraging me. My leg moves elegantly, my toe curved at the perfect angle. But then I wake up, and all I feel is the pain.

"Are you sure you get it?" Loki asks as he rinses off a pan. "Because sometimes I have the feeling that you seem like you hear things, but you really don't."

I poke a piece of soggy cereal, watching it bob up and down in the milk. "I said I was sorry yesterday and that I get what's going to happen to me if I don't behave. I'm not sure what else you want me to say."

He closes the dishwasher and presses the start button. "How about the truth for once? That's all I really ever want from you."

"You say it like it's so easy," I grumble.

"It used to be easy for you." He gathers his car keys, wallet, and a manila folder from the counter. "In fact, you were sometimes too honest for your own good. Like that one time when I asked you if I looked good enough for my date with Izzy Waltersen, and you told me I looked like a boy band wannabe."

The corners of my mouth twitch. "You did look like a boy band wannabe."

"And you know what? Even though I was pretty pissed off at you for making me feel like a douche bag, I was glad you pointed it out before I made an ass of myself in front of Izzy."

I prop my elbow on the smudged counter and rest my

chin on my fist. "I don't think I care enough to tell the truth anymore." But I know that I'm lying to him, and myself.

Yesterday, as I stood in the courtroom, listening to the judge reprimand me for my actions, I wanted to tell Loki everything. Explain to him why I've made so many mistakes. That I'll work on changing. But with all the stress he already has, how could I put that on him? How could I choose to make him feel the same way I do about our mom? So angry all the time. So bitter. And so guilty for feeling so angry and bitter.

"I know you don't mean that, and that somewhere deep down inside you, you still care about your family and your life, even if you don't want to admit it." He digs through a drawer full of paper clips, pencils, and markers until he finds a pen. "The physical therapist will be here in about an hour." He holds up his hand when I start to protest. "I know you don't want to get better, but this is the first step in helping you stop drifting. And you're going to be super grateful for it. Not everyone gets the luxury of having a therapist do home visits. You're lucky Easton's an old friend of mine and is doing us a huge favor. Zhara is going to keep an eye on you and has been instructed to call me if you so much as even step toward the edge of the property. I've also asked Tammy to phone me if she sees you trying to run. She might stop by and bring lunch to you guys, too."

I drop the spoon into the bowl and sit up straight. "Why are you bringing Tammy into our mess?"

"I didn't bring her into our mess. She offered to help after Miss Monelyson told her about our little predicament, which she heard from Mabel down the street." He shakes his head, annoyed. "God, I forget how fast gossip spreads around here. It makes me miss college . . ." he trails off, releasing a deafening breath. Every time he so much as mentions college he gets a really heartbroken look on his face. I can tell he misses his old life, but he refuses to ever say it aloud. "But, yeah, I'll be back around two. Stay out of trouble until then." He fans through a stack of papers in the folder, pulling out a letter-size envelope.

"What are all those papers for?"

"Doesn't matter. They're not important, except for this." With uncertainty, he places the envelope in front of me.

On the front of it, my name is written in my mother's handwriting.

"What is that?" I ask in a strangled whisper.

"It's from Mom and Dad . . . There was one for each of us with the will . . ." He clears his throat before continuing, "I was supposed to give it to you when you turned eighteen, but considering how things have been going lately, I thought it might be time for you to read it. Maybe it could help you deal with whatever you're going through."

I panic and flick the envelope away from me like it's made of poison. "I don't want to read it."

"That's your choice," he says with a disheartened shrug. "I'm just giving you the option."

"What else is in that folder you're carrying?" My gaze bounces between him and the envelope.

They wrote me a letter? When? Why?

"Just stuff I need to take care of." He winds around the counter, striding toward the back door. "I'll be back around two. Stay out of trouble. *Please.*" He waits for me to agree, and with reluctance, I nod. "Okay." He seems thrown off by my willingness. "Thanks, Anna, for not putting up a fight this time."

"It's not a big deal. I can't go anywhere or the police will show up, track me down, and take me to jail." I lift my leg and jiggle my ankle the bracelet is locked around. "I'm officially a prisoner in my own home."

"I know that, but I still need to make sure that you know you have to behave. The police can't show up here for any reason, understand?"

"I got it the tenth time you said it." My gaze zeroes in on the folder in his arms. "Are those papers from Family Services?"

"You don't need to worry about that." His jaw ticks, a habit of his when he's lying. "I have to go or I'm going to be late. Call me if you need anything." He waves at me then bolts out the door.

Silence sets in as I stare at the envelope on the counter. Finally, I get brave enough to pick it up and lift the edge with my fingernail, but chicken out and wrench my hand away.

I should just rip it up, but I can't seem to bring myself to do it. So, folding it up, I tuck it into my back pocket and pad across the kitchen. The hardwood floor feels cool on the sole of one of my feet but the other is numb. I camp out on the lumpy sectional in the living room and channel surf for something to watch. Since Christmas is in less than a week, all the shows and commercials center on the holidays.

Last year, our living room had been decked out with an oversized tree covered in tinsel and ornaments, and presents tucked underneath it. A wreath and stockings had hung over the fireplace, and twinkly lights had been wound around the banister. The entire place had sparkled. Now, it looks dull and lifeless with the *Charlie Brown* tree Loki brought home yesterday and the handful of presents Zhara stuck under it.

My head throbs achingly as my chest overflows with longing to have what used to be. I crave to get out of the house, run away, drink, swallow pills, anything other than feel this way. I glare at the ankle bracelet, hating my imprisonment, hating the judge who gave me the punishment, but worst off all, hating myself.

This is all your fault, so deal with it.

I watch TV, but don't really pay attention, getting lost in my thoughts. Things are so screwed up, and I realize all I can do is deal with it now, spend my time locked up in a home I've been running away from.

There's no place left to run.

Trapped Annabella.

My phone buzzes, and I distractedly fish it out of my pocket. I come too close to smiling when I read the name on the screen.

Luca: So, I'm staring at a picture of you right now.

I drop the remote onto the coffee table to text back.

Me: What r u talking about?

Luca: U look really cute in a tutu.

Me: Why r u at the dance studio?

Luca: Now why would I tell u that? It's more fun if u guess.

Me: No way. U clearly texted me to tell me you were there, so now u have to fess up.

Luca: No way. I texted u because I saw a picture of u hanging on the wall . . . U look cute when u smile. U should do it more often.

Me: No thanks. I prefer frownie faces.

Luca: Why? Does smiling not go with your emo rebellion thing?

I roll my eyes as I type.

Me: Yep. How'd u guess?

Luca: Like I said, I'm super perceptive ;)

After the candy thing, I think I believe him.

Me: R u really not going to tell me why ur hanging out a ballet studio?

Luca: Not over the phone. This gives me an excuse to come over and tell u in person :)

Me: I can't hang out. I'm grounded, remember?

Luca: I'm coming over when my mom brings lunch, so technically it's not hanging out.

Me: Trust me, u don't want to come over. It's super boring here.

Luca: It's better than spending another day in my bedroom, watching re-runs.

Me: If u say so.

Luca: I do say so. I find u interesting . . . I'd say make sure to be there when I come over, but I don't think that's really necessary since u can't leave ur house.

I'm not sure if he's joking, and I have no clue what to text back. Clueless Annabella, an old trait of mine.

When I don't reply, another text pings through.

Luca: Ok, so I just reread my text and realized I might've sounded like an asshole. I swear I was kidding. I told you I have a twisted sense of humor.

I decide to mess around with him, blast him with a dose of his own medicine.

Me: I'm glad u find my messed up life so funny.

Luca: I'm so sorry, Anna. Seriously. I didn't mean it. Let me make it up to u.

Me: I'm not sure u can. That was really a low blow.

Luca: I know. I'm such an ass. C, this is why my mom says I have issues with saying too much.

Me: She's right. U kinda do.

Luca: I know. I'm working on it . . . So, do u forgive me?

Me: Only if u do me a favor.

Luca: U name it and it's yours.

Me: Take down that picture of me and bring it to me.

Luca: Isn't that stealing?

Me: Nah, not technically since it's a picture of me. But u might not want to let anyone c u.

Luca: R u sure it's okay? I feel like I'm being watched.

I bite back a giggle and slap my hand over my mouth in shock.

Me: Yeah. Just grab it and put it in your pocket. No one will notice.

Luca: Wow. Instructions from an expert thief. I feel so lucky.

Luca: Dammit, I did it again, didn't I? I'm such an ass.

Me: Yeah, but I'm used to it by now.

I wait for him to answer, but he doesn't.

Me: Did you get the pic?

Luca: Running out of the studio right now with it in my pocket.

Me: Walk. Don't run. It'll make you look more suspicious.

Luca: Too late for that.

I restrain another damn laugh.

Me: And FYI, I was never upset by anything u said.

Luca: Wow, I totally got schooled. I feel like a sucker.

Me: Sorry. But I really wanted that pic down. It doesn't belong there anymore.

"Who are you texting?"

My gaze rises to Zhara who's standing in the doorway. "No one."

She nervously fiddles with the bottom button of her cardigan. "You looked really into it."

"It's just a text." I toss the phone onto the cushion when it buzzes, even though my fingers itch to read the reply Luca sent.

"Okay, if you say so," she says, but her tone is scrutinizing.

"I do say so." But really, I was so caught up in texting that I forgot about everything going on in my life.

She sits down on the armrest and crosses her legs. "I just came down here to check on you. Are you okay? Do you need anything?"

"I'm cool, but thanks."

I hear a man on the television yammering about his undying love, so I reach for the remote to change the channel.

"How about something to eat?" she asks. "I think there might be some pizza in the fridge that I could heat up."

"I'm fine, Zhara. Stop worrying so much."

She angles her head to the side, her cat eyes analyzing me from head to toe. "Are you sure? Because I can cook you something if you want. Just name it and it's yours."

"You don't cook, though."

"I used to not cook, but I took home ec last semester and I did really well. Plus, Jessamine's been giving me a lot of tips over the phone."

"How often do you talk to her?"

She seems shocked by my question, and honestly, so do I. It's been a while since I've showed any signs of caring about anyone.

"Every couple of days." She gives me an encouraging smile. "You should call her. I know she misses you. Plus, she heard about what happened and is super worried."

"She doesn't need to be." I surf through the channels again. "I'm perfectly fine."

"No, you're not," she whispers, her eyes wide.

I train my gaze on the screen, unblinking, and it takes all my strength not to cry.

Zhara springs to her feet, her face lit up like a firecracker. "You know what? I'm going to go cook some chocolate chip fudge brownies for you." She pats my foot. "I know they're your fave, so just stay put, and I'll let you know when they're done."

"Those aren't my favorite anymore—" I start, but she's already gone.

I concentrate on the movie until I get a whiff of freshly

baked brownies then I get up and sneak outside to get a breath of fresh air.

I stare at the road as the wind blows through my hair. God, what I'd give to just take off and run.

"Plotting your escape?" Luca asks as I'm edging toward the front lawn. He trots down the front steps of his house and strolls down the sidewalk toward the fence that divides our properties. "Or are you just living up to your wandering tendencies."

I gather my hair into a ponytail and secure it with an elastic from my wrist. "A bit of both actually."

He stuffs his hands into the pockets of his jeans, assessing me with his head tilted to the side. "You know that's a stupid idea, right? The police would find you the moment you stepped out of range."

I cross my arms over my chest. "You say that like you're an expert."

He shrugs. "I'm just giving you a warning. Trust me, don't try it."

"Have you had an ankle bracelet before?"

He gazes dazedly out at the street, his jaw set tight. "No, but I know someone who has."

"Your sister?" I wonder, thinking about what he said the other night.

He swings his gaze to me, and I almost fall back from the intensity in his eyes. "Can you keep a secret?"

I panic. *No, no more secrets.*

But when he frowns, looking deflated, I sputter, "Fine. Y-yeah."

"Good, because I really need to talk to someone about

this." He grabs onto the fence and leaps over it with the grace of a high jumper.

There used to be something magical when someone trusted me with a secret. Although I was never a huge fan of them, I was so great at keeping them. I heard a ton of whispered stories and wishes that my friends and family told me over the years. But that was then and this is now, and the secret I'm carrying for my mom is hard enough to lug around with me all the time.

I open my mouth to retract my answer, but his eyes zone in on my leg, and I'm reminded of another problem. Feeling super lazy this morning, I'd thrown on a pair of cut-offs. I haven't worn shorts since the accident. Right now, my scars are on full display, telling my story without my permission.

I splay my fingers over my scars, concealing them the best I can. "Did you bring my pic?"

"Yep. I sure did." He retrieves the crinkled photo from his back pocket. "Just so you know, it was way more complicated to steal it than you said."

"Hmm . . . really?" I ask, but I'm not surprised. My old dance instructor watched anyone who wandered into her studio like a hawk.

He nods, handing me the photo. "The dance instructor chased me down and almost made me give it back. She thought I was being a creeper, when she was the one who chased me down in ballet shoes and tights, doing some sort of weird shuffling thing."

I rub my hand across my face to erase a smile. "That'd probably be a chásse."

"Well, whatever it was, she looked ridiculous and super creepy doing it down the sidewalk."

My fingers wrap around the photo, curling the edges. "Sorry to break it to you, but the fact that you were hanging around a dance studio, with no intention of dancing, makes you a creeper, too."

"Hey, I was there for a good reason. I swear."

"Okay. What's the reason then, creeper?"

He chuckles at me then shakes his head before glancing from left to right then lowers down to the bottom step. "It's part of the secret." He pats the spot next to him then rests his hands on his knees. "Come sit with me for a minute."

My heart pitter-patters as I keep my hand over my scars and plant my ass on the step beside him. "Before you go spilling your guts, you should know that I suck at keeping secrets."

His gaze glides to me, and he raises a brow. "For some reason, I have a hard time believing that. You seem like the kind of girl who knows a whole lot more than she lets on."

I ease against the step behind me. "Believe what you want, but it's the truth, so don't say I didn't warn you."

"Warning taken and dismissed." He removes his glasses and cleans off the lenses with the bottom of his shirt.

"Why do you only wear glasses half the time I see you?" I ask, wanting to avoid hearing his secret for as long as possible.

"Because I'm only this awesome half the time," he jokes, slipping his glasses back on. I shake my head, stifling a smile, and he winks me. "I wear contacts when I'm trying to impress someone."

"So you're not trying to impress me now?" I aim for a bored tone but fail epically.

"You don't need to sound so sad about it." He playfully

nudges my shoulder then tucks a strand of my hair behind my ear.

The movement is so casual—so comfortable—that my muscles lock up. He did the same thing to me when I vomited on the road. I have no doubt Luca is a nice guy, and, god, what I wouldn't give to have met him six months ago, when I was the nice girl he deserves to be with.

"I'm not sad," I say, which causes his grin to expand. "And if that's the real reason, then you tried to impress me that night you picked me up."

He holds up his hands in front of him, the goofy grin still on his face. "You caught me. But the question is, did it work?"

I kind of prefer the glasses, but I'm not about to tell him that.

He gives me a knowing smile, like he can read my mind, and my heart does another pitter-patter, only quicker—more intense. It freaks the shit out of me.

I scramble to my feet. "I need to get back inside."

He snags the bottom of my t-shirt and pulls me back down. "Wait, I haven't even told you my secret."

"You're still stuck on that?"

"Of course. I won't be unstuck until I get it out."

I exhale exasperatedly. "Fine. Spill it. Tell me all your secrets, Luca Benton."

"Wow, I got a freebie secret pass. I feel so special."

"You should be. I never hand them out."

He skims over the two-story homes and grassy lawns around us before leaning in toward me. "I need you to pinkie swear that you won't tell a soul."

"Didn't we already go over how bad of a secret keeper I am?"

"I know. That's why I'm getting collateral."

"By getting me to pinkie swear?" I question with cynicism. "You do get that there aren't any real consequences if you break the promise."

He presses his hand to his heart, amusement playing at his the corners of his lips. "Pinkie swears are like the most unbreakable vow ever, Anna. Seriously. Never, ever question the bond between two people and their pinkie promises." He sticks out his hand with his pinkie hitched and waits with the most serious look on his face.

I roll my eyes at his absurdity, but hook my pinkie with his. "Fine. I pinkie swear I won't tell anyone your silly, little secret."

"It's not a silly secret." he says, aghast. "Take that back."

I give an exaggerated sigh. "Fine, tell me your dull, normal sized secret."

He smiles, but his lips falter when he glances at my thigh, completely exposed again. I pull away to cover the scars, but his pinky tightens around mine. I awkwardly cross my left arm over my right and place my free hand over my thigh.

"It's about my sister," he says in all seriousness. "And my mom and dad. I guess it includes me, too, if you really want to get technical." His entire mood has plummeted in the snap of a finger. "I was at the dance studio with my mom today because she was looking into classes for my niece since she's coming to live with us in about a week."

That secret doesn't seem too bad. Although it does hurt thinking about how lucky his niece is that she gets to dance, learn to live and breathe music.

I clear my throat as sadness sweeps over me. "Is your sister coming, too?"

He shakes his head. "That's where things get really complicated. My mom's still being really persistent that no one knows Rowan exists . . . Rowan's my older sister. She has . . . some problems."

We still have our pinkies latched, so I pull away again, but his fingers clamp down on mine as he lowers our hands to his leg, trapping them there.

"Since she was about sixteen, she's struggled with drug addiction." He scratches his forehead. "Bria—her daughter —used to live with us, but then Rowan got pissed at my mom one day and took off with her. My parents searched everywhere for her for over a year. It was crazy. They even filed a police report and everything." He cracks his knuckles against his leg. "Rowan's not a good mom, so I get why my parents were so dead set on finding her, but I felt like I was invisible half the time."

"I feel that way sometimes, too," I say without thinking, and he offers me an empathetic look. "Don't feel sorry for me. I bring the feeling on myself."

He squeezes my hand. "Still, you should never feel that way."

"So, why'd you guys really move here, then?" I put the focus back on him, not wanting to fixate on me.

"That part was actually true—we really did need a change . . . Our lives got too caught up in Rowan. Even though I loved L.A., I was kind of excited to get the hell away from that house where all the shit went down. But then, about a week ago, Rowan called, crying to my dad that she couldn't handle being a mom anymore and that he needed to come get Bria, but in Rowan style, there's a stipulation before she hands over Bria." He sucks in a breath, and I wonder if he's on the verge of crying. "She calls every freakin' night, trying to blackmail my mom and dad into giving her money before they can have Bria." He shakes his head, grinding his teeth. "We all know she only wants the money to buy drugs."

"I think I've heard your dad talking to her at night," I tell him, because I can't think of anything else to say.

His Adam's apple bobs up and down as he swallows hard. "Yeah, he talks to her outside because he doesn't want to upset my mom . . . She's not the best person at handling the hard stuff. She has this real issue with being overly nice and cheerful all the time."

"That doesn't sound so bad." My pulse thuds madly when he strokes the back of my hand with his thumb, and butterflies flutter inside my stomach. It's the exact opposite of how I felt with Miller. I hate that Luca makes me feel this way. Loathe him for it. But most of all, I despise myself for wanting him to do it again.

"It doesn't sound bad, but it is. Imagine never getting angry over anything and holding it all in." He stares down at our hands as he caresses the back of my hand again. "Eventually, you're going to explode."

I shiver from his touch, from his words. *Is that what's going to happen to me?* "Has she ever done that before? I mean, exploded because she held too much in?"

"Yeah, a couple of times, and it's really started to take a toll on her. Plus, when she's in one of her crazy nice modes, she almost becomes too helpful and turns into Rowan's crutch." He finally frees my hand, and I breathe in a huge gulp of air as the butterflies settle down. "Can you believe that she actually wants us to tell everyone that Bria's her daughter? It's fucking nuts."

"So, they're giving Rowan the money?"

"It's not really a choice. Crutch or not, this isn't about Rowan. It's about Bria . . ." He shudders. "God knows what she's gone through over the last year."

"Luca, I get why they're letting Bria live with them, but won't it seem really weird for you to suddenly have a little sister when your mom's been telling everyone you're an only child?"

"That's pretty much what my dad and I told her." He picks up a pebble and chucks it across the grass. "But, like I said, my mom's sanity is really questionable sometimes. She hates people knowing about Rowan. She says it's because she doesn't want anyone to know about our problems, but I think she really does it because it makes it easier for her to ignore the problems."

I trace my bumpy scars. "I can kind of see where she's coming from."

"You don't really mean that." He adjusts back on his elbows, his gaze following the movement of my fingers. "When people act like that, the people around them suffer. My dad, even me, has suffered from the crazy choices she's always making. It makes it hard to be happy sometimes."

His words strike me hard. I know that's what I'm doing to my family. Making them suffer because I won't deal with my problems; instead, I get arrested, refuse to go to physical therapy, and run away from my feelings. But hearing what it's like from the other side of the fence, makes me realize just how bad it's probably been for my brothers and sisters. I thought they weren't happy because our parents died, but maybe I'm the cause behind some of their misery.

I shake my head then shrug, not sure what to say, what I believe anymore. "Luca, I'm sorry you're life's been hard, but I need to know . . . why are you telling me this? It doesn't make any sense. You don't know me very well, and it's not like I've been very nice to you."

"You've been a lot nicer than most of the people around here."

"If that's the truth, it's sad."

"Sad or not, it's the truth," he says. "They don't seem too welcoming to new people."

"They just need time to warm up," I explain. "That's just how people are around here."

"Okay, but still. I feel like I kind of owe you a secret after what you told me the other night."

My eyes widen. "Oh, my god. What'd I tell you?"

"You can't remember, huh? Interesting." He seems way too pleased about it.

I sort through my memories of the other night. "I remember a lot of things, like wandering around, puking in front of you." I wince, my cheeks heating at the memory.

"That definitely wasn't one of your finer moments," he says. "But I did enjoy hearing you tell me how good I smelled when I was helping you into the car."

"I did not say that."

"Yeah, you kind of did. You even sniffed my chest."

I lower my head into my hands. "I swear to god, I can't remember doing that."

"Don't worry, it was kind of cute," he promises me. "You

looked totally out of it, too, so I mostly shrugged it off. I do wonder if you meant it, though."

I tip my head to the side and peer at him between my fingers. "Wonder what? If you smell good."

He nods, resting his arms on his legs. "It's not every day I get a compliment like that from an extremely beautiful girl, just to realize she probably doesn't even know what she's saying."

I make a gagging face. "Luca, do you want me to smell you and see if you smell good?"

He bobs his head up and down then leans toward me. A smile plays at his lips, and I know he's messing around with me. Still, I lean in toward him, so close his shirt brushes against my cheek. Miller always smelled like cigarettes and booze, which I was never a fan of. Luca smells amazing, like cologne and soap and earth.

Sneaking another sniff, I lean back. "You smell okay."

He frowns. "Just okay? Seriously? Well, that sucks."

I roll my tongue in my mouth. "Fine, you win this one. You smell great. Way better than any other guy I've ever smelled."

"Do you do that a lot?" he teases. "Go around smelling guys?"

"Sometimes when I get really bored," I retort.

He grins. "Well, thanks for the compliment. And I'm going to do you a favor in return and let you know that that wasn't the only thing you told me that night."

"Crap, really?"

"Unfortunately, yes."

The quietness that follows is maddening.

I clasp my hands in front of me. "For the love of god,

would you please just tell me what I said, or it's going to drive me crazy."

"*Going* to drive you crazy?"

I lightly shove his shoulder. "That's not funny."

He laughs. "I'm not trying to be funny. Some of the stuff I've seen you do makes you come off a little . . ." He rotates his finger in a circle at the side of his head, making a cuckoo motion.

I suppress a laugh. "Are you going to tell me what I said or not?"

His hand falls to his lap with his forearm up. He's wearing a short sleeve black t-shirt, and I can see his tattoo clearly in the daylight. He said it means strength, but what does he need strength for? The stuff going on with his sister?

"You told me about throwing the rock at the shop owner's window," Luca reveals, observing my reaction.

An image of me sitting in his car, babbling god only knows what to him, appears in the forefront of my mind. "I kind of remember . . . Vaguely, anyway." But I worry just how much I told him. What if it was *everything*?

"You were a little out of it. You never said why you did it, though. Only that the store owner was an asshole."

Avoiding his gaze, I stare at the back of my hands, flexing my fingers, evading the question in his eyes. "You never told me how you guessed which candies I wanted."

"That's a secret for another day," he says, sounding a tad disappointed that I'm shutting down.

"But you will tell me one day, right?" I glance up at him. "Because it'll drive me crazy if you don't."

His lips pull to an adorable half grin. "I thought we already decided you were already crazy." I playfully shove him again, and he laughs softly, fiddling with his leather wristband. "Can I ask you something?"

The change in his tone sends warning flags popping up. When his attention travels to my thigh, my body goes as rigid as a board.

Please don't ask me about my scars. Please don't ask. Please.

"Why purple?"

"Why purple . . . huh?"

He coils a strand of my hair around his finger, and I study the way he looks at me, totally mesmerized by how fascinated he seems to be with my hair. "Is it your favorite color? Because I've really been wondering, why purple? I mean, why not blue or pink or green?"

"Because purple's awesome," I joke, then shrug. "But if you really want to know, it was the first box of hair dye I picked up when I decided to steal one."

He unravels my hair from his finger and points at me accusingly. "You really are a little thief."

I hold up the crinkled photo. "So are you."

"I guess we're perfect for each other, then."

"Do you come up with those cheesy lines all on your own? Or steal them from movies?"

"Those are one hundred percent original cheesy lines," he quips. "And don't pretend like you don't like them. I can totally tell that you do."

The really sad part is sometimes I do. "Don't flatter yourself."

"I don't have to. You do it for me every time you smile at something I say."

I stare at him, unimpressed.

He chuckles amusedly. "You know, I knew the first time I

saw you that you were going to be hard to impress, but I didn't expect it to be this tough. Seriously, it's a workout trying to get you to smile."

"Maybe you should give up, then," I suggest. "It'd be easier."

"Because it's fun watching you try to stay pissed at me." He touches his thumb to the corner of my lips, and my breath hitches in my throat. "Your mouth gets all twitchy when you're trying so hard not to smile."

A nervous exhale puffs from my lips, and I cringe, knowing he had to have heard it. "Luca, I t-think we should take it easy . . ." I stutter over my words, just like I did when I invited Ben to my birthday party.

But I can't breathe, think, do anything as Luca's gaze lingers on my mouth. "I'm really confused right now and I…" And I what? I have no idea.

"We can do that, if that's what you want," he says, but then contradicts himself when he starts to lean in.

I gulp as my stomach somersaults. Holy hell, my heart is racing so rapidly I swear it's going to leap out of my chest. I don't know what to do with how I'm feeling. Don't know if I hate it. Like it. What.

I'm the most confused girl in the world.

Lost Annabella.

Right before our lips connect, I unexpectedly let out a cough, shattering the moment into pieces.

Feeling stupid and confused, I mutter, "Sorry."

"It's okay." Luca turns away, scratching at his tattoo.

Why is this so hard? It was always so easy with Miller.

An uneven breath eases from my lips as I realize why that is. With Miller, it never meant anything. With Luca, it means something because I like the idea of kissing him. Like silly, dreamy, girly crush kind of like.

But what would happen if I did it? Would I get the same numbness I did when I kissed Miller? I don't think so, since the idea of a kiss with feeling makes my pulse race, in a good/bad kind of way because I fear feeling too much, yet it feels so nice at the same time—so full of possibilities.

Goosebumps sprout across my arms as I recollect my birthday, the excitement and hope of experiencing my first kiss with Ben. I wanted it to be perfect but then everything changed, and that perfect first kiss ended up being just a kiss with Miller a couple of weeks later. Another dream gone that I'll never get back. Unlike my leg, though, I chose to give up my first kiss dream.

"Can I ask you something?" Luca asks, breaking the silence.

No, no more questions. I can't handle anymore.

I start to shake my head, but thankfully, a silver Honda rolls up into my driveway and saves me the trouble of being a bitch.

Easton, my physical therapist, gets out of the car, grinning at me. "Aw, you waited for me. How sweet of you, Anna."

Easton is the same age as Loki and likes to wear a lot of track pants and t-shirts, at least when he's working. He has what Luca would probably call a "twisted" sense of humor in the sole fact that his jokes seem to center around making me uncomfortable. Loki knows Easton from high school and chose Easton as my therapist knowing he won't put up with my bullshit. Personally, he drives me insane.

When I push to my feet, my legs feel like Jell-O, and I

have an irritating suspicion that has to do with Luca and our almost kiss. "Don't flatter yourself. I wasn't waiting for you. I was trying to think of a way to escape you."

"Kind of hard to do when you can't go anywhere," he jokes, popping the trunk.

Luca glances back and forth between Easton and me, then his brows furrow. I know he's wondering who Easton is, but I don't want him getting involved in this—he's already been involved in too many things.

"I'll meet you inside," I tell Easton, then turn for the front door.

"Aren't you going to introduce me to your friend?" he calls, humor lacing his tone.

I reel around too quickly, my knee buckles, and I grasp onto the railing tighter to keep from falling.

"I'm her neighbor," Luca introduces himself. "Luca Benton. We were just . . . hanging out." He sneaks a peek at me, and his eyes sparkle mischievously.

"I'm Easton. I help with Anna's physical therapy. Well, when she shows up for our appointments, anyway." He adjusts the strap of his duffel bag over his shoulder. "You wouldn't want to hang around and help me, would you? Anna gets kind of feisty, and I could use someone to guard the door and tackle her in case she decides to try and bolt." He shoots me a grin, and I retaliate with a glare. "She has a knack for doing that sometimes."

"Yeah, I've noticed she's kind of a wanderer." Luca shoots me an impish grin.

"Oh, my god. I'm in sarcasm hell." I open the screen door. "I'll be inside. When you two finish with your Anna jokes, feel free to join me."

The screen door bangs shut behind me as I step inside. The smell of brownies and chocolate engulfs me the moment I reach the living room, and potent memories swirl around me. My gaze drops to the flakes of glitter still stuck in the cracks of the hardwood floor, right there for everyone to see, yet no one seems to notice.

"Oh, my god, you so have to try these." Zhara skips up to me with a brownie in her hand. She has flour in her hair, chocolate on her shirt, and a huge smile on her face. "They're so good."

My mouth salivates at the gooey dessert, but I shake my head, knowing I can't handle any more memories for the day. "I'm not really that hungry."

Her expression sinks. "Oh, okay." She turns away, looking as sad as a kicked puppy.

Just let her go. She'll get over it.

The glitter still stuck in the cracks of the floorboards sparkle under my feet.

"It's a birthday miracle." Giggles float around me, and I laugh.

Everyone used to be so happy . . .

"If you're going to sulk about it, then give me the damn brownie," I say, sticking out my hand.

She spins around, perking up as she hands me the dessert. "You're going to love it. It tastes just like Mom's."

Mom's brownies were full of lies, baked with secrets, cooked by a woman who didn't really exist.

I lift the brownie to my mouth and take a bite. They're not great, but they're definitely edible.

"They're good, right?" she asks, eagerly waiting for my answer.

I take another bite just to make her happy. "They're great. You did a good job."

A massive smile lights up her face. "You know, that's the first nice thing you've said to me in months."

I lick a drop of chocolate from my bottom lip, unable to shake off the truth of her words anymore. I know how mean I've been to her lately, but with all the crap I was ingesting, I didn't feel enough to care. Now, standing here, fully aware of everything I've done, I hate myself. I think of Luca and his mom, who runs away from her problems, and how sad he looked when he told me.

"I think I just heard a timer go off." I struggle to keep it together. I want to cry. I want to scream. I want to apologize for everything. "Did you cook two batches?"

"Crap." She smacks her forehead, leaving a chocolate handprint, before she rushes off to the kitchen. "I forgot about them."

I nibble on the brownie while sorting through my ever-growing guilt. It's not just about my dad anymore. It's about Zhara and Loki—my entire family—and the hell I've put them through. My head feels like it's going to combust as I think of one bad decision after another that I've made over the last several months.

I'm the most horrible person in the world.

Thankfully, the screen door creaks open and offers me a distraction from myself before I end up bawling on the floor.

Easton and Luca step inside the house, chatting about something.

"I so want to try when I turn eighteen," Luca says, looking giddy. "I probably would've done it already, but my mom's got this thing about doing risky shit."

"They give classes down at Honeyton Sport Shop that are completely safe," Easton tells him. "You should check it out. It's a start, and it's good practice for the real thing."

"Thanks. I'm going to do that," Luca tells him, and then they do this knuckle bump, weird, guy-only handshake thing.

"What are you two getting all giggly about?" I prepare to get them back for all the teasing they've done to me.

"Easton was telling me about his rock climbing adventures," Luca explains to me, readjusting his glasses into place. "Which is so cool because I've always wanted to try it."

"You mean like you've always wanted to *explore* the town and have *adventures*," I say sinisterly as I lick a drop of chocolate off my finger.

His eyes turn to slits, but his lips curve upward. "I never said that. You're remembering wrong."

"That's not what your mom said." I stuff half the brownie into my mouth and smirk at him.

"Glad to see you found your sense of humor again." Easton pats me on the shoulder as he whisks by me and into the living room. He drops his bag onto the floor then places his hands on his hips. "Now, where's an office chair I can use?"

"Upstairs in the family room." There's actually one in the kitchen closet, but I want to procrastinate for as long as I can.

"I'll be right back." Easton jogs up the stairs, calling over his shoulder, "You better be ready for some pain."

The moment he's out of earshot, I zero my gaze in on Luca. "You have to leave." When he doesn't budge, I add, "Please leave. You can't be here for this."

He juts out his lip, pouting. "Easton said I could stay."

"I don't care what Easton said." I shoo him toward the door. "I don't want you here for . . ." I rub my injured leg, feeling so self-conscious I want to hide. "No one gets to see me like this."

"Okay, I'll leave but I'm coming back when your therapy's over. I'm not going to go back to sitting in my house alone again." His tongue slips out of his mouth to wet his lips. It's not an intentional move or anything, but it reminds me of the almost kiss and makes my stomach do all sorts of crazy things.

"You can't come over later . . . I'm doing stuff."

"Then I'll help with the stuff."

"What if it's super girly stuff?"

He glances at me with skepticism. "Yeah, I doubt that. You don't seem like the girly type."

"I used to be," I say softly, then cough into my hand, giving myself a moment to pull it together. "Look, I'm just not sure if it's a great idea for us to hang out."

"Good thing for us I know it's a great idea if we do." He steals the half-eaten brownie from my hand. "See you in a bit, Anna."

"Don't you dare eat my brownie," I warn, lunging for him.

He winks at me then stuffs the brownie into his mouth, wolfing it down in one bite. "Mmm. That was yummy." He grins arrogantly before sauntering out the door.

My chin pretty much smacks the floor as the butterflies in my stomach come to life again. I never felt them with Miller, but I felt them with Ben and countless other crushes I had before . . .

My parents died.

My fingers fumble as I retrieve the envelope from my pocket.

When I was twelve and had my first crush, I asked my mom about the butterflies.

"I feel them every time I see him," I told her in a giggly tone.

She was sitting behind me, leaning against the head-board, braiding my hair. "I felt that way with your dad, too."

"Really?" I peered over my shoulder at her, and she nodded. "Was he the only guy that ever made you feel that way?"

Her fingers stopped moving through my hair. "Of course."

Looking back, I now know she could have been lying. Maybe the guy at the antique store made her feel the same way. Perhaps there were more guys. More secrets. More than I could ever, or will ever, understand.

Shoving the envelope back into my pocket, I sniff back the tears, wishing she were here with me so I could just ask her. I could even talk to her about how I'm feeling now. A year ago, she would've taken me into my bedroom and told me to pour my soul out. Eventually, I would've told her everything about the way I felt because I trusted her.

I glance around at the banister nicked with memories, the glitter stuck in the cracks, and the gouges in the floor-boards, mainly from me dancing around in tap shoes when I was younger.

I slide the photo out of my pocket. It was taken about a year ago, right before I was about to go on stage. I was decked out in a swan costume, covered in feathers, sequence, and tulle. Standing in fifth position, my posture was perfectly straight, my legs strong, unscarred.

But that girl doesn't exist anymore.

I crumple up the photo and chuck it in the trash.

All that's left of my life now is a scarred leg and an empty house.

THIRTEEN
HORROR MOVIES, PROM DANCES, AND BURIED SECRETS

IT SEEMS LIKE IT TAKES FOREVER FOR CHRISTMAS EVE TO arrive. I spend most of the day watching horror movies and munching on the snowman sugar cookies Tammy brought over, trying my best to curb the need for pills and alcohol with sugar. She had set aside one that was covered in purple Skittles, and for some reason, that cookie ended up tasting the best.

The house is empty and extremely quiet today. My family went out to visit my parents' graves and decorate the headstones with wreaths Zhara made. It's really bothering me that I couldn't go with them. I usually don't care, but today, it's got me throwing myself a pity party. I miss the numbness from the pills I used to pop and the nights of getting drunk and forgetting. Those nights used to be so uncomplicated. But it was those nights that got me trapped in my own home.

I grow desperate enough that I ransack the house for alcohol and pills, but Loki did too good of a job clearing out everything. Weirdly, I'm relieved when I come up empty handed. As numbing as it was to be out of it all the time, now that I'm not anymore, I realize it gets exhausting trying to stay high to escape. All the emotions, pain, the past, the future I was running away from, still existed under the sea of painkillers and booze.

I return to the sofa, but the second my butt hits the cushion, the quiet unsettles me again. I contemplate texting Miller and asking him to come over to distract me like he used to do.

I haven't spoken to him since the cabin incident, but from the rumors Alexis told me, he hasn't gone to jail yet, but there's a good chance he will. I don't feel bad that he might; after everything that happened, he kind of deserves whatever punishment is headed his way.

Just like I deserve my punishment.

Growing way too emotional again, I open a new text message.

Me: Hey, I've been thinking about what happened, and I just wanted to say that

Say that I what? Still feel super pissed that he forced me down on the bed and left bruises on my arm. That I want to vomit every time I think about it. That I'm glad he got arrested because he deserves it—deserves more.

"What am I doing?" I hammer my finger repeatedly against the delete button and switch to a different message feed.

Me: Saw u leave the house this morning. FYI, u look super dorky in a Santa hat.

Luca: Yeah, right. If I looked dorky, then u wouldn't be looking.

Me: How could I not look? U looked ridiculous.

Luca: Keep telling yourself that. We both know that's not true. U secretly liked it. Just like u secretly like me.

A smile tickles my lips. I haven't seen much of Luca since the day he told me the secret about his sister, even though he did say he was going to come over. But he never showed up. I thought some time away from him would make the ridiculous grinning and butterflies vanish, but clearly that isn't the case.

I set the phone down on the coffee table and tuck my hands under my legs. "Don't text him anymore." The phone buzzes. "Don't pick it up." It vibrates again, and growling at myself, I scoop up the phone.

Luca: U want to see something really crazy?
Luca: Check this out.

Attached to the message is a picture of his mom decked out in a red sweater with bells sewn on it. On the top of her head is a green elf hat that's embellished with pointy ears. Her cheeks are painted pink, and she's grinning as she hugs a man dressed up as Santa.

Luca: And that man she's hugging is my dad. This is how I've spent the entire morning— hanging out at my dad's store with these two weirdoes.

The two of them look silly, and the photo should make me laugh, but for some reason, a wave of sadness washes over me. My parents used to do goofy stuff like that around the holidays, but now that I think about it, it was more my dad than my mom who encouraged it.

Me: They look really happy. Ur lucky.

Luca: Anna, I didn't mean to make u sad. I'm so sorry.

Me: I'm not sad. I promise.

Luca: Don't lie to me. Perceptive. Remember? Now tell me what's wrong.

I force down the lump wedged in my throat. He wants me to tell him what's wrong? Is it that simple? To just type it? Say it? Just throw out the secret I've been carrying around for seven months now?

Me: I have to go. Easton just pulled up.

I toss the phone onto the table, flop back on the sofa, and focus on the woman running for her life across the television screen. But my attention keeps drifting to the sad looking, undecorated tree in the corner. It makes the room feel cold and empty, still, like a graveyard. If my dad were here, he'd be so sad that this is what we turned Christmas into.

The last time I saw my dad flashes through my mind, and without even thinking, I stride to the garage to get a box of Christmas stuff. I tell myself *just one box of ornaments. For him.* But then I come across the matching stockings my dad bought everyone a couple of years ago—purple for the girls and green for the guys—and end up grabbing those, too.

I return to the living room and drop the boxes onto the floor. Then I dust the dirt off my hands and crank up the iPod that's on mantle. "6 Months" by Hey Monday, a song Alexis listens to sometimes, blares through the speakers.

I open the first box and dust puffs out along with a cloud of memories so strong I almost back out. But I push through the pain for him, because it's the only thing I can do. There's no going back in time, no rewinding and doing things differently. I can't go back and tell him. Can't erase my love for dancing. Can't run from the pain and anger I feel over the loss of my parents. Whether I can run or not, the past happened. All of it. The good days and the stormy ones.

By the time I'm finished, the tree branches are drooping down with the weight of way too many ornaments, and the stockings hang crookedly above the fireplace. It's not perfect, but it makes the living room less cold and empty.

Wiping away a few tears that managed to escape my eyes, I settle in the sofa and continue watching my movies until Easton shows up for my third session this week. The moment I hear him knock on the door, the pain in my leg amplifies, as if it knows reality has finally arrived. But since I can't escape from it, I have no choice but to open the door and face the inevitable.

———

"I don't want to do this anymore," I complain to Easton as he makes me continuously push the chair around the couch. I can only use my injured leg because, according to Easton, I rely too much on my good leg. "My leg feels like it's going to fall off."

"That's how it's supposed to feel," Easton says, eyeing the gory movie on the television. "Do you really watch this stuff all the time?"

"What can I say? I have a morbidly twisted fascination with fear." I groan as the chair crashes into the corner of the sofa. "This sucks. My leg hurts so badly."

"No one said physical therapy was supposed to be fun."

"Um, yeah, you did. At our first appointment, you said,

'I promise you're going to have fun, Anna,'" I deepen my voice, mimicking his, while making air quotes.

"I said that to bring positivity to the atmosphere, but since it didn't work on you, I'm trying a more blunt approach," he replies, patting me on the head.

My lip curls. "I'm not a dog."

"You kind of are, though, with how much growling you do." He grins at me. "Kind of like a feisty little Chihuahua."

I don't give him the benefit of a growl. "Can I do something else now? All the spinning in circles is making me dizzy."

"I was so hoping you'd ask that." Bending over, he rummages around in his duffel bag for something.

I don't like how happy he's suddenly gotten. "Maybe you should go easy on me. I'm getting tired."

He glances over his shoulder at me. "Going easy on you won't help you get better."

"Can we at least take a break?" I ask, clasping my hands in front of me. "It's Christmas Eve, and we're supposed to be celebrating."

He stands up with a silvery bow in one hand and an old school CD player in the other. He sticks the bow on top of my head. "There. Now you're all decked out for the holidays."

I pluck off the bow and press it to the back his shirt as he walks off. He sets the CD player down on the end table and leans over to plug in the cord. He presses the play button then spins around, rubbing his hands together as "Bright" by Echosmith comes on.

"Let me guess. You listen to this in your car on your way

to work. I bet you even dance around in the seat." I roll my shoulders and shimmy my hips.

"Actually, I do." He flashes me his pearly whites as he snaps his fingers. "Now, stand up. It's time to have that fun I promised."

I know where he's going with this, and I don't like it at all.

I curl my fingers around the chair. "No way."

"Anna, this is important." He gently grabs my arm and drags me to my feet. "When we had our first visit, Loki really stressed that he wanted you to be able to dance again." His expression softens. "Now, I can't promise you that you'll be able to dance like you used to, but we can at least work on dancing again."

"Then what's the point?" I wiggle my hand from his hold and inch back.

"The point is that this is part of the healing process," he says.

Shaking my head, I inch back until the backs of my legs smash into the table. "I'm not dancing, especially with you."

He chuckles, offering me his hand. "I promise I'm really good. I won't even step on your toes."

I scrunch my nose. "It's too weird."

"It's only weird if you make it weird."

The last thing I want to do is *try* to dance when I used to be able to effortlessly twirl and leap. "You're too . . . old." It's a lame excuse, but it's all I can come up with at the moment.

He shuffles back with his hand pressed to his heart. "That was a low blow."

"I just mean that you're older than me, and it'd be weird if we danced together, because we're from different eras."

"I'm only three years older than you. That's not a different era." When I waver, he puts his hands up in front of him, surrendering. "Fine, I won't make you dance with me."

I calm down, breathing freely again. "Seriously, thank you. That might be, like, the nicest thing you've ever done for me."

He leans back, peering out the window. "Hang on. I have an idea."

"No! No ideas. I don't even want to dance, anyway . . ." I trail off as he runs out the front door.

I sink into the chair and let my head fall back. I won't do this. I can't. I need to find a way out. Running away isn't going to work this time. Throwing a fit might help, but it's a fifty-fifty chance with Easton.

Panic overwhelms me, and without warning, I'm back in that damn car, hanging upside down, blood rushing to my head. Everything feels so fuzzy, so distant, so nonexistent.

The Doctor looks at me with pity. "Let's just worry about getting you walking properly again, okay?"

I realize I'm not breathing, and I gasp for air. The song ends, but Easton must've put it on repeat because it plays again. I stand up to change it, but halt when I spot Easton and Luca heading up the porch steps.

"Oh, my god, he didn't." I spin around to bolt for the stairs, but move way too quickly, and my feet fly out from under me.

I land flat on my back and blink back tears.

"You dance while I cook," my mom says while cracking eggs and mixing batter.

I pirouette around the kitchen on my toes, my arms forming a perfect circle in front of me, my long brown hair whipping around and around. "I love dancing."

"I know you do, sweetie."

"When I grow up, I'm going to be a ballerina."

"Of course you are."

When Easton and Luca enter the living room, I'm still sprawled out on the floor.

"What happened?" Easton runs over to me and extends his hand to help me up.

"I'm fine." I shoo his hand away as I sit up, stretching my legs. "I was just taking a break."

He doesn't buy into my bullshit, but he doesn't call me out on it either. "Ready for the last exercise of the day?" he asks me.

"When you put it like that, then yeah." Grabbing hold of the table, I grit my teeth and hoist myself up. When I get my feet under me, I turn to Luca. "Whatever he promised you in exchange for doing this, just know they're all lies."

Luca's gaze skims across my sloppy ponytail, baggy shirt, shorts, and knee brace. I wonder what he thinks of my messy look then realize, more often than not, he's seen me looking like a hot mess.

Luca glances at Easton then inches toward me. "He didn't promise me anything, other than I'd get to spend time with you." When I fold my arms across my chest and arch a brow, he looks at me innocently. "What? I'm being serious."

"You so aren't." I assess him closely. "What'd he promise you? Free rock climbing lessons?" Luca shifts his weight, shoving up his sleeves, seeming twitchy, and I feel like I've won a prize. "That's it, isn't it?"

"I would've done it, anyway," he insists. "The rock climbing lessons are just an added bonus."

"It's cool," I say, waving him off. "It makes it easier on me that he had to bribe you, anyway."

"Why would that make it easier?"

"Because it means you really don't want to be here."

"But I want to be here," Luca protests, tugging the beanie off his head. Strands of his dark brown hair stick up everywhere, and he runs his fingers through it, trying to tame it.

I visualize my own fingers there, playing with his hair, which I bet is super soft.

I blink from the daydream, realizing Luca is still talking to me. "Huh?"

His forehead creases as he studies me closely. "I said I offered to help before Easton even asked for the favor." He sticks out his hand for me to take. "Honestly, he probably should've bribed you." He leans in and whispers, "I suck at dancing."

My heart pounds like a drummer rocking out and a thin trail of sweat drips down the back of my neck as I eyeball his offered hand with reluctance.

Just take his hand. A simple hand hold. Don't let it mean anything more.

I'm not sure I can do this, and I hate myself for acting weak.

It's just dancing.

But it's so much more.

As if sensing my panic attack, Luca gently threads our fingers together then reaches for my other hand. He lightly places my palms on his shoulders then steps closer to me until the tips of his sneakers brush my toes.

"See, not so bad," he says, looping his arms around my waist. His fingers tremble the slightest as they spread across my lower back, contradicting his words.

I try not to notice the smell of his cologne or that he's not wearing his glasses. But I notice. A lot. "Not so bad? We're being forced to dance in my living room. I feel like I'm at a middle school prom."

"Just be thankful there's no one watching us," he jokes with a half smile.

"Yeah, right." I raise my voice loud enough so Easton can hear me. "There's a creepy old dude watching us in the corner."

"I'm not that old," Easton argues, crossing his arms. "Now, come on. Move faster and do a few spins."

Panic seizes my throat. "I can't spin. I'll fall on my ass."

"Just go slow," he instructs, sitting down on the armrest of the sofa. "And let Luca hold most of your weight." When I hesitate, he adds, "You can do this, Anna. Otherwise, I wouldn't push you."

"I'm going to fall," I whine, my fingertips stabbing into Luca's shoulders.

"No, you won't." Easton props his foot on his knee and sits back, completely at ease. "Just trust Luca, and you'll be fine."

"Yeah, just trust me," Luca teases, softly pinching my side.

A shiver tingles up my spine. "Please, just don't let me fall," I beg, our gazes locking.

Luca's expression softens. "I promise I won't."

I shove down the lump in my throat and nod. We start swaying, turning in a slow circle. Luca leads and supports most of my weight. I feel like someone's strangling me, and I can't get air into my lungs as my head spins with a foggy memory.

"Anna, you look so beautiful on stage," my mom says, pulling me in for a hug. "You're becoming such an amazing dancer. I'm so proud of you."

"Thanks, Mom." I wrap my arms around her and breathe in deep, feeling so loved. "And thanks for supporting my dream and always driving me to lessons. I know you're busy."

"I'm never too busy to support your dreams." She kisses the top of my head then steps back to look at me. "You'll always come first, no matter what. All of my kids will."

I breathe in and out as my blood boils with anger.

Lies! All lies! Where are you now, Mom? Not here to drive me to lessons, to help Alexis with her art, to watch Nikoli play football, or to obsess over books with Zhara. That's all been put on Loki.

"Anna, are you okay?" Luca asks, concerned.

I nod my head up and down and step closer to him, holding on tighter than I probably should. But I'm afraid if I let go, I'll fall, and I might never want to get up. His breath tickles against my skin, and quickens the closer we get. His fingers are unsteady on my back, and I feel sickly gratified that I'm not the only one who's nervous.

We continue to dance through the entire length of the song, and I gradually calm down enough to rest my head on his shoulder. We're so offbeat, though, that the dancer hiding inside me just about loses her mind. I want to take over, show them how it's done, but I'm scared to death to step into those shoes again. They no longer fit on the foot of my scarred leg that doesn't move as flawlessly as it used to.

"So what's up with the zombie movie on the TV?" Luca whispers in my ear, brushing my hair out of the way. "Seems like an odd choice, considering it's Christmas Eve, but I'm betting you have your own weird reasons."

"I find it calming." I shudder from the feel of his fingers sketching a path back and forth across my back.

A low chuckle reverberates through his chest. "For some reason, I'm not surprised. I mean, we did establish that you were a little crazy."

I close my eyes, and a faint smile touches my lips. Fortunately, my head is turned to the side so no one can it. "You don't know me that well, Luca Benton, so don't assume you do."

"But I do, *Annabella Baker*. You're the girl who likes to wear leather jackets and sweaters in ninety-six degree weather, who hates getting help, who wanders more than anyone I've ever met, who loves Snickers and M&Ms mixed together, and who secretly likes classic rock and guys who are old school." He leans back, looks at me, and grins.

I suck my bottom lip between my teeth. He knows more about me than I thought.

His grin expands, and he tugs me back against him, crashing our bodies together.

There's something intimate about the way our chests and legs are aligned, how my head is resting against his shoulder, and how he grazes his fingers across my back. I can tell he's nervous by his faltering exhales and it makes me like him. And I mean, really, really like him. I like the way he smells. The way he doesn't offer me a chemical escape from reality.

The way he teases me. The way he sends me little texts. They're all little things, but they're the little things I always imagined the guy I dated would do. Cute and sweet instead of sloppy and rushed. Just like how I believed my parents were. Their relationship may not have been what I thought it was, but I still want what I thought they had. And I don't know what to do with that.

Luca trips and stomps on my toe. "Sorry," he apologizes as a flush creeps across his cheeks.

"You're fine." I heave a sigh and glance at Easton. "How long do we have to do this?"

He's messing around with his phone and singing the lyrics under his breath. "I'll let you know when time's up."

Knowing Easton, he'll make me do this until my leg hurts so badly I'm in tears. I make a choice, mostly blaming the decision on Easton, but just thinking about it breathes life into my lungs for the first time since the car wreck.

Loosening up, I move left and right, then back and forth with flawlessly timed steps.

Luca stares down at our feet. "What are you doing?"

"Dancing." My fingernails dig into his shirt when my leg wobbles. *I won't fall. I won't fall.* "What're you doing?"

Our gazes collide, and his lips quirk. "Apparently, taking the chick's role."

I snort a laugh, and Easton's head whips in our direction, his face contorted in confusion. "Are you okay?" He looks at me like my laugh is on the endangered species list or something.

To distract Easton, and myself, from my temporary loss of sanity, I tell Luca, "Spin me."

He pulls a wary face. "Are you sure? I kind of suck at all of this."

I'll do anything for Easton to forget about my laughing because he'll tell Loki and then Loki's going to make assumptions about the nerdy guy next door and how he makes me feel.

I bob my head up and down. "Do it. Just don't let me fall."

"I promised I wouldn't," he reminds me as his hand skates up my arm.

His fingers circle my wrist right above my hammering pulse. He has to know I'm nervous but, thankfully, doesn't comment. Lifting my arm above my head, he braces his hand on my back and guides me around in a circle. I lean into him, keep my scarred leg straight, and holding my breath, I spin around on my good foot.

When I make a full circle, relief sweeps over me. I clutch one of Luca's arms and free the air trapped in my chest.

"You good?" Luca asks, wrapping his arms around my waist.

"I-I think so."

"I'm impressed," Easton says, clapping his hands. "I didn't think you'd do it."

"I knew you'd bug the crap out of me until I did." I feel like I'm going to vomit. Feel like I'm going to cry. Feel so much I almost fall to the floor.

Luca pulls me against him as I sway dizzily. "You going to make it there?"

I shake my head but then nod, confusing the hell out of him and myself.

"No, you're not okay," he says gently. "Anna, tell me

what's wrong."

"I can't." My voice is hoarse.

I try to suck it up, but sadness consumes me. I miss dancing so much. Miss the past. The future I once had. Miss my parents. My family. But most of all, I miss the sunshine and rainbows girl I used to be. The one that could only see the sunshine because she'd never noticed the clouds until they completely covered the sky.

"Sit down and take a break." Easton rises to his feet and turns off the song.

I wipe my sweaty palms off on the side of my shorts and sit on the edge of the coffee table. I can feel Luca's and Easton's eyes on me, but I'm too close to crying to look up.

Breathe in. Breathe out.

Just breathe.

"Just breathe. I know it's hard getting onstage, but you'll do great," my mom says as we wait backstage.

Sounds of violins and the light brush of pointe shoes fill the air. My hair is pulled into such a tight bun my brain hurts. But all I can focus on is how terrified I am to go out there and dance in front of the crowd.

I fold my arm around my stomach and hunch over. "I feel like I'm going to throw up . . . I don't think I can do this."

"Stage fright is perfectly normal." She smoothes her hand down my back. "With time, you'll get over it."

I tilt my head back and look up at her. "What if I don't? What if I stay this way and never get over it?"

"As long as you push past the fear and make it up onstage every time, then you'll be just fine," she says. "Having a fear doesn't make someone weak. It's letting the fear control you that does."

I drown in memories and all I can do is *remember*.

No matter what she did, I really miss her.

I breathe in and out until my heart rate settles then lift my head up and meet Easton's and Luca's worried gazes.

"I'm fine," I assure them. "I just needed a moment."

Looking worried, Luca opens his mouth. "Are you sure—"

Zhara bursts into the foyer, waving her hands in the air, belting a Christmas carol at the top of her lungs with a bitter looking Alexis stepping in behind her. "Hey, Anna and Luca," she sings but her skin pales when she sees Easton. "Oh, hi, I um, yeah . . . Oh, my god." She slaps her hand across her face and sprints up the stairway.

"What was that about?" Easton looks at me with his brows dipped as he unplugs the CD player.

Alexis leans against the doorframe with her arms folded. "She has a crush on you and is totally embarrassed that you saw her acting like herself."

"Alexis," I warn, massaging my sore leg muscles. "Stay out of Zhara's business."

"I didn't do anything but tell the truth, which is more than I can say for you." She stands up straight. "You know, everyone walks around trying to stay out of each other's business, but all that's done is let this family fall apart. It's tragic." She turns away muttering, "No one even cares about anyone anymore."

I start to chase after her as Loki and Nikoli walk inside.

"I can't believe you didn't say anything," Loki says, slamming the front door. He has a few presents in his hand and a scarf wrapped around his neck. "You could have at least warned me, Anna."

"What're you talking about?" I ask, genuinely perplexed this time.

He drops the presents on the bottom stair before striding into the living room. He blinks in shock at the decorated tree and stockings I hung up, but swiftly shakes his head. "You're really going to pretend that you don't know."

"I . . ." I try to think of what on earth he could be referring to, but still draw a blank. "I'm sorry," is all I can think of to say.

He's furious, his hands balled into tight fists. "The other night, when you went out, were you at the antique shop?"

My gaze snaps to Luca. "Did you tell someone?"

He shakes his head, his eyes begging me to believe him. "I swear to god I didn't, Anna. I'd never out you like that."

"There were security cameras there, Anna," Loki snaps. "And they captured a pretty fucking clear picture of you, and you know that everyone knows everyone around here." He wrangles his scarf off then turns to Easton and Luca. "Can you guys give us a second?"

"Sure," Easton says, looking more than eager to get the hell out of here. "You want me to go get started on that thing?"

Thing?

Loki hesitates then nods. "Yeah, I'll be there in a minute to help."

Luca offers me a sympathetic look. "I actually need to get home."

Yes, run. Run while you still can.

"I'll see you later." He hesitates, glancing at Loki before stepping toward me and leaning in. "Call me later, okay? I want to make sure you're okay."

"I'll be okay," I try to assure him.

"Still, call me so I know for sure if my new best friend

has been grounded again," he says, leaning back. "You seem to have a knack for that."

"If you're going to be my friend, you better get used to it."

"I already am." A smile graces his lips. "Talk to you in a bit." He walks out of the room and out the front door.

Once everyone's cleared out, Loki fixes his attention on me, looking madder than hell. "You're so goddamn lucky the owner isn't going to call the police."

I grind my teeth. "Was the owner a guy?

"Yeah . . ." His forehead creases, but then he shakes his head, his anger shooting up a notch. "That doesn't even matter. What matters is that you're out of control and this has to stop." He paces the floor. "As soon as that bracelet comes off, you're going to go over and apologize to Dennis. He wouldn't take any money for the window, but I want you to make it up to him . . . Offer to help him around his store or something."

"*Dennis?*" Blood roars in my eardrums.

"Dennis is the owner." Annoyance simmers in his tone as he grinds to a stop in front of me. "And you better memorize that name because you're going to be doing a hell of a lot of apologizing to him."

I pierce my fingernails into the palms of my hands until my flesh splits open. *I won't explode. I won't explode.* "No, I'm not," I say as calmly as I can.

His face reddens. "Don't give me any bullshit. You're going to do this, Anna. I'm not just going to let it go. You need punishments—need to understand that there's repercussions for the stuff you do."

"I won't apologize to that man!" My. Heart. Explodes.

Into. A. Thousand. Pieces. "I'll fucking go to jail before I do!"

He blinks at me in shock. "What the hell's gotten into you?"

"You wanted me to feel something. Well, I do! I hate that man!" I fight the tears back and take off for the stairs before he can get another word out.

My instinct is to run out the door, run away, but I can't because of the ankle bracelet. So I limp up the stairs, moving way too fast, but pigheadedly refuse to slow down. When I make it to my room, I lock the door and crank up my music. "Sugar" by System of a Down comes on, and I pace the room with my hands on my hips.

I want to punch a hole in the wall.

Want to break every single thing in my room.

Want a pill.

Want a drink.

Want. To. Be. Numb. Again.

But I do the only thing I can. I open my mouth and scream at the top of my lungs until I run out of oxygen.

Panting for air, I feel the slightest bit better. I grab my father's journal from off the shelf and lie down on my bed. My fingers tremble as I open the book and peel off the envelope taped to the inside of the back cover.

I can't take the unknown anymore.

It's killing me inside.

I start to open it, but fear soars through me and I wrench my hand away.

No, I can't do this. I'm too afraid of what I'll find in there.

I drop the envelope onto the bed and scoot away from it.

"As long as you push past the fear and make it up onstage every

time, then you'll be just fine," my mom says. *"Having a fear doesn't make someone weak. It's letting the fear control you that does."*

If she knew what I was contemplating doing right now, would she have given me the same advice?

Picking up the envelope, I slide my finger under the flap and take out the piece of paper inside. My fingers shake as I unfold it. There are several creases on it, as if someone has refolded the letter over and over. Maybe my dad. Or my mom. I'll never know.

Dennis,

I find it so funny that I'm actually writing you a letter, like I'm living in the 19th century. I can almost hear the fire crackling in the corner and the quill scratching against the paper as I write. I'm so glad you suggested doing this. You were right. This is so much more fun than simply sending a text.

I worry, though, what it means. Letters are so much more personal, and I feel like we've crossed too many boundaries as it is. What happened the other day . . . I didn't mean for that to happen. I just got caught up in another life . . . another time . . . Got caught up in you. I've been struggling with accepting what my life has become, and you were so distracting.

Don't get me wrong. I love my kids and being a mother. I would never, ever give that up. Sometimes it feels like there's something missing and when I'm with you, that missing part doesn't seem so bad and I feel . . . well, happy. But I worry what it means about me, about my future, about the choices I'm afraid to make.

I honestly don't know what to do. Or maybe I do and that's the problem.

But anyway, I don't want this letter to be completely depressing. I can't wait to see you again. My daughter's birthday's coming up soon, and I'll be heading out of town, but I might stop by before I do, just to say hi and see you for a few minutes—get my much needed smile. I swear that's all we can do, though. No more crossing boundaries!

Love,

Beth

Love Beth? Oh, my god, did she love Dennis? Did she love Dennis more than she loved my dad? And how was I so oblivious that I didn't know she was unhappy?

I ball the paper up, throw it on the floor, then curl up in a ball. Hot tears spill from my eyes as I hug my dad's journal. Reading that letter must have almost killed him. He loved my mom so much.

But how could he have possibly loved her after reading that?

More tears cascade down my cheeks. *Fight the pain. Fight it back.*

Searing hot rage and sadness simultaneously whip through me, potent and strong. I pinch my leg to erase the emotional pain, but it doesn't work this time. I hug the journal so tight my arms begin to shake.

I wonder how my dad got the letter. Wonder if my mom knew he had it. Wonder how many times he read it. Wonder how long my mom was with this Dennis. Wonder why my dad stayed with her. I wonder so many things, and I'll never get answers.

Sliding my hand under my pillow, I feel around until my fingers brush against the envelope Loki gave me. But I don't take it out. I'm not ready to read anything else my mom wrote.

I'm not ready to forgive her.

But maybe, just maybe, I might be ready to find a way to forgive myself.

FOURTEEN
CAKE AND SPARKLERS

I WAKE UP THE NEXT MORNING FEELING HUNGOVER AND disoriented, just like I used to. Only, instead of feeling like shit from consuming too much alcohol or drugs, I feel like shit from all the crying I did. My lips are dry, my eyes are swollen, and my head is throbbing. For a moment, I can't even remember why I stayed up all night bawling like a baby, but then I feel the journal in my arms and everything rushes back. Dancing with Luca. Loki yelling at me over the window. Me shouting at Loki about Dennis. The letter.

That stupid letter.

Rolling out of bed, I bend over to pick it up. I'm not sure what to do with it. Burn it? Keep it? Show it to someone?

Uncertain what to do, I fold it up and hide it in my dresser drawer under my socks. Then I pull my hair into a messy bun, slip on a pair of yoga pants and a tank top, and check my phone.

One text message.

Luca: Just seeing if u r ok? U didn't call me last night.

Such a simple question, but it makes me feel overloaded with emotion.

Am I okay?

I have no idea.

I decide to be truthful.

Me: I'm still trying to figure that out, but I'll let u know.

Luca: Well, I'm here if u need to talk.

Me: Thanks. I'm not ready for that, though.

Luca: Maybe one day, though.

Me: Yeah, maybe one day.

Leaving the phone on my dresser, I go downstairs. My muscles groan in protest with every step, and my heart hurts with remnants of how it felt to dance again. I long for the days where I could just run away.

In the living room, Zhara has entered cleaning mode, vacuuming the rug as if her life depends on it.

"What are you doing!" I shout over the humming of the vacuum.

"What!" she shouts, continuing to roll the vacuum back and forth.

I inch closer to the doorway. "What are you doing!"

She cups her hand to her ear. "I can't hear you!"

I wind around the sofa and pull the vacuum cord out of the outlet. "I said, what are you doing? It's Christmas morning. You don't need to clean."

"I know, but the Bentons are coming over for breakfast this morning, and I," she gives a shrug, "I thought it'd be nice if the house looked clean. Mom would've wanted it that way, you know."

I think about blurting out what I discovered about our mom, but instead I force a smile, and she turns on the vacuum again.

With the weight of the world on my shoulders, I enter the kitchen, and my chin nearly smacks the floor. Have I somehow ended up in wrong house?

In the center of the island is a ginormous cake stacked high and shaped like a Christmas tree, just like the cake my mom used to bake every Christmas Eve.

"Pretty cool, huh?" Loki yawns and stretches as he walks in. He's wearing a long-sleeve shirt and a nice pair of jeans, and his hair is tousled like he used to wear it.

I look back at the cake. "Who made it?"

He gets a bag of coffee beans from the cupboard. "Easton."

"*Really*? Easton can make cakes?" I say, grinning wickedly. "Wow, I'm so going to use that against him one of these days."

"Be nice to Easton." He starts up the coffee machine then fastens his gaze on me. "You and I need to talk."

"About what?" I ask, even though I already know. But I'm not ready to talk about it yet. Maybe ever.

"Anna, don't play dumb with me. We need to talk about what happened last night," he says, collecting two mugs from the dishwasher. He slides one to me. "I know you're going through some stuff, but I'm a little confused as to why you got so pissed off when you were the one who broke the window."

I pick up the cup. "I'm just moody. You know that."

"This was more than just moody. You've been so unemotional lately I seriously thought you'd turned into a zombie or something . . . But after last night . . . I'm worried you might be holding in more than I thought."

I swipe my finger across the cake, stealing a drop of icing. "You thought I was a zombie? Seriously?"

"I'm speaking metaphorically."

"Aw, I get it. The philosopher side of you is rising from the dead."

"Don't try to make this about me," he says, reaching for the coffee pot. "I want to talk about you for a minute." He pours himself a cup of coffee then fills my cup to the brim. "You want to tell me what got you so upset?"

I plant my butt on one of the barstools. "I'd rather not."

He adds two spoonfuls of sugar to his coffee. "Well, you need to give me something."

I gather the steaming mug of coffee and sip the hot liquid, trying to decide what to tell him. I'm faced with a choice. Out my mom and let everyone know what kind of person she was? Or keep the secret to myself and let them remember her as the loving woman she was? Which would mean living with the burden of the secret forever, taking it to my grave.

"Will you settle for parts of the truth?" I ask.

He stirs milk into his coffee. "That depends. Let's hear it, and I'll decide from there."

"I hate this Dennis guy," I admit, staring at the steam rising from the cup. "But I can't tell you why. Just know that it's for a good reason."

He remains silent for a while, stirring his coffee absentmindedly. "You're keeping something from me . . . I can tell."

"I think that's all we do anymore. I know you are with those papers you're always carrying around and those phone calls Nikoli's overheard."

He raises the mug to his mouth but then lowers it without taking a drink. "I'm responsible for this family and all that stuff going on . . . That's my problem. You guys don't need to worry about it. You already have too much to worry about. Like graduating before ending up in jail."

My cheeks puff out before I exhale loudly. "So, how about this? I keep my secret to myself, and you can keep yours."

He frowns with hesitancy. "I don't think that sounds like a good idea. It's too, I don't know, adult-like. And you're only seventeen."

"I'll be eighteen in, like, six months." Picking up my cup of coffee, I stand to my feet. "And we all kind of grew up the day . . . the day Mom and Dad died."

"Hate to break it to you, but your actions haven't been very mature lately."

I stare at the floor as guilt gnaws inside me. "Yeah, I know, but I'm going to try and change that."

"You're acting strange . . . This thing that you're not telling me . . . You're not in more trouble, are you?"

"No, but I'm still not going to go over and apologize to Dennis. You can punish me or whatever, but I won't do it."

"If that's what you decide to do, then fine." He turns on the faucet and begins rinsing off the dirty dishes from last night's dinner. For the first time since the accident, he made everyone sit around the table together, and it was more than just awkward—it was painful. But we're all still standing, so I guess that's a plus. "Go get cleaned up. We're having breakfast this morning with the Bentons."

I clasp the mug in my hands. "Who invited them over?"

He reaches for a dishtowel. "I did."

"But how did it even come up?" How did they become friends so fast? "I mean, they don't have kids your age or anything."

"Tammy's been helping me with some really important stuff," he says, scrubbing a dirty plate with a sponge.

I study his overly jarring movements, as if he's trying to scrub a hole though the plate. "What kinds of stuff?"

He shrugs, dismissing our conversation, and because he didn't pry into my business, I let the subject go.

I turn to leave when Loki says, "I'll let you know what your punishment is later."

"Fine by me." The punishment doesn't matter, anyway.

It won't change my decision. I won't apologize to the man my mom was having an affair with. Just the idea of seeing him causes my blood pressure to skyrocket . . . I know I can't face him.

I go up to my room, feeling dizzy with confusion, and get changed into a pair of black jeans and a violet shirt that matches my hair. Or used to, anyway. I haven't dyed it in months and the purple has mostly grown out, so half my hair is the plain brown color it used to be. I want to dye it but need to figure out how to get my hands on a box of dye.

I braid my hair to hide the streaks then apply some lipstick and eyeliner before slipping on my boots. As I'm getting ready to walk out, I get a text.

Cece: Merry Xmas, Anna. I know u won't reply

but I just wanted to say that I hope u have a great day. I know how much u used to love the holidays.

Used to.

With Cece, everything always reminds me of the past. It might always be that way with her because she's part of my past. It's why I chose to go with Miller that day. But that didn't work out for me very well, either. Temporarily, sure. But the escape I found in the pills I took by the handful, the bottles of alcohol I drank, and the time I spent with Miller is no longer an option. And I'm stuck trying to figure out who I am in this world without Miller. Without dancing. Without my mom and dad. It makes me feel so . . . alone.

Me: Merry Xmas, Cece.

That's all I can say for now.

By the time I make it to the living room, Luca and his parents have arrived and are chatting with Loki, Zhara, and Nikoli. A fire is crackling, the air smells like pine needles with a hint of bacon, and there are more presents under the tree than there was last night.

"Hey, I was just about to come get you," Loki says when he spots me lollygagging in the doorway. His feet are kicked up on the coffee table, he has a plate of bacon and eggs on his lap, and he seems more relaxed than he did a half an hour ago.

I shrink back when everyone's eyes land on me.

"Hey, Annabella." Tammy greets me with a warm smile and a wave.

Today she's wearing a red dress, silver earrings, and a jean jacket. It's completely opposite of the jazzed up holiday outfit she was sporting yesterday, and I wish she would've worn the crazy bell sweater, because in these clothes, she looks like my mom.

Tammy turns to a man sitting beside her. "Jack, this is Annabella, the girl Luca's been talking our ears off about."

From the window seat, Luca bursts into a fit of coughs, nearly hacking up a lung. "Mom, don't exaggerate."

I place my hand over my mouth to hide my laughter.

"I'm not exaggerating," she protests. "Jack, tell him I'm not exaggerating."

Jack, who looks like an older version of Luca, gives me an apologetic look. "It's nice to meet you, Annabella. We've heard a normal amount of stuff about you."

Luca presses his palm to his forehead and mumbles something under his breath.

"Likewise," I say, and even manage to sound like I mean it.

"Breakfast is in the kitchen. We did sort of a buffet style thing," Loki tells me, glancing at the paper plates on the coffee table. "We were waiting for you to eat before we dig into the cake."

"We can eat it now," I suggest, hyperaware that Luca is staring at me. He has on the knitted cap he seems to like to wear, and a plaid shirt and jeans. But what I really notice the most is that that he isn't wearing his glasses. "Cake for breakfast actually sounds awesome."

Loki shakes his head and points toward the kitchen. "Eat some eggs and bacon first."

"Kids these days, right? Always wanting to eat sugar," Tammy chuckles, looking down at the floor. "Like this little one."

At first I can't figure out who she's talking about, but

then a little girl wearing a pink dress, who looks around six or so, pops up from the floor. "When do we get to open presents?" she asks impatiently.

"Soon, Bria." Tammy pats her head. "But we need to wait until everyone's ready."

So that's Bria, Luca's niece. After what Luca told me, I wonder how Tammy will introduce her.

Bria sulks as she climbs onto the sofa beside Tammy then her eyes land on me. "Who's she? Her hair looks like bubble gum. The grape kinds that tastes really bad."

Luca chokes on another laugh, and I shoot him a death glare but have to wrestle back a smile.

"That's Annabella." Tammy twists around to look at me. "Annabella, this is Bria." She doesn't specify who Bria is, so I'm left wondering if she decided to go the crazy route and call Bria her daughter or not.

"It's nice to meet you, Bria." I offer her one of my rare smiles.

Bria looks unimpressed, though. "Why'd you do that to your hair? It looks weird."

"Bria," Tammy warns, guiding the little girl onto her lap. "Remember how we talked about saying too much?"

I catch Luca rolling his eyes before he rises to his feet. "I'm going to get something to eat," he tells his mom, then crosses the room toward me. When he brushes by, he links our arms together and tows me along with him. Once we're in the kitchen, he frees my arm and lets his head fall back. "God, she's driving me crazy today," he mutters, pinching the bridge of his nose. He breathes in and out and wiggles his shoulders, shaking off his aggravation, then raises his head. "So, how's your Christmas morning going?"

"Super obvious subject change." I head for the platter of eggs and bacon sitting on the counter near the stove.

"Yeah, I know, but I don't want to talk about my crazy mom," he says, trailing at my heels.

I get a paper plate and hand him one, then pick up the silver serving spoon and scoop up some eggs. "We have to talk about her for a minute, though."

He juts out his lip, pouting. "Why? I mean, there's so much else we could talk about, like nasty purple gum and why your hair looks like it."

I stick out my tongue, and he grins. "Ha, ha, you're so funny."

"I know." His fingers brush through my hair, and I lean in unintentionally. "It does look really nice today, though, pulled back like that. It looks like the old you."

My heart crashes against my chest so forcefully it nearly knocks the wind out of me. "What do you mean the old me? You didn't know me before. . ." I flick my wrist, waving at myself. "I looked like this."

He hitches his thumb over his shoulder. "There's photos of you hanging on the wall. I'm guessing they're old since you have brown hair." His lips tug to a dorky smile. "Brown like a Hershey's bar."

"What's with you and all the candy references?"

"I like my sugar." He ogles the Christmas tree cake, licking his lips. "I can't wait to dive into that."

"Me either," I say absentmindedly. "My mom used to bake a cake every holiday."

He presses his lips together, as though he's contemplating his next words. "Anna, I meant what I said. If you ever want to talk, I'm here. I'm a super good listener. I promise."

What I wouldn't give to tell him—anyone—what I've been holding onto for months. But how could I when even I don't know the entire truth?

I turn away and pile pieces of bacon onto my plate. "So, who is Bria? Did your mom decide to tell everyone she's her daughter?"

"That's still undecided." He steps up beside me, and his chest brushes across my back as he moves around me.

I'm not sure if he did it on purpose or not, but the butterflies make their grand appearance. "Okay, so do I pretend I have no clue who she is?"

"Yeah, probably." He shovels a mound of eggs onto his plate. "As of now, I guess my mom's just introducing her as Bria. But when someone finally asks, she'll have to decide." Instead of picking up bacon from the platter, he steals a piece of mine and stuffs it into his mouth.

"Thief." I smack his arm.

"I learned from the best." He winks as he pulls out a chair and takes a seat at the table.

I sit across from him and set my plate down. "Did your dad give Rowan the money she asked for?" When Luca tenses, I quickly add, "You know what, never mind. It's none of my business."

He stuffs a strip of greasy bacon into his mouth. "No, it's fine . . . I'm just trying to decide how I feel about what happened." He dazes off into empty space, chewing on his food. "I didn't even get to see Rowan. She made my dad meet her at a secret location with the promise that he would come alone with the money. Even though no one wanted to give her the money, because we all know where it's going to go, he did it for Bria, so I guess it's worth it."

I stab my eggs with a fork. "It sounds like something straight out of a movie."

"Knowing Rowan, she probably got the idea from a movie." He distractedly pushes the eggs around on his plate. "We used to be close, but now I feel like I have no idea who she is anymore . . . Maybe I never did."

"I think I know what you mean," I whisper, squeezing the life out of the fork in my hand.

He looks at me expectantly, and I have the sudden the urge to tell someone—spill the beans to him like he did to me.

"My mom." I stare at the cracks in the table. "I just found out some stuff about her that makes me question if I ever knew her at all. It felt like I did, but I don't know . . . now it feels like I was pretty clueless all along."

I feel guilty.

Confused.

So lost.

But the weight on my shoulders feels the tiniest bit lighter.

He nods understandingly, his gaze dropping to the tattoo on his forearm. "A couple of years ago, Rowan got her act together for a little while and got sober. That's when my mom and dad took us to get the tattoos. She wanted to get something that'd symbolize her strength. She seemed so happy to be getting better, but then suddenly she wasn't. There was this one night where she flipped out and said no one knew her at all—never did—and that she was moving out to live with this guy who had a rep for selling drugs . . . That was pretty much the last time I saw her."

I deliberate telling him about the last time I saw my

mom, how she had me lie for her, and how I wish I hadn't. "Do you ever wish you could have a do over . . . do it all different . . . say more?"

"I guess. But I know I can't, so there's no use thinking about it. I don't think there's anything I could've said that would've changed my sister's mind. And even if I did, I can't go back in time, so . . ." He shrugs, then takes a bite of his eggs.

I nibble on a piece of bacon with his words replaying in my mind. Even if I could go back in time, which I can't, it might not have changed anything. My dad might've already known about the affair, anyway, and we still might've ended up on that road, heading to the university at precisely the same moment the driver of the semi-truck lost control of his vehicle.

"It's nice to have Bria around again. It's distracting my mom, too, which is always good." Luca rubs his hands together, grinning wickedly. "It gets her attention off me and gives me more time to do stuff I want to do, like rock climbing lessons."

"Good luck with that." Collecting my plate, I scoot the chair back from the table, the legs grinding against the floor. "Easton totally exaggerated on how awesome the rock wall is here in Honeyton. I took Nikoli there once, and it was seriously maybe ten feet high."

"It doesn't matter." Luca picks up his plate and heads to the sink with me. "I just want to get out of the house and do something fun."

"When are you going to do it?" I ask, tossing my paper plate into the trashcan.

"Probably when school starts up again." He drops his fork into the sink and the plate into the garbage, then casts a glance at the doorway as Bria shouts something about wanting to open presents. "That way I can just drive there straight after school without having to answer an endless amount of questions." He pulls off his knit cap and tucks it in his back pocket. His brown hair is askew, and again, I have that compulsion to run my fingers through the strands and fix them back into place. "What?" he asks, amusedly curious.

I become embarrassingly aware that I'm gawking at him, so I start moving the dirty pans on the stove into the sink to distract my fingers from acting on my crazy thoughts. "Nothing. I was just thinking how we're not going to be friends anymore once school starts."

"So, you're finally admitting we're friends?" he teases. "Man, when did that happen? And how the hell did I miss it?"

"I don't know. Probably because you were so focused on trying to weasel your way into my life," I retort, setting the griddle into the sink.

"Yeah, you did make me work really hard." He pauses, considering something. "But why don't you think we'll be friends when school starts? Because, with how hard I had to work for this awesome friendship," he flashes me a light-hearted smile, "I don't think I'm going to let it go very easily."

"It won't be your choice." I turn around and tense when I realize how close he's standing to me. He stares down at me, his gaze flicking to my lips, and all I can think is, *holy shit, is he going to kiss me?* And then I think, *holy shit, I want him to kiss me.* Panicking, I stumble back. "I don't have friends at school, not anymore, anyway."

He seems disappointed but tries to hide it, carrying on the conversation without missing a beat. "What about the guy who picked you up that day? You're not friends with him at school?"

"He's not in high school." I rub the spot on my arm where Miller grabbed me. The bruises have faded, but every time I remember the feel of his fingers on my skin, I get nauseated. "And we're not really friends anymore . . . We haven't been since you picked me up from the party."

"What? Did you finally realize he's an asshole?"

"More or less," I say in a tight voice.

"You never really explained to me what happened that night." He struggles for words, scratching at his tattoo. "You said he almost did something, but never explained."

My heart rate quickens. "Because it doesn't need more explaining. What happened with Miller . . . it's in the past."

"I know, but sometimes if you don't deal with stuff, even if it happened in the past, then it can seriously mess you up."

"You sound like you're speaking from experience."

"Maybe I am." He steps closer, and I want nothing more than to eliminate the small space between us.

I grip onto the counter. "Then maybe you shouldn't be lecturing me about not dealing."

"I tell you what. If you tell me what's going on with you, I'll tell you what happened to me," he says, like it's that easy.

"I don't know if I can handle anymore secrets . . . yours or my own." My gaze is glued to the floor. I'm too afraid to look at him, too afraid that my expression will give away how terrified I am when I think of that night. "I will tell you that I found out just how big of an asshole Miller is."

"Did he . . ." He shifts his weight, seeming uneasy. "Did he hurt you?"

Our gazes collide, and my voice comes out all wobbly. "Even if he did, I'll heal."

His eyes dart up and down my body, as if checking for wounds. "A guy acted like an asshole to my sister once, and she said she'd heal, but she never really did."

"Luca." The ice around my heart momentarily melts. "What you're thinking happened, didn't. I told you in the car that something *almost* happened, but that's why I left and was walking down the road."

It takes him a moment to speak, and when he does, his voice is gentle. "You promise you're not friends with him anymore?"

"Even if I wanted to be, it wouldn't matter. He's probably going to jail."

"But you shouldn't want to be."

"I know I shouldn't, but sometimes life is easier when I'm with him, at least for a while, and when life gets hard, I want to be with him . . . If that makes any sense." I tug at my pant leg and point at the bracelet around my ankle. "But it doesn't really matter. Whether I want to see him again or not, I can't because of this lovely thing. My very own Scarlet Letter."

"Hate to break it to you, but you've never come off as a rebel to me, even though you've tried," he says right as Bria hollers something about presents again.

I lower my pant leg over the ankle bracelet. "Sometimes I am."

"Not with me, though." He laces his fingers through

mine, startling me, not just from his touch, but from the truth of his words. "Now, come on. Let's go open presents before Bria throws a fit."

"It sounds like she's already throwing one." I want to jerk my hand away from his, yet I don't. Do. Don't. Can't. Can. Have. Want. Need. What do I want? Him. So stinking badly. "And my hair doesn't look like grape bubble gum. I can't believe she said that."

"Me either. It's like grape Skittles, not gum. Speaking of which," he stuffs his hand into his shirt pocket and pulls out a baggie filled with yellow, red, orange, and green skittles. "These are for you, for eating your delicious brownie the other day."

For unknown reasons, my skin turns lukewarm. "Where's all the purple ones?" I ask, taking the bag from him.

Grinning, he retrieves another bag from his pocket. That one filled with all purple. "Those are for me." He opens the bag and pops a handful into his mouth. "I don't care what you say. Purple tastes the best."

My skin goes from lukewarm to flaming hot. Feeling way out of my element—way too much like the old Gets-Easily-Embarrassed Anna—I slip my hand from his and limp into the living room.

I hear him chuckle from behind me but don't look back, mostly because I'm afraid I'll want him to hold my hand again.

We spend the rest of the morning sitting in a circle around the Christmas tree, opening presents and eating the cake Easton made. It'd be just like old times, except my mom and dad aren't here, Jessamine is in London, and Alexis refuses to join us. A huge chunk of the life I once had

—the family I once knew—is gone, and celebrating feels wrong.

How are you supposed to be happy after you lose someone?

Like Zhara who's handing out presents with a huge smile on her face. Whether it's fake happy or not, she hasn't sunk into a bottomless pit of self-destruction like I have. And Loki seems pretty content eating his cake and cracking jokes with Luca's dad. Even Nikoli doesn't seem as sulky when he opens the present Zhara got him.

Watching them without a veil over my eyes makes me sick to my stomach, and guilt gnaws at me from the inside as I think of all the shit I've put them through. I should make it up to them somehow, try to do something nice.

For the day, I decide that I'm going to try and act like a normal person who isn't burdened by loss and secrets. I don't need to be the old Anna to do so, just a nicer version of whoever the hell I am now.

"And this one's from me and Jack," Tammy says as she picks up a small box from beside her feet and hands it to Loki.

"You didn't have to get me anything." Loki looks happily surprised as he plucks the glittering red bow off and sticks it on Zhara's head. Then he rips off the silver and gold wrapping paper and lifts the lid off the box. His expression warms as he reaches in and removes a navy blue tie. "Thanks, you guys." He clutches the tie in his hand, one step away from tearing up.

Tammy leans over and gently pats his knee. "I remember the other day how you said you didn't have any that weren't your dad's. We thought having your own would come in handy for . . ." She glances at Nikoli, Zhara, and me. "Stuff."

Loki nods his head up and down. "Thanks." He clears his throat then quickly stands up. "I just remembered I forgot to turn the stove off." He ducks out of the room with his head down, squeezing the life out of the tie.

Zhara starts to get up to go after him, but I grip onto her knee and shake my head. "Give him a minute, okay?"

Reluctantly, she nods and takes a seat back down on the floor.

The room grows quiet until Bria jumps up. "I want to go outside and play with my bubbles!" she exclaims, fist pumping her bubble wand into the air. She does a strange little dance that looks like a mix between disco, tap dancing, and a chicken running around.

We all exchange a look and then bust up laughing. It's not even that funny, yet it is. Just like laughing feels wrong, yet it doesn't. Nothing really makes sense at the moment, other than I don't feel so heavy, so maybe I'll stop trying to figure it all out.

"Our Bria," Tammy sighs with a content smile. "She's always loved to dance. That's why we put her in dance lessons."

"My mom and dad did the same thing with Anna." Zhara peeks over at me to assess my reaction.

"Yeah, I heard Anna was quite the dancer. One of Stella's most promising students . . ." Tammy presses her lips together, glancing at me worriedly.

Stella is my former dance instructor, and I can almost hear her saying, *The girl that used to have so much potential, if only her leg wouldn't have gotten messed up . . .*

"She'll like it," I say, glancing at Bria bouncing up and down. "And it'll be a great way for her to get her energy out."

Tammy smiles, glancing at her granddaughter. "Bria's always been a really wound up girl. Her mother was like that, too, when she was younger."

My gaze darts to Luca who's sitting on the step in front of the fireplace with his legs bent and a plate balanced on his knees.

He rolls his tongue in his mouth, containing a smile, but I'm sure he's relieved his mom decided not to go with the whole I-suddenly-have-a-daughter story.

"Bubbles! Bubbles!" Bria chants, tugging on Tammy's arm. "Come on, Grandma."

If Tammy didn't just out it herself, Bria would've just done it for her.

"All right, I'm getting up." Tammy gets Bria bundled up in a coat before the two of them and Jack head outside, saying they'll be back in a bit to help clean up the scraps of wrapping paper laying around the living room.

"I'm going to go watch the game," Nikoli announces, pushing to his feet. "You want to come?" he asks Luca.

I observe Luca's reaction, wondering if he's a football kind of guy. In fact, I wonder a lot of things about him, what he likes other than candy and teasing me.

He doesn't seem all that eager, but still says, "Yeah, give me a bit. I need to give Anna her present first."

Nikoli gives me a perplexed look. "You can come, too, if you want," he tells me, tossing and catching the football Loki just gave him.

Ever since he came into my room, asking me to do our

family a favor, we haven't spoken. And since we hardly talked before that, his offer catches me off guard.

"Maybe I will." I shrug, scraping up the frosting on my plate. "In fact, I probably will."

Some of Nikoli's anxiousness alleviates, and he heads for the stairway with a bounce in his step.

Zhara goes right into cleaning mode, jumping up and picking up pieces of wrapping paper.

"Just leave it for a while." I snatch hold of her hand when she reaches for a bow near my foot.

She shakes her head anxiously. "I need to clean. This place is a mess."

"Mom never cleaned on Christmas," I remind her. When she looks torn, I press the issue, "Just let it go for today, and I'll help you clean it up tomorrow."

She tucks a curl behind her ear, and her cat eyes bore into mine. "Why are you being so nice?"

I shrug, flicking a few stray pine needles off my legs. "Call it an act of insanity due to too much cake and candy today."

She sneaks a glance in Luca's direction, and I can see her wheels turning. I want to demand that she stop overanalyzing my change in behavior, but I'm not about to do that in front of Luca.

"Fine. I'll leave it until tomorrow, but only if you'll watch a movie with me tonight. A happy one." She cringes, but sticks out her hand to shake on it. "None of that blood and guts stuff you've been watching lately."

I run my thumb along the leather-studded watch on my wrist that she just gave me. Clearly, she took into account the things I like. "Fine." I shake her hand and seal the deal despite how much I don't want to watch a happy movie

"Thank you, Anna." Her smile goes *poof.* "I have no idea what to do with myself now."

"You can stay here and watch Anna open her present," Luca suggests, scooting down onto the floor beside me with a gift in his hand. "Maybe, if you're lucky, she'll share one of them with you." He sets the box on my lap then rests back on his hands, looking totally entertained by my befuddlement.

I tentatively shake the box wrapped in purple wrapping paper, and it rattles. "Hmmm . . . Let me guess. A huge ass box of candy."

"You'll have to open it up and see." His eyes sparkle mischievously.

I pick at a crease in the paper, but finally grow inpatient and just tear into it. "It's . . . Sparklers."

Like the Fourth of July sparklers my dad used to give me for my birthday. I glance up at him, grasping the box in my hand, and he smiles, but I can tell he's nervous by the way he keeps wiping his palms on his pant legs.

"I just wanted to get you something fun," he explains, sitting up straight. "I thought maybe we could go out and light them up in the driveway."

I want to toss the box into the fireplace and run away as it explodes. Forget about Christmas and presents and Fourth of Julys, but then what the hell would I do? Sit up in my room and feel every emotion, all alone.

"Okay?" It sounds like a question.

"We don't have to," he says quickly. "We can just hang out and watch the game if you want."

"Didn't peg you for a football fan," I mock with a grin.

He lifts his shoulders, giving an *eh* shrug. "I'm not." He flicks the box in my hand. "I'm more of a let's-do-something-adventurous kind of guy, but I'm always up for anything."

I stare at the box. What do I want to do?

What do I want?

I have no damn clue.

"We can light a couple," I say with a shrug, pretending to be more composed than I really am.

"Are you sure?"

"Positive." I stumble to my feet, just to prove that I'm completely and totally sure.

"Awesome. Let's do this, then." Luca picks up the box of sparklers and follows me to the foyer.

I slip on my boots while Luca zips up his hoodie then we head outside to the driveway.

"Where's your mom, dad, and Bria?" I ask, glancing at his empty yard next door.

"Who knows? Maybe they took off to the park for a while, like Bria wanted to," he answers, kicking the tip of his sneaker against the concrete.

"She's a lively one," I remark, buttoning up my leather jacket.

He sighs, lifting his gaze to mine, seeming uneasy. "She's been running around, jumping on everything since she got here the other night. I think she might be starved for attention or something."

"It's good that your mom decided to say she was her granddaughter, though, right?"

He nods, loosening up. "That was probably the best present I could get from her."

"Speaking of presents. What's up with your mom giving Loki a tie? And when did they get so close? I don't get it. They act like they've been hanging out or something."

"Maybe they have." He fiddles with his zipper, dragging it up and down.

"You know something, don't you?" When he refuses to meet my gaze, I inch to the side and step in his line of vision, forcing him to look at me.

He sighs. "I can't tell you."

I put my hands on my hips. "Why not?"

"Because I promised I wouldn't."

I should just back off, let it go, but with all the secrecy, I'm getting worried. Just like I sensed something wasn't right with my mom on my birthday, I can tell something's up, but unlike my birthday, I'm not going to look the other way.

Stepping closer to him, I place my hands on Luca's shoulders. "Please tell me. I need to know; otherwise, it's gonna drive me crazy."

"I don't know if I should." He stares at my lips, and his fingers shake as his palms mold around my waist.

"Please." I jut out my lip, using a move Cece used to do all the time when she wanted to get her way. I honestly don't expect it to work—I've never been all suave and perfect like Cece—but Luca seems fixated with my mouth, and slowly, he caves.

"She's been helping him make sure he has everything in order for Family Services," he says quietly. "I guess they've been keeping an eye on you guys, and with all the . . ." he winces, "stuff going on, they're questioning if he can handle the responsibility. Since my mom's gone through some similar stuff with Rowan, she's been helping him out. Although, your brother's a hell of a lot more responsible than my sister ever was."

My scars blaze as guilt eats me from the inside out. "This is all my fault." I move back, my hands falling to my sides. "God, everything's so screwed up." I slump against the side of the garage, staring at the tire tracks permanently stained on the pavement from the time I braked too hard when my father first taught me to drive. "I wish I could go back . . . and make different choices."

"But you can't." Luca offers me a sad smile. "You can change what you do from now on, though."

I shut my eyes as the cold breeze stings my cheeks. "You say that like it's easy."

"It's not, and some people are never able to do it, even when they try . . . like my sister." He pauses, and when I open my eyes, he's standing closer than I anticipated. "Some people do, though. And you don't have to do it alone . . . you have a ton of people who can help you. Loki, Zhara, even my mom would be more than happy to help you." With a pucker at his brow, he presses his lips together and cups my cheek, smoothing his thumb across my skin before pulling away. "And yeah, I kind of want to help, too."

I swallow hard, pressing my hands to the garage as my legs turn into noodles. "It seems crazy, wanting to help someone when you don't even know them . . . Your life would be easier if you didn't."

"My life's never been easy, but do you know what's really easy?" he asks, and I shake my head. With a hint of a smile on his face, he reaches out, and I think he's going to grab me, but instead he taps the box of sparklers I'm holding. "Lighting sparklers."

I frown warily at the box. "That's actually harder than it seems."

Suddenly, a gust of wind scatters the dead leaves across grass, and the cloudy sky grumbles, warning us of an impending storm. Clasping the lighter in one hand, I open the box and wiggle two sparklers out.

Can I do this?

I give one to Luca then fumble to light the lighter.

Am I really going to do this?

Blame it on my nerves, but I can't get the damn thing to work.

Maybe I shouldn't do this?

Finally, Luca pries my fingers off it, flicks the top, and creates a steady flame. He lights his first then, holding it out as if it were a magic wand, silvery sparks shoot out.

"Put yours up to mine," he instructs, stuffing the lighter into his back pocket.

With a deep breath, I kiss the tip of his sparkler with mine. *Oh, my god, I'm really doing this.* They hiss as the flames aglow.

I move the sparkler in a circle in front of me. "Wow." I forgot how magical a simple firework could be, and for a moment, I see the world through my old eyes, lit up like fire-flies that I swear I could catch if I just stick out my hand.

For the next few minutes, Luca and I play around in the driveway, going through sparkler after sparkler, giggling like a couple of kids as we clumsily skip around. When it comes down to the last one, he lights it up and hands it to me.

As the sparkler reaches the halfway point, Luca moves up

behind me and circles his arms around my waist, covering my hand with his so we're both holding onto it. His breath tickles my ear as he laughs and traces letters in the air. My hand moves with his, but I can barely focus on what he's writing. I'm too distracted by his chest pressed against my back, his warm fingers covering mine, how very alive I feel in that moment, and how terrified I am.

"Luca, I think . . ." I trail off as he stretches our arms out to the side and fixes his finger under my chin. Turning my head toward him, his eyes search mine, then slowly, he leans in.

When our lips brush, the sparkler crackles, but I hardly hear it as the beat of my racing heart fills my ears. He tastes like frosting, and his lips feel so good against mine that it's mind-blowing because I can feel it. Feel *everything*. The softness of his mouth. The little breaths he keeps taking. The warmth of his fingers against my cheek. This kiss is so different from kissing Miller. Less numbing, more devouring, consuming, more of a connection, more feel-and-breathe-the-moment.

I turn around, press my chest against his, and fall into the kiss. Still holding the burning sparkler out to the side of us, he slides his tongue into my mouth, backing us up. I grasp onto him, letting him slowly guide me backwards until my back brushes against the side of the house.

Pressing his chest and hips against mine, he deepens the kiss, his tongue softly tangling with mine. It's everything I've always wanted in a kiss. Everything I thought I couldn't have and still don't know if I deserve. I don't know what I'm doing. Don't know what I'm going to do when it ends. But right now, I don't care. That control I always felt with Miller doesn't exist with Luca. There's no control at all, over my emotions, over my mouth, over anything.

I kiss him back, biting his bottom lip, and he groans in response. His free hand cups the side of my neck, and he murmurs my name as his lips trace a path down my jawline to my neck. When he sucks on my skin, I tip my head back and stare up at the clouds right as a raindrop splatters across my forehead.

I shut my eyes. *I'm not going to let the rain ruin this.* Putting a sliver of space between us, I cup his face and move his lips back to mine. We kiss as the clouds rain down on us. Kiss until I can't breathe. Kiss until the sparkler hisses, shooting its final spark, which ends up landing right on the back of my hand.

I jerk, gasping for air as my flesh burns.

"What's wrong?" Luca asks, breathing raggedly, an arm on either side of me.

"It's nothing. I just . . . ." A blister is already forming on my hand. The storm kicks up. Rain drizzles over me—reality crashes over me. How perfect this kiss really was and how this is what I wanted my first kiss to be. How I wish my mom were here, so I could tell her about it. How much I really, really enjoyed the kiss. How much I'm really here, in this moment, feeling everything. All of it. The good. The bad. *Everything.* "I-I'm sorry," I sputter, then hurry for the house, running away from what I'm feeling like I always do.

But like with my leg, I've done too much too fast, and now every part of me aches.

By the time I stumble into my bedroom, I'm sobbing so hard I can't get any oxygen into my lungs. I collapse to the floor and crawl toward my bed. But I have no energy left inside me, and I end up curled up in a ball, crying on the floor.

"Anna," Zhara says as she cracks open the door.

I roll toward my bed to hide the tears in my eyes.

"Is everything okay?" she asks tentatively.

I shake my head while tears stream down my cheeks.

"Oh, Anna." She lies down on the floor and wraps her arms around me.

My shield ruptures and everything trapped inside me bleeds out.

"I miss Mom," I whisper through my sobs. I miss the mom I grew up knowing. The one who took care of me. The kind, caring person I once wanted to be like. I miss the mom I wasn't ever so angry with. The mom that would have held me, hugged me, told me she loved me. The mom I loved.

"Me too," she says, hugging me tightly.

I sob uncontrollably again, and my body trembles.

"It's okay," Zhara says. "Just let it all out."

I do exactly what she says, and let it all out because in the end, it's either shut down and rot away more.

Or just let go.

Just let go, Anna.

FIFTEEN
LEARNING TO WALK AGAIN

I SPEND THE NEXT FEW DAYS STAYING AWAY FROM THE GUY next door. Not because I'm blowing off Luca. I just haven't figured out what to say to him. Over the next few days, he texts me a few times and tries to call once, but on New Year's Day I don't hear a peep from him.

For most of the morning, I lounge around on the couch with Zhara, streaming movies, comedies per her request. Today, Easton gave me a break from physical therapy, and I'm glad just to spend time sitting on my ass because my leg hurts, maybe even more than it did pre-therapy. Then again, I'm completely, one-hundred percent sober, which means everything—my mind, my body, my senses—is crystal clear. Too clear sometimes, especially when it comes to all of the horrible stuff I've done, like getting arrested, getting drunk, refusing to show any sympathy to my brothers and sisters who've been going through the same stuff I have.

"So . . . What's up with you and Luca," Zhara says unexpectedly as the credits roll across the screen.

"Nothing. Why are you askin'?" During my meltdown on my bedroom floor, I accidentally let it slip out that I was crying over kissing Luca. I learned that Overly Emotional Annabella sucks at keeping her lips zipped.

"No reason." She sits up and tucks her feet under her butt. "I just haven't really seen him since Christmas."

"But it's not like we hung out that much before Christmas," I say, bending my knee underneath me.

"Oh, Anna." She gives me a look as if I'm the younger sister who's dense about guys. "Really?"

"Don't 'oh, Anna, really' me," I slip out the elastic in my hair and comb my fingers through the strands. "I think, at least for now, maybe Luca and I should just be friends."

She flicks a popcorn kernel off her lap. "Have you told him that?"

I shake my head. "But I will."

"Promise?" she asks, shoving the sleeves of her pink thermal shirt up. "Because he seems like a really nice guy who likes you a lot and cares about you. I know you're not used to that."

"I know." I lightly rub my hand over my thigh where the elevated scars are hidden below my plain pajama bottoms. "And, Zhara, I'm not dating Miller anymore. I never really was."

"Good." She beams happily, scooping up a handful of popcorn from the bowl that's in between us. "I'm glad you two are over. I never liked him that much."

"No one did." But there are times when I miss the freedom Miller gave me.

It's not really Miller himself that I miss, just the numbness, drinking, and drugs he provided for me. Those feelings of longing to self-medicate come in sporadic spouts when life gets really unbearable, like after a nightmare or an agonizing therapy session, where I work my ass off, or when I think of my mom and dad and how they're not here with us.

But there's also another part of me that's almost . . . relieved to be out of the world of drugs that leads you to nowhere but down, down, down, until you finally crash.

"And just so you know, I really like Luca." Zhara points the remote at the TV and clicks off the screen. "He seems like he'd be a really good boyfriend, when you decide you want one."

"Zhara, you saw me the other night," I say. "I'm not sure I'm ready for a boyfriend."

"And that's okay, too." She bounces in the cushion as she turns to face me. "Okay, I have an idea, and you can totally say no, but I want to ask just in case you feel, I don't know, like doing something different." She pauses, and I motion for her to spit it out. "I'm going to FaceTime Jessamine this morning, and I want you to do it with me." She holds up her hand, silencing me before I can even get a word out. "I know what you're going to say, but you're wrong. Deep down, you want to talk to her. And just think, whatever you tell her stays all the way over in London with her. No one will know but Jessamine."

"But what if I don't really have anything to say?" I nibble on a few pieces of buttery popcorn, remembering what caused me to pull away from Jessamine.

Right after my parents' funeral, she was getting into a taxi to go to the airport so she could fly 'home.' I hated that she called London her home, hated that she was leaving us, but most of all, I was jealous because she could leave her old life while I was stuck in it, even when I no longer felt like I belonged. Yes, I was selfish. Yes, I messed up. But I was confused about life and what I was supposed to do from there.

"Then you can just wave and sit with me while I talk." Zhara seizes my hand and lifts me to my feet as she leaps up. "Come on. I promise you won't regret it."

I begrudgingly let her lead me up to her bedroom where I sit down in front of her laptop opened up on her bed and attempt to figure out what I'm going to say to Jessamine. It's been months since we've spoken, and I have no excuse other than I was confused about myself, my family, life.

With a few clicks of the mouse and couple of taps on the keyboard, Zhara sets up the video chat. The computer makes a dinging nose, and then I'm staring at my older sister.

She looks the same as she did at the funeral, except her hair is shorter now and her mascara isn't running. "Anna?" She squints at the screen, leaning in closer to get a better look. "Is that you?"

"Yep." I muster up a smile. "Hey."

"Oh, my god!" Her earsplitting squeal is so loud that the speaker shorts out. "I'm so happy you're talking to me. It's been way too long."

"Yeah, I guess it has." We stare at each other for a minute until I grow uncomfortable over who she's seeing. Stoic Annabella, or the real, raw, Doesn't-Have-a-Clue Anna. "You cut your hair."

"Yep. A couple of days ago, actually." A devious grin spreads across her face. "But, dude, what's with the purple hair?"

"Hey, don't mock the hair. I like it." I collect the laptop, balance it on my lap, and sit back against the mounds of pillows on Zhara's bed.

"I actually do, too." She taps her finger against her chin. "You do need to touch up those roots, though."

"I'm waiting until I decide what color I want to dye it." I lift a strand of my hair in front of my face. "I was thinking maybe a different color, but I can't decide which one."

Zhara reclines back beside me with a bottle of nude nail polish in her hand. She stretches out her legs and swipes the brush across her toenail. "I think you should do brown and leave a few streaks of purple."

Old and new? Is it really that easy? I don't know what to think, if I love the idea, hate it, want it.

"We'll see." I let my hair fall back to my shoulders. "I can't dye it until after Christmas break's over, though, since I can't leave the house."

"Yeah, I heard about that." Jessamine folds her arms on her desk. "You want to talk about what's been going on with you?"

"Life." I shrug, because I can't think of anything else to say.

"You seem like you're struggling with it."

"I am . . . was . . . confused."

"Is it anything I can help with?"

I shake my head. "I don't think so. I just need to figure out who I am, I guess."

She gives me an understanding smile. "That's probably one of the hardest things to do, especially at your age. I remember right after I graduated, I had no clue what I wanted to do, other than I didn't want to stay in Honeyton."

"I used to have it all figured out." I stare down at my toes, pointing and flexing them. They use to curl so prettily, but now the left foot can hardly move. "But not so much anymore. And I think . . . I think maybe that's why things have been so hard."

"That's okay . . . Stuff happens and sometimes we have to change our plans, right?" She stares at something to the side of the screen, and I wonder what she's looking at.

"Are we talking about me or you now?"

Sighing, she directs her attention back to me. "I'm not sure." She perks up, squaring her shoulders. "But if you ever feel like doing something really crazy, you can come hang out with me in London. It gets lonely sometimes."

"I'll think about it." I glance at Zhara as she swipes the brush across my toenail, painting the nail a shimmering pink. "Really, Zhara? Pink?"

She applies a stroke of nail polish to another toe. "What? It looks nice on you. And you used to wear pink all the time."

Deciding to pick my battles, I concentrate on Jessamine. "Can we talk about something that doesn't have anything to do with me, please? Tell me something cool or happy going on with you. Because I haven't heard much happy or cool stuff in a while."

"Hmmm . . . Well, I'm seeing a guy. He's from the States, actually."

"Tell me about him. Is he crazy and mysterious, like that one guy you dated, or is he more like Milo, all happy and positive all the time?"

"He's nothing like Milo," she says, getting a faraway look

in her eyes before blinking back at me. "And besides, Milo and I were—are—just friends."

"That's what you guys always said, but there were a couple of times that I'm pretty sure I walked into your bedroom and caught you guys fooling around."

She jabs a finger at the screen, biting back a grin. "I know what time you're talking about, and I swear to god, we weren't fooling around. Milo was just showing me his scars."

A conniving grin spreads across my face. "Were his scars on his—"

Zhara's hand covers my mouth, her cheeks flushed. "Anna, watch your mouth." When she removes her hand, Jessamine and I laugh at her. "You guys are ridiculous and so gross."

"Oh, my sweet, naïve Zhara." Jessamine sighs. "One day, there's going to be a guy you'll like enough to want to see his," she makes air quotes, "scars."

Zhara huffs, working to get all riled up, but it doesn't go very well for her, and she ends up simmering down and returning to toenail painting.

"What about you, Anna?" Jessamine says. "You dating anyone?"

Curious, Zhara watches my reaction.

"How much have you heard?" I ask Jessamine, resisting the urge to touch my lips as I remember the kiss.

He tasted so good, like cake and Skittles, and I swear to god, I can still taste it now.

"Zhara told me about some guy with blue hair getting you into a lot of trouble," Jessamine's tone carries caution, "but she wasn't sure if you were really dating him."

"That would be Miller. And he didn't get me into trouble. Everything I did," I pause as Zhara's elbow bumps the bracelet around my ankle, "I chose to do."

"That's a very mature thing for you to say," Jessamine tells me. "Now, if you could stop choosing to get into trouble, things would be great."

"I'm working on it." My tone wobbles, raw with the truth.

"Good." Intrigue twinkles in her eyes. "Now, tell me about this Luca Zhara says you've been hanging out with."

I glower at Zhara, but smile so she'll know I'm partially joking.

I spend the next twenty minutes giving Jessamine a few details about Luca, how we met, his fascination with candy, and our kiss. Then the three of us talk about Zhara's plans for college, even though she doesn't graduate for over a year and a half, but she already has everything planned out.

By the time we say goodbye, it's late afternoon. We decide to clean the house while Nikoli is at football practice and wherever Alexis wanders off to during the day. Loki is at the store until eight, so we start to make dinner, preparing to ring in the new year with chips and salsa and chicken quesadillas.

"Remember how Dad always made these every New Year's?" Zhara asks, skipping around the kitchen island and toward the fridge.

I push the chicken around in the skillet with the spatula. "I remember how he burned them every year."

Zhara giggles as she grabs a bag of shredded cheese. "I never really got why he was the one who cooked so much when he clearly sucked at it."

The peppery smoke funneling from the sizzling pan makes my eyes water. "Because Mom didn't like cooking."

"She didn't? I never knew that. I thought she loved cooking. That's why she was always baking cakes and brownies and pies." Her mood plunges. "How could I not know that about my own mom?"

"Don't beat yourself up." I twist down the heat of the burner and sprinkle a little salt and pepper on the chicken. "Sometimes it's better not to know everything about your parents."

"You think so?" she wonders, setting the bag of cheese on the counter beside the stove.

I keep my back to her. "I know so. The only reason I knew she hated it is because I overheard her talking to Dad once about it. She said the kitchen was starting to feel too stuffy and she needed a break." *A break from all of it,* she had told him. But I don't tell Zhara that.

About a week later, my dad took on the responsibility of cooking, even though he sucked at it and worked at the store all day. I didn't think much of it until now, but he almost seemed desperate to please her.

"Do you think Mom and Dad were happy?" Zhara sputters, sounding terrified.

I reel around, clutching onto the counter for support. "Why would you ask that?"

She shrugs, examining her fingernails. "Sometimes, I just wonder if they—if anyone—is truly happy."

Where's this coming from? I haven't told anyone about the letter. The more time that passes, the less it feels like I should. But I still haven't brought myself to burn the piece of paper yet, wanting to hold onto it for some insane reason.

I've read it so many times, obsessing over each word, and wonder if my dad did the same thing.

"Are we really talking about Mom and Dad?" I ask, getting a knife and fork from the drawer to cut up the cooked chicken. "Or you?"

"I'm not sure." She angles her head forward, staring at her feet. "It's just hard sometimes, you know, to always put on a happy face."

"You don't always have to put on a happy face, Zhara. No one expects anyone to be happy all the time, and no one should be happy all the time."

I used to think my mom was happy all the time, but I was so wrong, and looking back, I realize I was extremely blind. Through the way she always seemed to be searching for a hidden talent and all sorts of hobbies. How she tried salsa dancing but hated it. How she'd disappear for hours in her room sometimes. How she'd get these sporadic impulses to get out of the house.

"Let's just go do something," she'd say. "Anything at all, as long as it's not sitting around in the house. I can't take being bored any longer."

"Someone has to be happy in this family," Zhara mutters, interrupting my thoughts. She tucks a brown curl behind her ear. "No one else seems to want to smile anymore."

"You're allowed to be sad sometimes—we all are. And trust me, crying can be . . ." I search for the right word that sums up how I felt the other night after I let it all out. "Kind of therapeutic, I guess."

"Mom wouldn't want me to be sad," she mumbles, her hand falling to her side. Then like lightning, she goes from cloudy to sunny, forcing a bright smile as she looks up at me. "Dinner smells delish."

I want to pry more out of her, but before I can even start, someone knocks on the front door.

"I bet it's Luca," she singsongs as she tears open the bag of tortilla shells.

"Maybe." My nerves are a jumbled mess as I cross the kitchen to the foyer.

What do I say to him? How do I explain that I wasn't really crying over the kiss without going into detail about my whacked out brain.

When I open my door, I realize I have bigger problems than cute neighbor guys I've been ignoring.

The wind is howling, the air chilly from a storm brewing, and in the middle of the madness, is Miller. He's standing on my front porch with his hands stuffed into the pockets of his torn jeans. His blue hair is flattened on one side, dark circles reside under his eyes like he hasn't slept in days, and red lines cover his cheeks, as if he's been scratching at his skin.

"What're you doing here?" I ask through the screen door.

He rubs his hand over his eyes, then scratches his arm. "I just wanted to see you." His gaze darts over my shoulder then lands back on me. "Can I come inside?" Without waiting for me to answer, he reaches for the screen door.

Shaking my head, I grab the handle and hold tight. "You need to leave. Now."

He grunts in frustration, dragging his hand down his face and stomping his foot. "Come on, Annabella. I really need your help."

"I'm not giving you any money, if that's what this is about."

He scowls at me but quickly tries to dazzle me with a grin. "Look, if you loan me a hundred bucks, I'll give you half of what I buy. I can even get you some of those pills you like." He waggles his eyebrows at me. "You gotta be going super fucking crazy at this point, being locked up without anything."

"I'm fine," I lie through my teeth, and I know he can hear the unsteadiness in my voice. "Now, go away." I step back to close the door when he grabs the handle of the screen door and yanks it open.

"I just need a hundred bucks." He shoves me into a wall as he pushes his way inside, tracking in mud and leaves all over the floor. His eyes drink in the marble fireplace in the living room, the stairway, and the chandelier hanging from the ceiling. "Fuck the hundred bucks. I want five hundred."

"I'm not giving you any money." I square my shoulders and stab my finger in the direction of the door. "Now get the hell out of my house."

"You're such a greedy bitch," he snaps, his gaze flitting from me to the front door, then he shuffles right and bolts for the stairs.

I skitter around him and block his path, spreading my arms out to the side of me. My legs are trembling. My heart is erratic. I'm scared to death. And all I can do is feel it—feel it all. "Get the hell out!"

"Anna, what's going on?" Zhara appears in the doorway of the kitchen, clutching a tortilla shell in her hand.

Miller's attention zones in on her, and that sick feeling in my stomach that I felt the night he held me down spreads throughout my body.

"Who's this?" A silent threat blazes in Miller's eyes as his lips curl to a smirk. "That your sister?"

I hold his gaze. "She's just a friend."

"You're such a liar." He looks me dead in the eyes, and I can't see anything but hunger in them. A hunger to feed whatever's rotting inside him, the addiction for the next hit, the need to numb whatever it is he doesn't want to feel.

Is that what I looked like a month ago?

"Always have been." He shoves me back and barrels up the stairs.

"Call the police," I yell at Zhara as I scramble up the stairs after him.

Where did he go? Where did he go?

I dash down the hallway, peeking into every bedroom and my dad's office. When I find him in my parents' bedroom, I just about lose it.

"Get out!" I yell, storming inside.

My outburst only seems to encourage him. He frantically dumps out the dresser drawers, pouring watches, wallets, old clothes, and photos all over the floor.

"There has to be some money in here somewhere." He pokes his head inside the closet. "Poor people don't live in houses like this."

"Dead people don't have money," I say in a desperate attempt to get his attention.

He stares at me like he's seeing me for the first time. "Your parents are dead?"

"Yes." I sink down onto the edge of the bed, which is still

made exactly how it was seven months ago. "So, please, just get out."

He rubs his jawline. "Maybe I should just be asking you where the money is. I mean, if they're dead and you still live here, then they must've left you some." He gets amped up as he paces the floor. "Dude, this is so much better than I thought. I totally lucked out with you."

I hate Miller in that moment, more than I think I've ever hated anyone. Even worse, I hate myself for ever letting him touch me, for thinking that it was better to be high and in his arms than living in reality with my brothers and sisters.

"I'm not giving you any money," I say, rising to my feet.

He stops pacing, and his brow cocks. "You wanna bet?"

My chest heaves as I struggle to breathe normally. "Yeah, I do."

My gaze darts to the door. *One . . . two . . . three . . .*

Ignoring the pain in my leg, I run for the doorway. My muscles knot in protest, but I make it out of the room and sprint down the hall. It feels like I'm learning how to walk again, one foot in front of the other, my leg in so much pain I see spots. Just like how life has felt for the last seven months. Like I'd forgotten how to live, and was drifting around blind, and now suddenly, I'm here, seeing everything, and all I can do is take it one step at a time.

As I almost reach the stairs, bony arms enclose around my waist, and I'm jerked back.

"Let me go!" I shout, slamming my head back.

His grip tightens as he trips toward my parents's room. "Not until you give me some money! I need it! Don't you get it!"

We crash into walls, step on each other's toes, and finally

stumble to the floor. I flip over onto my stomach and clamber to my feet.

Miller jumps up and chases after me. "You're making this more complicated than it needs to be, Annabella!"

"It's Anna," I growl, whirling around and backing up toward my parents' room with my gaze locked on him. "And I'm not about to give *you* any of *their* money."

I'm not about to let any part of my parents fix this mistake for me. No matter how much I loved my mother and wanted to be like her, I refuse to be like her, refuse to make any more mistakes without thinking about the consequences they have on others. I won't give Miller any of my family's money, won't give him a reason to come back asking for more.

I am my own person.

Enraged, Miller lunges and topples over me. Blood rushes to my head as we tumble to the floor. I blink through the dizziness, preparing to fight when he's pulled off me.

"Are you okay, Anna?" an officer asks from above me while another drags a fighting, furious Miller down the hallway.

Nodding, I sit up and press my hand to my tender forehead. "I think so . . . Wait, how do you know my name?" I squint at the officer who has hazel eyes, cropped brown hair, and looks around the same age as Jessamine. *Is he one of the cops who arrested me?* It clicks. *"Milo?"* Jessamine's Milo. "When did you become a cop?"

Milo chuckles as he offers me his hand and helps me to my feet. "Since about a month ago. Heard a lot of things about you, too, but I didn't think I'd get called out to your house this quickly."

"I didn't . . . It wasn't me." I massage my leg, knowing by morning it's more than likely going to be swollen. But the fight was worth the pain.

"I know. I'm just messing with you. Zhara explained what was going on." He nods toward the stairway. "How about we go downstairs and sit down, so I can take a statement from you."

I do what he says and limp down the hall for the stairs. Zhara hugs me the moment I step foot into the foyer and cries against my shoulder.

"It's fine. Everything's going to be okay," I tell her, just like my mother used to do when we were hurt or scared.

I feel strangely calm, but I think it might be shock setting in. Miller was never the nicest person in the world, but he was never as angry and desperate to get drugs as he was tonight. It makes me fear what I would've turned into if I'd stayed with him that night in the cabin, if I hadn't said no and walked away.

If I'd chosen to keep giving up.

After we sit down, Milo asks a few questions, and I give him the details he asks for.

Loki shows up toward the end of questioning and immediately flips out when he sees Milo sitting with us, in full police uniform. "What happened?" he asks, rushing up to Zhara and me.

"We're all fine," I assure him, and then give him a quick recap of what I just told Milo.

"Good god, you scare the shit out of me." He loosens the tie around his neck—the one Tammy gave him. "When I saw the cop car outside . . ." He shakes his head. "Well, I thought they were here because of you."

"Anna did good tonight," Zhara says, defending me.

"It's fine," I say. "I deserve it."

"No, you don't," she argues, dabbing her eyes with a tissue. "You've been doing well the last few weeks."

"But I've been doing shitty for the last seven months." I take a deep breath and look at Loki. "I think I have some making up to do."

"I like the sound of that." Loki tosses his tie onto the armrest. "How about I go finish up with Milo, and then we'll talk about it some more."

I nod, and Milo and Loki head outside into the windstorm to fill out some paper work and get everything wrapped up.

Zhara rubs her puffy eyes and stands up, smoothing her hair into place. "I'm going to go check on Nik."

"Where is Nik?" I ask worriedly. "Shouldn't he be home by now?"

"He got home when all that stuff was going on upstairs so I sent him next door."

"Good idea." I'm glad Nik wasn't around while Miller was losing his shit.

She hesitates to leave the room. "I'll be right back, okay?"

"Zhara, I'm fine," I assure her, kneading my tight thigh muscle with my knuckles. "Go check on Nik."

"I'll bring you some ice for your leg."

"Sounds good."

She reluctantly leaves me and the break gives me time to prepare myself for whatever punishment Loki is going to give me for screwing up again.

When Loki returns to the living room, he looks

completely worn out, as if the last seven months have crashed over him at all once.

"I think after this, Miller's not going to be a problem for a while. He's probably going to be spending a long time in jail, since, yes, we are pressing charges." He waits for an argument that never comes. Plopping down on the sofa across from me, he spreads his arms across the back. His head tips back, and his eyelids close as he mutters, "I'm so tired. I just wish I could sleep for, like, an entire day.

"I'm sorry," I say, blinking back the tears.

Confusion swirls in his eyes. "For what?"

For everything. "For you being tired. For being a pain in the ass. For bringing Miller into our lives." I align my fingers across four pink marks on my arm where Miller roughly grabbed me. "For everything that happened tonight."

"What happened tonight wasn't your fault. Miller chose to come here on his own and forced his way in." He kicks off his shiny shoes and they hit the hardwood floor with a thud. "The only thing you did wrong, though, was getting in his way. Seriously, Anna, you should have let him just take whatever he was looking for and stayed downstairs with Zhara until the cops showed up."

"He wanted money—Mom and Dad's money. And he didn't deserve it." I massage my temples as my head pounds.

"You okay?"

"Yeah, I just have a little headache."

"Why don't we go find you something to eat and then get you some painkillers?" He gets to his feet, adding sternly, "The over-the-counter kind."

A soft laugh escapes my lips, even though it's not funny.

But it feels so good to be able to laugh without feeling as though I'm doing something wrong.

We spend the rest of the night eating the dinner Zhara and I made and playing board games. Even Alexis joins us, but only because Loki told her she'd be grounded if she didn't.

Just before midnight, we gather around the television and count down the seconds until midnight, taking turns, carrying on the Baker tradition even though we usually started at seven.

"Five," Zhara says, clapping excitedly as she spins toward the end table.

Nikoli chucks his football in the air, stretching out his legs across the floor. "Four."

Loki reaches for his soda on the coffee table. "Three."

Alexis flops back in the sofa. "Two," she grumbles.

I'm lying on my back with an ice pack on my leg, reading a message Luca sent me when it's my turn.

Luca: Happy New Year, Skittles Girl

"One," I say with a trace of a smile on my face.

Me: Happy New Year, Skittles Freak

"Happy New Year!" We all shout while Zhara tosses a splash of glitter into the air that floats to the floor and gets wedged in the cracks.

Tearing my attention away from the glitter, I look at the five of us and feel a saddening sense of peace hover over me.

From now on, this is it. The five of us here, together, holding onto what's left of our family. I can try to run away all I want, but the reality will always be here, waiting for me when the day is done. The house may be emptier, but at least there's a roof over my head and four people here to fill up the space and remind me that Anna's still here. That I might not ever be that silly, happy girl who had big dreams and loved to dance, that naïve girl who had crushes and once worshipped her mother, but a part of her exists somewhere underneath the purple hair, dark eyeliner, and ankle bracelet.

And I can either choose to keep fighting who I am now or learn how to live with just being me.

SIXTEEN

THE SECRET TO CANDY, TO LIFE

THE REST OF THE WEEK PASSES BY WITHOUT ANY MORE drama. Before I know it, Friday arrives and my ankle bracelet is removed, giving me two and a half days of freedom before I have to return to school on Monday. Still, standing on the sidewalk in front of my house, the air tastes better than it ever has. My leg feels lighter and my shoulders less weighed down.

"Now, remember," Loki says as he hikes across the lawn toward me. "Just because it's off, doesn't mean you can go back to wandering around. You still have physical therapy during the week, and school. And I want you to start going to a counselor, too."

I draw my hoodie off my head and inhale another breath of freedom-kissed air. "How long do I have to go to a shrink?"

"Until I feel you're okay." He undoes the button on the sleeve of his shirt and rolls it up then repeats the movement on the other side. Ever since he's been spending time with the Bentons, he's started dressing more professionally. I don't think he's doing it because he wants to, but because he feels like he has to appear more responsible. "I just want you to feel okay again without self destructing."

I dig the toe of my bulky red boots into the dirt just in front of the curb. "I've been okay for the last few weeks. Well, compared to how I have been." I glance up at him. "I meant what I said, Loki. I really am sorry. It may not seem like it, but I've been trying. I just need to figure some stuff out."

"I know you've been doing okay, but I want you to do great. I want you to be that girl who used to smile all the time." His voice conveys such passion, as if he whole-heartedly believes that I can do it—be the old Ballerina, Ray of Sunshine Annabella.

I don't have the heart to tell him that even if I bring some of the sunshine back, the ballerina in me might be gone forever, that my leg will never be exactly how it was before the accident. Just like me. And I have to learn to accept what is and move on; otherwise, I'll end up down that dirt road again, throwing bricks at windows, popping pills, stealing, and getting arrest.

He shoves his hands into the pockets of his tan cargo pants and rocks back on his heels, his gaze fixed on the hill line just behind our neighborhood. "I know I can't take the place of Mom and Dad, but I'm going to try my best to make things as normal for you guys as possible. I know I suck sometimes, but I'm trying my best to do better."

"Loki, you're doing a good job." A twinge of guilt seizes the center of my heart. "This thing with Family Services . . . Is everything okay?"

"Yeah, I think so." He crosses his fingers with positivity gleaming in his eyes, but he looks so defeated with the dark half circles under his eyes and pale skin. "Let's hope I can keep it that way." He lets out a hollow laugh.

"I have a feeling things are going to get better," I say with genuine positivity. "In fact, I had a dream about it."

He peers up at the sunlight glistening through the clouds. "I thought you stopped remembering your dreams."

"I did for a while, but my mind's been a lot clearer these last few weeks without all that crap in my system. Painfully clear sometimes."

He steps forward and clasps my shoulder, giving it a squeeze, just like my dad used to do to all of us when he was trying to give us a pep talk. "It'll get better eventually."

"You're the expert, so you'd know."

He backs across the grass. "Hey, I only smoked, like, a couple of times. That doesn't make me an expert."

I throw a joking grin in his direction. "Is that why you spent half your senior year with your bedroom door locked and your smoke alarm shoved under your pillow?"

"That was a science experiment." He spins on his heels and strides for the front door. "Dinner will be ready in, like, an hour. Don't wander off, please."

"Yes, boss." I salute him then return back to the curb.

I glance left and right, up and down the cozy, quiet neighborhood. All I would have to do is start walking until I made it to the bench three blocks down. I could get on the bus and just go, ride it until I felt like getting off. Nothing's stopping me anymore. Except that part of me doesn't want to. Part of me wants to stay right where I am, where I feel safe, loved, even if it means I have to deal with the guilt, the agony, the regret—everything I feel inside.

I slip my hand into my jacket pocket and graze my fingers along the trim of the envelope that has my name written on it. I still haven't opened the letter, but ever since New Year's, I sometimes carry it around with me, conjuring up all kinds of ideas of what it'll say. I know once I open it, that's it, though. Whatever I read, I'll have to accept whatever's in there. Whether her words are encouraging, discouraging, there's no going back from reading it, and I need to make sure that I can handle it.

Even though I've decided that I want to forgive myself, want to heal and change, I still haven't exactly figured out how to do so. How do I become that strong, happy person again?

My phone buzzes from inside my back pocket, and I dig it out.

Cece: Hey, I was wondering if we could have lunch on Monday during lunch break. I really want 2 talk 2 u again.

My fingers hover over the buttons to type back, but then I tap her contact number and put the phone to my ear.

"Hey," she answers, sounding as shocked as the day she saw me with my purple hair. "I'm so glad you called."

I lower myself down to the curb, racking my brain for something to say. "I'm sorry I haven't talked to you in a while . . . I've just been going through some stuff."

"Yeah, I heard about that. Are you okay now?"

I look down at my bare ankle. "You know what? I think I might be."

"Good, because I miss talking to you."

"I miss talking to you, too." I need to get everything out in the open, instead of holding it all in like I have been. "But I need you to understand that I'm not the same person as I used to be. The accident . . . It changed me. And I'm not just talking about my hair . . . Sometimes it's hard to talk to you because you were such a huge part of my old life."

"Is that why you've been blowing me off for the last few months?"

"Partly . . . Sometimes it's hard to be around you, too, because you're so happy."

"You used to be happy with me," she whispers. "I miss that."

"I miss that, too," I say. "But I'm not like that anymore. Sometimes I get sad and that's just how it is. There's nothing I can do about it except let it pass."

"I'm so sorry, Anna, that this happened to you."

"Me too." I inhale and exhale. *Deep breaths. Get through it.* "I want to have lunch with you, though. If you still want to."

"Of course I still want to," she says, like I'm being silly. "And, Anna, I just want to say that I'm not dating Ben. I know that's what it looks like, but we're just friends."

"It's okay if you are." And I mean it. Ben belongs in the past with the glitter stuck in the cracks and the boxes of ballet slippers and leotards. "I don't think of him that way anymore."

"But I'm not."

"But you want to."

"Kind of, but I'd never do that to you."

"Maybe we can talk about it at lunch," I suggest. "And figure it all out."

"I'd like that," she says, then in Cece style, she lets out a squeal that makes my ears ring. "I'm so glad you finally called! I've missed you so much!"

We talk for a while about guys and school, who's dating whom. I even tell her a little bit about Luca. By the time I hang up, I'm still unsure where things with Cece will go. I don't think we'll ever be as close as we used to be, the best friends who spent every waking hour together talking about guys, makeup, school, dancing. Even though I still have no idea who I want to be, I know those things are no longer important to me, but maybe we can be friends.

"Thinking about running away so soon?" Luca's voice sails over my shoulder. "Man, I know you like to wander, but I thought you'd at least give it a couple of days."

The sound of his voice makes me both giddy and sullen as I remember the amazing, breathless, perfect kiss we shared and how I lost it right afterward.

"I might give it a few days, but I haven't decided," I joke without turning around. "It all depends on how bored I get."

"Guess we'll have to make sure you don't get bored, then." He moves up behind me, so close I can smell the cool, woodsy scent of his cologne. "Happy Ankle Bracelet Goodbye Day, by the way. We so need to celebrate this ever so awesome, once in a lifetime occasion. I mean, it's not every day I get the honor of being part of a criminal's initiation back into society."

"I know. You're so lucky." I erase my silly smile, push to my feet, and face him. "I'm guessing you already have something weird planned to celebrate."

He has on a blue hooded jacket with a logo on the front, dark jeans, and a black knitted cap. The glasses are MIA, and I wonder if he'll ever wear them around me again. A hundred butterflies come to life in my belly just thinking about him no longer wearing the glasses around me, because he wants to impress me.

He feigns hurt, jutting out his lip. "My ideas aren't weird."

"They are, too, and you want to know why? Because you're weird. Like super weird. Like Skittles, guessing games, stealing brownies kind of weird."

"So are you. In fact, you're probably the strangest girl I've ever met."

"I know."

Unsaid words float between us. The wind picks up, blowing dirt and debris in the air. Strands of my hair veil my face and get stuck against my lips. As I pluck it out, he becomes obsessed with my mouth, wetting his lips with his tongue as he stares at it. I wonder if he's even conscious that he's doing it. That he's looking at me like I used to want to be looked at, as if he wants nothing more than to kiss me. My stomach feels as if it has turned into a bouncy house.

"So, about the other day with the sparklers . . ." I decide to be brave and address the big fat elephant dancing around between us.

He cups the back of his neck, staring at the bare branches of a tree lashing around. "Huh, didn't expect you to say that. I thought we were just going to pretend it didn't happen."

I'm so ridiculously nervous. That kiss with Luca meant something to me, and whenever I'm around him, I feel giddy, scared, lost, and sometimes even happy. It makes me want to run. Makes me want to stay right where I am. Makes me want to do a lot of things that involve our lips.

"Do you want to pretend it didn't happen?" I ask coyly, kicking at the dirt.

His eyes pop wide open as his gaze whips back to me. "*What?* No, not at all . . . Do you?"

I bite on my thumbnail and shake my head. "No."

The tension in his body gradually evaporates. "Thank god."

"But," I start, and his mouth curves downward, "I really like you, but right now I'm kind of, I don't know, lost, I guess. There's so much stuff that's happened lately, and I think I need to take things slow, just until I can get my feet under me again, if that makes sense."

"It makes perfect sense." He glances over at his house, like he's going to leave, most likely because he thinks I suck. "You wanna see something I haven't really shown anyone before?"

"It wouldn't, by chance, be how you miraculously guessed what candies I wanted? Because I'm still waiting for that."

"Actually, it kind of has to do with that." He holds his finger and thumb a sliver apart. "A little bit, anyway." He extends his hand out for me to take. "Come on and I'll show you."

I think twice before lacing my fingers through his. Is this taking it slow? I'm not sure, but it feels so good, okay, right, so I stop analyzing and go with it.

We hold hands as we wind around the fence and cross the yard to his house.

"It smells like a burnt Christmas tree in here," I say when I get a whiff of the charcoal scent lingering in the entryway that's covered with Barbie dolls and glittery princess stuff.

He lets go of my hand to shuck off his jacket. "That's because the tree almost burnt down."

"*Seriously?*" I ask right as I get a good view of the half singed Christmas tree leaning against the living room wall.

"Yeah, my dad was trying to light some candles close to the tree, and the tree was too dry and, well, one thing led to another." He drapes his jacket on the coatrack then nudges some toys out of the way with his foot. "You'd think a grown man would know better, but surprisingly, he seemed pretty confused as to why it happened."

"My dad almost burned down his store once, with fireworks he always kept stashed in the office closet," I tell him. "My mom flipped out and yelled at him, even though she always joked about wishing he'd get rid of the store."

"My mom was pretty upset, too, but my dad usually just laughs her off."

"My dad does, too . . . or, I mean, did." I pretend to have something in my eye and duck my head so he won't see my eyes bubbling with tears.

He threads his fingers through mine, our palms conforming, and he sketches his finger across the back of my hand. "You think you're ready to hear about my magical mind reading gift?

Sucking back the tears, I meet his gaze again. "If you could mind read, you wouldn't be hanging out with me. Trust me. One look into my thoughts, and you'd be running the other way."

He brushes a strand of hair out of my eyes, his knuckles grazing my temple as he tucks it behind my ear. "I doubt that. I find you fascinating. Always have."

I shiver from his touch and cross my fingers that he

doesn't notice. "There you go again, talking like you've known me forever." But the intense, butterfly-inducing look on his face has me worried that he somehow has.

He leads me up the stairs toward the second floor.

"Where is everyone?" I ask.

"At the store," he says.

So it's just him and me?

My stomach does a double back flip, but I shake off the feeling and focus on walking up the stairs, taking in the family portraits lining the wall. One in particular captures my attention; a younger Luca sits with a girl around my age wearing baggy clothes and a stud in her nose. She looks thin, her frail arm is around Luca's shoulder, and the sunlight beaming down on them highlights the shadows under her eyes.

"Is this Rowan?" I ask, pointing at the picture.

"Yeah. It was taken a few years ago." His voice grows thick with emotion. "My mom thinks it's one of the better pictures of Rowan when she wasn't high . . . I don't know why she can't see it."

"Sometimes people only see what they want to." Like I did with my mom.

Looking back, I see it now, in the way she decided she didn't want to cook anymore, how she never was a fan of my dad's store, how she drove to the antique shop on my birthday, to do god knows what with Dennis. The woman, who I thought had been the perfect mother and wife, had her flaws —everyone does, I guess.

We silently finish climbing the stairs then step into a room with an unmade twin bed, a pile of clothes on the floor, and a cluster of snapshots tacked to the dark blue accent wall. The air smells like sugar and cologne with a splash of charred pine needles.

Luca slips his fingers from mine to turn on the lamp and tug off his beanie.

"Did you take all of these?" I turn in a circle, looking at all the photos of him, of the mountains, the beach, trees, people I've never met. Some are in black and white, others in color, but the one thing they have in common is they all tell a story of the life Luca's lived, where he's been, what he's seen.

"Yeah. I pretty much started taking pictures since I was old enough to work a camera. But I took a lot of my best photos during the year Bria was missing, when my parents were pretty much nonexistent." He scoots a pile of clothes aside and sits down on his bed. "I was actually kind of a pain in the ass back then."

"You were, huh?" I find the idea of him being a pain in the ass amusing for some reason.

"I spent a lot of time being . . . well, depressed." He grabs an album from his nightstand and places it on his lap. "You remember how I told you my parents were caught up in finding Bria?"

Nodding, I examine a photo he took of himself. He's leaning against a chain-link fence with a hood pulled over his head. His glasses are off, and he looks so miserable. "This one looks familiar," I say. "Where'd you take it?"

"Here actually." He opens the album. "Last summer when we came to visit."

I look at him. "You were here last summer?"

"We've spent summers here almost every year for last ten years or so."

"Were you here on June sixth?" I have no idea why I ask,

or why it matters. It really doesn't. That's the past. This is the now.

I need to start focusing more on the now.

"I was." His head's tipped down as he examines the photos taped to the pages.

"I'm guessing you heard about the accident, then?"

He bobs his head up and down with his gaze glued to the photos. "I was actually in town that day with my mom, and we drove right by it on our way back to the house we rented . . . I saw you being lifted into the ambulance."

My chest constricts thinking of the days I can't remember, the days I lost drifting in and out of consciousness. Days were lost as I drifted in and out of consciousness. "How did you know it was me?" I take a seat on the bed beside him and straighten my injured leg to ease some of the tightness in the muscles. "I don't even look like the same person anymore."

"Yeah, you do. You just wear more makeup and have crazy purple hair." He gently tugs on a strand of my hair. "I saw you before that, though, lighting off a sparkler in the parking lot of the grocery store."

"Oh, my god." I don't know whether to frown or laugh that he saw me that day, before the dyed hair, thick eyeliner, and scars. It's overwhelming to know that all this time he recognized me and I had no idea. That he knew my don't-gives-a-shit-attitude was a fraud. "That's how you knew what candy I'd pick. Because I was eating Snickers and M&Ms right before I decided to light the sparkler."

He chuckles, a deep husky sound. "It was pretty funny watching everyone stare at you like you were crazy."

"I was bored, and it was my birthday, so I thought, what

the hell." I scrape at the pink nail polish Zhara put on me the other night. "My dad gave me sparklers every birthday." Another thought dawns on me. "Is that why you got me some for Christmas?"

He nods, his fingers curling around the corner of the page. "You looked so happy that day. I wanted to see you that happy again."

"I was happy." An uneven breath falters from my lips as I remember what it felt like to be that freely happy.

Like standing on the edge of a cliff with the wind in my hair and my arms spanned to the side, something I did with my dad once after a hike. Or right after an extremely hard dance practice, when my toes were numb, blisters covered my feet, and every one of my limbs ached; all that pain represented every ounce of what I had into dancing my best.

"I was kind of jealous when I saw you," he says. "Of how happy you were. I was sulking on the hood of the car, waiting for my mom to stop talking to some random stranger she cornered at the store. I had my hoodie up because I knew it'd piss her off."

I bite down on my tongue to stop myself from laughing at the memory. "I remember her yelling at you. I think you even looked at me while she was."

"I did look at you. A lot, actually."

He looks down, and when I follow his gaze, my heart nearly stops.

There are a few pictures of me on the page. Some were taken recently while some were older, taken a couple of years ago, when my parents were alive. There's one of me reading on the bench in front of my dad's store. Another of me sitting in the shade of that ridiculous gnome statue. There's even a photo of me dancing underneath the fireworks at the park, with my arms stretched out to the side and a huge ass grin on my face, as if every single second was perfect.

"The first time I saw you, you were fourteen." He looks at the photo of me dancing under a shower of sparks. "I was pissed off at my dad because he forgot to play baseball with me, or something stupid like that. It was the Fourth of July and I had wandered down to the park. I swear, almost the entire town was there. It was crazy."

"They probably were. It's a thing around Honeyton, something you'll soon learn."

"You were there, too, you know . . . And your family." His smile doesn't quite reach his eyes. "You all went so crazy when the fireworks started going off. You took off running, yelling something about fireflies."

"It was something we did every year . . ." I find myself smiling, yet wanting to cry over what'll never be again. "It was one of my favorite holidays."

"I wanted to have that," he says softly. "That's what kind of caught my attention. How happy your family was. Mine was so messed up all the time. My mom with her meltdowns, my dad with his grumpy, you-need-to-grow-up-and-be-responsible-don't-be-like-Rowan attitude, and Rowan . . . well, she'd been doing drugs for a couple of years by then. I thought about joining you, but just sat back and took pictures instead."

"You should have. Joined us, I mean." The idea makes me smile just a bit. I would've been so stoked if a guy as cute as Luca would've wanted to hang out. "I was super nice back then."

"I know you were. I saw you a couple of times after that,

and a few times over the next couple of summers. I thought about talking to you, but you looked too nice and sweet. You were always smiling, and it was a little intimidating when I felt so depressed all the time."

I feel like I'm seeing an entirely new side of him, just like he's seen an entirely different side of me. But maybe that's how everyone is, carrying around so many layers, and you never fully get to see all of them unless you get close enough that they let you.

"It's hard to believe you were sad," I say. "You seem so happy all the time."

He closes the album and sets it aside on the nightstand before turning to me. "I had a revelation about seven months ago that kind of changed my life."

Seven months ago? "The day of the accident?"

He nods, intertwining our fingers, and I can feel his pulse racing through his grip. "When I saw you on that stretcher, being put into the ambulance, all I could think was I might have lost my chance at ever meeting you. Then, a week later, I heard that you were okay, and that's when I decided that I needed to stop watching life and actually live it. I went back home and started doing more of the things I wanted to do. Hanging out with friends, going to parties, biking in the mountains, hiking, seeing places I never knew existed. And I also made myself a promise that when we came back for our next summer trip that I'd finally talk to you." His lips tilt to a lopsided smile as he struggles to conceal his nerves. "But then we ended up moving right next door to you. I swear, I seriously about lost it when I found out."

I think back to that day I first met him and how stunned he appeared when he saw me. I thought it was because of my purple hair. The idea that he knew me, knew the real me, this entire time is mind-blowing.

"I can't believe you even recognized me. I look so different."

"I know you don't want to hear this, but you still look like you." His grin broadens, pretty much taking over his entire face. "Well, a crazy, rainbow version of you."

I roll my eyes but a tiny raindrop of a smile sneaks through. "This is so weird. All this time you've known me and I didn't even know it."

"I didn't really know you. I just took pictures of you sometimes."

"When you put it that way, you kind of sound like a stalker."

He scrunches his nose. "Wow, I kind of do. It wasn't in a weird way, though. I just like taking pictures of people, and you take really good pictures, and I—"

I put my hand over his mouth to stop him from rambling. "I don't really think you're a stalker. Trust me. I used to watch people all the time, especially tourists. That's how I noticed you." I lower my hand. "I just didn't take pictures. But I did dance around in parking lots with sparklers in the middle of the day, so I've got the crazy thing going for me."

The stiffness in his body alleviates. "I'm sorry I didn't tell you right away. At first it was because I was worried you'd think I was too weird, and then I didn't because . . . ." He rakes his fingers through his hair with his free hand. "Well, because it seems as if you don't like to be reminded of the past." He traces the folds of my fingers. "If you ever want to talk about anything, just know that I'm here."

Anything at all?

God, it must've been hard for him to tell me his secret, yet he did. Just like that, gave it up. I try to make sense of it, how he knew me, how he *saw* me, how he used to be so depressed—so sad—and then one day just deciding he wasn't going to be.

"I decided that I needed to stop watching life and actually live it."

If I'm ever going to forgive myself and move forward then perhaps living life is where I should start. Luca may have brought me up here with every intention of telling me how he knew about the candy, but really he told me so much more.

He reminded me that I used to *live* life.

And now I'm about to try it again, only with purple hair and a scarred leg.

"You want to do something fun?" I'm jittery with all the adrenaline pumping through my veins. It's been too long since I felt this way, and I swear my heart's going to leap right out of my chest. "I should warn you, though, it's kind of crazy, and maybe just a little bit dangerous."

Wariness floods his eyes. "Is it illegal?"

I waver. "Nope. Not really."

"Then count me in," he says with zero hesitation.

A bundle of nerves, I stand up, telling myself I can do this. If for no other reason then to remember the man my dad was.

One foot in front of the other, Anna.

Time to live again.

SEVENTEEN
FIREFLIES REALLY DO EXIST

"WHAT ARE WE DOING HERE?" ZHARA ASKS FROM THE backseat of Luca's Jeep as she stares out the window at the park.

Nikoli is sitting beside her with a football on his lap and the hood of his jacket pulled over his head.

After Luca agreed to go with me, my initial instinct was to get in the car and just leave. That's what I would've done a month ago. But that was then and this is now, and being in the now, I made myself ask for permission. The only way Loki would allow me out of the house past seven was if Zhara went with me, and I was pretty okay with that. On the way out, though, we ran into Nikoli, who looked depressed and lonely sitting on the steps, playing catch with himself, so Luca invited him, which made me like Luca even more.

"And what did you guys get from Dad's store?" Zhara adds, unbuckling her seatbelt.

Luca and I exchange a look, silently agreeing not to tell

her what's about to happen. Then we open the doors and hop out. The sky has cleared up and is dusted with handfuls of stars.

"Are you sure this isn't illegal?" Luca double checks as we meet around the back of the vehicle.

"Not on New Year's or the Fourth of July," I say as he pops open the rear door.

"Wait. We're doing something illegal?" Zhara asks as she climbs out of the backseat and joins us. She pulls her fleece coat tighter around herself, anxiously glancing around at the trees surrounding us. "Anna, I can't get in trouble."

Nikoli climbs out with the football tucked under his arm. "Zhara, would you relax. You're stressing me out just listening to you." He hikes across the grass, tossing the ball into the air.

"We won't get in trouble," I tell Zhara, grabbing one of the smaller firework boxes from the back of the Jeep. "Dad used to do this all the time."

Her mouth sets in a firm frown. "In January?"

"One year he did." A faint smile rises on my lips at the memory. "As a belated Christmas present to me."

"We should have an escape plan, just in case." Luca gathers up the rest of the fireworks and bumps the rear door shut. "We are harboring an ex-felon here."

He grins at me, and I stick out my tongue.

"We're going to get in trouble," she whines, close to tears. "I know we are."

"Relax. Everything's going to be fine." I pat her shoulder as I pass by her and head for the open grassy area where Nikoli has sat down.

"So, fireworks, huh?' he asks, and I nod.

"I thought it could be fun," I say.

Nikoli shrugs. "I guess it sounds cool."

Luca walks up with a stack of fireworks in his hands. "So, where are we doing this?"

I point toward a flat area, then we head over and begin setting up the first fountain.

"How far will they shoot?" Luca wonders, glancing around at the grass and then the sky.

I read the back of the box. "It says that it just shoots a shower of sparks."

'That's not very specific."

I balance the stand on the grass. "That's half the fun. You never know what's going to come out of them."

"Okay, but if this backfires and does something crazy, like set the park on fire, I'm totally running and leaving you behind." He shoots me a grin so I'll know he's kidding.

"Yeah, right. I'll knock you down and steal your car keys before you can bolt," I retort, sticking out my hand. "Now, hand me the lighter."

He drops the lighter into my palm, brushing his fingers across my wrist in the process, and my heart slams against my chest. He smiles as he steps back, as if he knows exactly how uncontrollably excited and nervous he just made me feel.

I crouch down in front of the fireworks. "Ready?"

He folds his arms across his chest. "Whenever you are."

"Ready, Zhara!" I call out to her, because she's still huddling near the truck.

"I guess," she replies anxiously.

"What about you, Nik?" I ask.

He inches back toward the trees. "Sure. Get the show rolling."

"If all goes awry, there's a hose near the bathrooms," I say to everyone. Then I flick the lighter and the flame hisses against the wick. I shuffle back, giving it some room, waiting, waiting, waiting.

Boom!

Vibrant shades of purple, yellow, and blue shimmer through the air like a rain shower and light up the sky like the Fourth of July. Without even thinking, I clumsily chase after the sparks with my hands out, ignoring the limp in my walk.

It doesn't matter right now.

"There's something so freeing about lighting off fireworks," my dad says as an array of colors explode in the sky.

"You used to hate them," I remind him, spinning around and around. "What changed?"

"I did," he says simply. "Sometimes people do that over time."

"Is it a good thing? Change, I mean."

"As long as you're happy with yourself, then it is," he says, walking up beside me.

I pause. "Daddy, are you happy?"

He smiles down at me. "Right now I am." Then he lifts up his hands and spins around and around with me.

I twirl around with my hands in the air, getting dizzier and dizzier, but refuse to stop, to ever let go of that freeing, happy, heart warming feeling that the memory brings.

Luca laughs as he watches me. "If I'd known this was how I could get you to loosen up, I would've done it a long time ago."

Smiling, I keep whirling inelegantly around until the

sparks fizzle out. Then we light off another one, and unable to help herself, Zhara runs around with me while Nikoli and Luca stand off to the side, chatting about something. After we get through the larger fireworks, we move on to the sparklers. Eventually, my leg grows sore, so Luca and I wander back to the Jeep, leaving Zhara dancing around on the hillside with two sparklers and Nikoli lying on the grass, stargazing.

Luca opens the back of the Jeep and motions for me to sit down. Hoisting myself up into the back, I zip up my coat. The car radio turns on, to the classic rock station, of course. "More Than A Feeling" by Boston flows melodiously through the speakers as Luca returns and sits down beside me.

"So, now what's on the agenda?" he asks.

I shrug, swinging my legs dangling over the edge. "I don't know. I was thinking about stealing a box of hair dye on our way home." He gives me a grim look, and I steal his move and wink at him. "I'm just kidding. I think I'll take it easy on getting in trouble for a while."

Chuckling, he lies down with his hands tucked behind his head. "Sounds good; otherwise, I might have to go back to just taking pictures of you."

I lie down beside him and stare up at the roof of the car. "Was it hard for you to tell me about that?"

"It was a little nerve-racking," he admits, giving me a sidelong glance. "Mainly because I thought you were going to think I was a freak."

"You kind of are, though, but so am I."

He rolls over and props himself up on his elbow. "You're not a freak, Anna."

"What do you see when you look at me?" I ask, unable to stop myself.

"Honestly?" he asks, and I nod. "I see someone who's been through a lot and is a little lost . . ." He ravels a strand of my hair around his finger, hurriedly adding, "But that's okay. Everyone gets a little lost sometimes."

I don't know why I do it. Maybe it's because of what he told me earlier, or the fact that I'm here lighting off fireworks, something I thought I'd never do again, but I find myself opening up to him.

"Can you keep a secret?" I say, and he nods, his brows furrowing. I can't hold still—can't believe I'm doing this. I sit up, and he moves with me. I take a deep breath and another, feeling the fresh air saturating my lungs, something I wouldn't have appreciated a month ago because I would've been too high. Life's always changing, whether we want it to our not, and sometimes we have no choice but to change with it.

I stick out my pinkie, and he loops his around mine without so much as a second thought.

"The day we got into an accident, I found out my mom was having an affair." I pull my pinkie away from his and stare out at the parking lot illuminated with the glow of the lampposts that enclose the area. "It was the guy who owns the antique shop, actually. She went there that day with me in the car, and when she came out, she was acting strange . . . I knew something wasn't right . . . and she kind of asked me not to tell my father without actually asking me . . . When we picked him up, I swear to god he knew, but I hesitated and didn't say anything to him. Then a few minutes later, I didn't have a choice anymore." I blow out a breath. "I don't even know why I'm telling you this. No one else knows, but sometimes I feel like it's literally killing me on the inside. Like my body survived the accident, but my mind really didn't."

It takes him a few heartbeats to respond, and I worry I might have said too much. Maybe he wasn't ready to hear my family's secrets.

"Anna, you not telling your dad . . . That's not your fault," he says. "Your mom should've never asked you to keep that kind of a secret."

"I get that. And I think if there hadn't been an accident, I probably would've ended up telling him." I realize the truth as I say it.

If my dad hadn't died that day, I would've eventually said something. I may have wanted to be like my mother while I was growing up, but my dad was the one who cooked me burnt breakfasts, bought me fireworks on my birthday, took me to the park to light them off in the middle of the night. My dad was a good person, and he deserved to hear the truth, even if he already knew it.

"That's because you're a good person," Luca says, covering my hand with his. "Whether you want to admit it or not."

He's studying me with an intense, smoldering look, and all I can think is, I want to kiss him, right now, in this moment before it's too late. Whether this is fast or slow, I don't care. I just care about missing my chance and never being able to have this moment again.

I lean in slowly, the shy side getting the best of me, but I keep going until our lips connect. Sparks erupt, but I'm not sure if it's from the kiss or from Zhara and Nikoli lighting off another firecracker in the distance.

I giggle against Luca's mouth, thinking how I used to believe kisses could actually create fireworks.

"What's so funny?" he asks, breathless, his eyes glazed over.

"Nothing." I quiet him, deepening the kiss.

He cups the back of my head, pulling me closer and sliding his tongue into my mouth. He tastes minty, smells like fireworks, and his body feels so warm against mine as he lays me back into the Jeep. His hands roam all over my body, grazing my skin. I slide my hands underneath his shirt and feel the softness of his skin, get lost in the way he moans. This kiss is so different. This time I'm less afraid and more willing to let go. This kiss isn't about the past. It's about the present. It's about him and me.

I want this.

The song switches to "Disarm" by Smashing Pumpkins as I hitch my bad leg over his hip and press against him. Everything starts to move quickly after that. Out-of-control. I'm getting lost again, but in the most beautiful way possible. His shirt comes off, and mine ends up around my neck as we kiss each other almost frantically. He keeps letting out these moans that I've never heard a guy make, and I can't seem to get enough air into my lungs. But I don't really care. I just want more kissing. More lips to lips. Body to body. Skin to skin.

"Oh, my god! Sorry!" Zhara screeches right as Luca undoes the button on my pants.

We break apart, breathing raggedly as she takes off running. But when we look at each other, we both erupt with laughter.

Luca's head falls against my shoulder, and his breath

caresses my skin. "I hope we didn't just embarrass the crap out of her.

"I wouldn't count on that," I say, working to catch my breath. "She probably won't be able to look either of us in the eye ever again."

Luca rolls off me, ruffling his hair into place, and I readjust my shirt. Then I button up my jeans while he pulls his t-shirt back over his head and puts his jacket back on. Before we get out to search for Zhara, he tucks a few strands of my hair behind my ear and gives me a look that makes my skin warm. Even though I can't see into the future, I know there's going to be more kisses like that between us, because I plan on kissing Luca a lot.

With a quick brush of his finger across my cheekbone, he turns away and scans the parking lot for Zhara. "Where'd she go?"

I spot her lingering over by the bathrooms, looking everywhere but the Jeep. "Can you go get Nikoli and tell him it's time to go so I can have a second to talk to her?" I ask Luca, and he nods, hopping out of the car. I lower my feet out of the vehicle and hobble over to Zhara. "Hey, you okay?"

"Yeah, I'm fine." But she won't look me in the eye.

"Zhara, you don't need to be embarrassed," I say. "We were just kissing."

"It doesn't matter what you were doing. I'm just being silly." She glances over her shoulder at me, and her eyes are red and puffy.

"Then why are you crying?"

She shrugs, dabbing her eyes with the sleeve of her coat. "Not because you two were kissing. I was just thinking about some stuff."

"Want to talk about it?" I ask.

She turns around and wraps her arms around me, hugging me tightly. "I just miss them. That's all. Being out here reminds me so much of Dad."

"Me too." I hug her back. It's the first time I've willingly hugged one of my brothers and sisters since the accident, and I think I might need to start doing it more. "Did you know Dad told me once that he secretly dreamed of opening a firework stand?"

Zhara pulls back, her eyes wide in shock. "He did?"

I nod, laughing softly. "He said it'd be awesome and it'd save him so much money because then he wouldn't have to pay for the fireworks he bought all the time."

"He did buy a lot," she sniffs, wiping her eyes with her sleeve. "I always wondered why."

"Because it made us happy and his favorite moments in life were when he got to see us happy."

"Did he tell you that?"

I nod. "He actually told me while we were out here lighting off fireworks . . . I remember he looked so happy that day. He even let me light one of them, which he never did." I laugh, but my eyes water. "It was a great day."

"A lot of days were." She takes my hand and gives it a squeeze. "We're going to get through this, right? I mean, one day it's not going to be so hard?"

I smash my lips together, nodding. "You know what? I think so."

We both release a breath then return to the vehicle where Luca and Nikoli are waiting for us, talking about something that seems to be making Nikoli happy.

Luca straightens when he sees me approaching. "Everything okay?"

Is everything okay? It feels that way right now, but I can't be one hundred percent certain. Of anything really. Of where my life will go. If I'll always feel as good as I do right now. If Luca and I will work out. If I'll get that fairytale ending I used to dream about. All I can do is just take the good stuff and hold it in my hand for as long as I can.

"I think so," I say, glancing at Nikoli as he opens the door and hops into the back. "What were you two talking about?"

"Football," Luca says. "That kid really likes his sports."

"He always has," I explain, realizing that while things are different, not everything has to be.

"Is your sister okay?" Luca asks, glancing at Zhara as she rounds to the other side of the Jeep to get in.

I nod, tucking my hands into my sleeves. "She's just going through some stuff."

"You about ready to go?"

"Yeah, but can we stop at the store on the way. I need to buy some hair dye."

"That you're going to pay for, right?" Luca jokes, and I shove him playfully.

He catches my arm, tugging me closer, and shyly leans in to kiss me on the corner of my mouth. It's short and sweet, but I can feel it all the way down to my toes.

We break apart and I head around to the passenger side to get in, but I pause as I'm about to open the door. Out in the field, I spot a tiny glowing dot. At first I think it's a stray spark from a firework that hasn't burned out yet, but it's moving with purpose.

No way.

A firefly.

I hurry after it, rushing across the grass faster than I should, and trail its path with my hands cupped in front of me.

My mom once told my dad that there weren't any fireflies in Honeyton, but my dad argued that he'd seen a few.

"I've seen them before, honey," he says to my mom as Zhara and I bounce around the blanket they were sitting on, hyped up on sugar and anticipation for the firework show to get started.

"They weren't fireflies," she replies, sitting back and nibbling on a cookie. "They don't exist here."

My dad just shakes his head then winks at me. "Go catch a firefly for me, Anna."

I spring forward and cup my hands around the tiny, gleaming bug. My palms glow against the night as I stand on the middle of the hill, holding it in my hand, scared to let it go, but knowing that I have to eventually.

"Dad, you were right. They really live in Honeyton," I whisper as tears roll down my cheeks.

Then I summon a breath, open my hands, and let it fly away into the night.

When I get home, I go up to my room and take out the letter hidden under my pillow. I'm scared to death to open it, but I've been running away from my fears for too long.

It's time to let go.

With tears flowing down my cheeks, I slip the letter out of the envelope.

My dear Crazy Dreamer Annabella,

If you're reading this, then it means I'm no longer around to watch you grow into the woman I've always known you were going to become. When I imagine where you'll be, I see you dancing in some big city, under the lights, and you've finally cured your stage fright. But that might be the dreamer side of me talking.

Like you, I've always had big dreams, but unlike you, I've never really chased them. I always envied you and your bravery, to get over your fears and stand in front of everyone as yourself. It's a gift to be so free like that, to be whoever you want to be in the moment. I know you don't see yourself like that. That you think you're ordinary, but you're so very wrong. You're anything but ordinary. Always have been, from the time you danced your first step instead of walking it. You saw the world differently, full of sunshine and happiness even on the most dreary, rainy days. You were never afraid to feel every emotion, to savor every breath, to dream of all the possibilities waiting for you.

If I can give you one last piece of advice, it's to never let that go. Always be truthful to yourself, Anna, no matter what. Life will have a lot of storms in it, but if you remain true to yourself, you'll make it through.

Love,

Mom

My hands shake as I fold up the now tear-stained piece of paper and tuck it away in a box in my closet right beside my worn ballet shoes and crinkled posters that used to hang on my bedroom walls. Then I get out the letter to Dennis.

Even though she made mistakes, I love my mom. But that's not why I'm getting rid of the letter. I'm doing it so Loki, Jessamine, Zhara, Alexis, and Nikoli can always remember my mom as the loving, happy person we all saw her as. I don't ever want them to have to be burdened with this secret. She never should've taken me with her to the shop that day, never should've asked me to keep quiet. But what's done is done. I can't change it. But I can change it for everyone else.

Clutching the envelope, I shred the letter into pieces and toss them into the trashcan, letting the secret go.

EIGHTEEN
A NEW, OLD ANNA

"Your hair looks weird," Alexis says as I enter the kitchen the next morning.

"I like it," Zhara says, admiring our handy work from last night, when we rinsed out the purple and just high-lighted a few streaks.

"Are you sure you want to do this," she'd said as I sat in front of the sink with a towel around my shoulders.

Nervously nodding, I handed her the box of dye. "It's time for something different . . . time for something . . . new."

"You would," Alexis mutters, scooting back from the table and picking up her empty cereal bowl.

"Be nice," I warn as two slices of toast pop up from the toaster.

Alexis glares at me. "Just because you've turned into your freakin' overly positive, my-shit-don't-stink self again, doesn't mean you can act like the boss."

"I haven't turned into that person again." I grab the

slices of toast. "I'm just . . ." I trail off, trying to figure out how to put what's going on with me into words.

Even though my hair is different, I still have on eyeliner, but not as heavy, and I decided to wear a pink T-shirt to add a little color to my black skinny jeans and clunky boots. I feel strangely exposed, like I'm giving the world a peek at the person I used to be, the one who ran around chasing rainbows, who hated getting into trouble. The one who wasn't rotting inside from the guilt and the confusion of not knowing what to do with myself after the accident. It feels like I'm learning to walk again, and with one misstep, I could fall.

"She's just a new, old Anna," Zhara offers, looking at me.

"You know what? I think that works for now." I toss the butter knife into the sink, pick up my bag, and head for the stairway to wake up Loki.

But he's already up and dressed for work, drinking his coffee in the living room, watching the news.

"Wow, you're up early," I say, swinging the handle of my bag over my shoulder.

"I could say the same thing to you." He does a double take at my hair and pink shirt then rotates around in the sofa. "When'd you do that?"

I stuff half the slice of toast into my mouth, feeling self-conscious with my new look. "Last night, after I got back with Luca."

"Should I be worried about you two?" he asks, picking up his cup of coffee. "I mean, he seems like a nice guy, but I was thinking about Dad last night, and how he was with Jessamine and guys and, I don't know, I feel like I need to be more protective or something, and talk to you more about," he clears his throat, staring at the cup in his hands, "stuff."

By stuff, does he mean safe sex?

I swiftly shake my head, backing for the door. "You're doing great. I swear. And if it's cool with you, I'm going to get a ride to school with Luca since it's his first day."

"I guess it's okay, but don't forget you're supposed to meet with the guidance counselor this morning to talk about how you can get your grades up."

I frown. "Oh yeah, I forgot about that."

"Please make sure you go. This is important. You're in your senior year, and I know you don't want to think about it, but graduation is coming fast."

I nod, clutching the handle of my bag. "Okay, I'll go."

"Thank you." He studies me over with his head cocked. "Anna, I'm . . . I'm really proud of you. I know it's been hard for you, but it means a lot to me that you're trying to do better."

"I'm sorry I've been such a pain in the ass. You didn't deserve to have to deal with that . . . none of you did."

"It's okay. We've all had our pain-in-the-ass moments. Even I went through some shit."

"I know, but I almost got us taken away."

"But you didn't," he says pressingly. "And, like I've said a ton of times, you need to stop worrying. Everything'll be fine. Now get your butt to school so you're not late."

I glance at the wall clock. "I should probably be saying the same thing to you."

He looks at the time and jumps to his feet. "Shit." He hurries toward the kitchen. "Zhara, Alexis, Nik, we gotta go!" He pats his pockets to make sure he has his keys and wallet as I head for the door. "And, Anna, remember I'm picking you up a little early for your counseling appointment," he shouts as I step into the foyer.

"Okay." I feel a little apprehensive about seeing a therapist, but maybe it'll help me face the future a little better. At least that's what I'm hoping.

When I step outside into the chilly winter air, Luca is waiting for me by his Jeep bundled up in a coat and beanie.

His eyes nearly pop out of his head when he spots me coming around the fence. "Holy crap, you look . . ."

"Like the new, old me," I offer as I stop in front of him.

"Not exactly what I was going to say, but it works." His gaze scrolls up and down my body, making me feel super insecure.

"I thought I'd try something different." I shrug, but his gaze causes my heart to dance.

"You look good," he muses, opening the car door for me.

I hoist myself in, setting my bag on my lap as he climbs into the driver's seat. "So, are you nervous?" I ask.

"For what?" He appears genuinely perplexed as he slides the key into the ignition.

"For your first day of school."

"It's not like I'm in kindergarten, Anna," he teases, revving up the engine and cranking up the heater.

"Yeah, but you're not wearing your glasses." I draw my seatbelt over my shoulder. "Which means you're trying to impress the entire school."

"Nope, just the person I'm giving a ride to school." He grins at me as he backs out onto the street.

"You're such a dork." I turn my head toward the window so he can't see my dorky smile.

"I'm going rock climbing after school," he says as he steers onto the main road. "You should come."

I flex my fingers, staring at my father's store as we drive by it. "As fun as that sounds, I don't think I can climb a rock wall."

"Easton said the place has a beginner wall that's super small and easy, which probably was that ten foot wall you were talking about." He twines his fingers through mine, drawing my attention back to him. "He said if I could convince you to come, it could be part of your physical therapy." He eagerly waits for me to respond, his eyes carrying a question: *Are we together?*

It's been a long time since I've known what I wanted, but I realize how much I want to be with Luca.

"You've been talking to Easton about me?" I ask.

"I just want to spend time with you, so I brought it up, hoping he'd bite the bait and say it was cool for you to go." He shrugs, like it isn't the nicest thing a guy has ever done for me

"Okay, if it's cool with Loki, then I'll go." I smile at him to let him know I'm serious.

"Sweet." He gets as giddy as a cheerleader at a homecoming game, and it might be the most adorable thing I've seen. "This is going to be so awesome. I've been wanting to do this forever. In fact, it's on my list."

"You have a list? Like a bucket list?"

He nods. "I've had it ever since . . ." He trails off worriedly.

"That's good," I say. "It's good that you know what you want to do with your life."

"Well, I don't know everything I want to do. I just know there's a lot of stuff I'm going to try to do."

I contemplate what he said. "Maybe I'll make a bucket list, too."

"You should. And I could help you," he says, then smiles. "You should put rock climbing on it."

"Maybe I will." I lean back in the seat, thinking about all the things I could still do with a bad leg

He rambles about rock climbing and mountain biking and all the stuff I should try. He's so excited, talking animatedly with his hands. It's fun watching him get amped up, and I want to be right there with him, getting all stoked, but the closer we get to school, the more I sink into my worries.

I haven't walked the hallways as a fully sober Anna for almost eight months. People are going to stare, whisper, gossip about the ankle bracelet, and I'm not going to have my makeup, hair, and don't-give-a-shit attitude to hide behind.

This is it. This is reality.

"Are you going to make it?" Luca asks, yanking me back to the here and now. "You look like you're going to be sick."

We're parked at the school and the engine is off. The campus yard is bare, the cloudy sky and plummeting temperature forcing everyone inside. The hallways are going to be clogged up with people and their whispers.

"I'm fine. I'm just a little nervous." I open the door and slide my feet to the ground, getting my bearings before putting all my weight on my bad leg.

My legs wobble as I meet Luca around the back of his car, slipping on my backpack. He takes my hand, and we start across the parking lot. Everything feels fine until I stumble over a crack in the sidewalk right as we reach the entrance. I nearly turn around and bolt, just like I used to.

Luca strengthens his hold on my hand. "Don't worry. I won't let you fall, remember?" He winks at me.

Some of the pressure eases off my chest, and I manage a small smile, thinking about how I danced in the living room with him when I never thought I'd dance again. *I can do this. I've made it through so much already. This should be the easy part.*

Standing up straight, I open the doors and step inside with Luca, refusing to run away, to tumble into self-destruction, to be that lost illusion of myself.

When we enter the hallway, I notice every stare, hear every whisper, but I also feel Luca's hand in mine.

"I have to check in at the main office," he says, glancing around at all the people gawking.

"That's okay." I clutch onto his hand tighter. "I have to go to the guidance counselor's office, which is right by the main office."

We veer right and push our way through the people crowding the hallway. I see Cece standing with a few of her cheerleader friends, and when she waves, I wave back.

"So, do you want me to show you around after I get out," I ask Luca when we arrive at the main office."

"Of course." He slips the handle of his backpack over his shoulder. "Okay, you're right. I'm a little nervous. I've never started a new school before."

"You'll be fine," I assure him, feeling really freaking anxious myself. "And if not, then we can both be outcasts together. You can even put purple in your hair and wear dark clothes so we can give everyone twice as many reasons to stare."

"Sounds good to me." He leans in and kisses my cheek. "See you in a bit, Anna."

Smiling, I turn for the door and wipe my sweaty palms on my jeans before walking into the office.

Mr. Dalcebee glances up from a stack of papers. "Anna, please come in and have a seat."

I drop down in a chair in front of his desk and pick at my fingernails, restless and fidgety because I'm here, getting ready to talk about my future with a clean, unpolluted mind.

"So," he starts, adjusting his smiley face tie. "I wanted to discuss your grades again since it's a new semester, which means you have a clean slate. I really think you should take the opportunity to get your grades back up to what they were."

I stare at my hands. "I guess I could try that."

"Good. I'm so glad to hear that." He sounds mildly shocked. He leans over and retrieves a folder from the file cabinet. "Now, I'd like to discuss your plans for college. I know at the end of last year you had a few colleges you were planning on applying to. Are you still planning on applying to those colleges? Because a lot of the schools have deadlines."

I shrug, wringing my hands on my lap. "I'm not sure. Stuff's changed, you know."

"I know." He pauses then closes the folder and sets it aside. "I know you've been through a lot and life has changed for you, but I'd really like to see you focus on something, just to brainstorm more ideas of maybe what you want do with your life."

I'm not sure how to respond, and I have no idea what I want to focus on.

"How about this," he says, crossing his arms on his desk. "Is there one thing you're passionate about? Or maybe something that you've thought of doing after college?"

Seven months ago, I would've answered the question without a second thought. I want to be a dancer. Eventually, a wife and a mother. Happy. Healthy. Successful. In love.

Thinking about it right now, though, seems so overwhelming, so I decide to take it one step at a time.

"Honestly, I'm not really sure what I want to do in the future," I tell him. "But for now, I kind of just want to be Anna."

About the Author

Jessica Sorensen is a *New York Times* and *USA Today* bestselling author who lives in the snowy mountains of Wyoming. When she's not writing, she spends her time reading and hanging out with her family.

ALSO BY JESSICA SORENSEN

Other books by Jessica Sorensen:

<u>Tangled Realms:</u>

Forever Violet

Untitled (Legend's story) (coming soon)

<u>Curse of the Vampire Queen:</u>

Tempting Raven

Untitled (coming soon)

<u>Shadow Cove Series:</u>

What Lies in the Darkness

What Hides in the Shadows (coming soon)

<u>Mystic Willow Bay Witches Series:</u>

The Secret Life of a Witch

Broken Magic

Untitled (coming soon)

<u>Standalones:</u>

The Forgotten Girl

The Illusion of Annabella

Confessions of Luna & Grey

Rules of a Rebel and a Shy Girl

<u>The Heartbreaker Society:</u>

The Opposite of Ordinary

<u>Broken City Series:</u>

Nameless

Forsaken

Oblivion

Forbidden (coming soon)

<u>Guardian Academy Series:</u>

Entranced

Entangled

Enchanted

Entice (coming soon)

<u>Sunnyvale Series:</u>

The Year I Became Isabella Anders

The Year of Falling in Love

The Year of Second Chances

<u>Unraveling You Series:</u>

Unraveling You

Raveling You

Awakening You

Inspiring You

<u>The Coincidence Series:</u>

The Coincidence of Callie and Kayden

The Redemption of Callie and Kayden

The Destiny of Violet and Luke

The Probability of Violet and Luke

The Certainty of Violet and Luke

The Resolution of Callie and Kayden

Seth & Greyson

<u>The Secret Series:</u>

The Prelude of Ella and Micha

The Secret of Ella and Micha

The Forever of Ella and Micha

The Temptation of Lila and Ethan

The Ever After of Ella and Micha

Lila and Ethan: Forever and Always

Ella and Micha: Infinitely and Always

<u>The Shattered Promises Series:</u>

Shattered Promises

Fractured Souls

Unbroken

Broken Visions

Scattered Ashes

<u>**Breaking Nova Series:**</u>

Breaking Nova

Saving Quinton

Delilah: The Making of Red

Nova and Quinton: No Regrets

Tristan: Finding Hope

Wreck Me

Ruin Me

<u>**The Fallen Star Series:**</u>

The Fallen Star

The Underworld

The Vision

The Promise

The Lost Soul

The Evanescence

<u>**The Darkness Falls Series:**</u>

Darkness Falls

Darkness Breaks

Darkness Fades

<u>**The Death Collectors Series (NA and YA):**</u>

Ember X and Ember

Cinder X and Cinder

Spark X and Spark

<u>**Unbeautiful Series:**</u>

Unbeautiful

Untamed